PAMELA HARJU

The Truth about Tomorrow

KEEP UP-TO-DATE WITH NEW RELEASES FROM PAMELA HARJU.

I love to hear from my readers, and I hope they love to hear from me. The best way to make sure that you don't miss any new releases from me is to sign up to my mailing list – but more on that later. You are keen to get reading my book, aren't you?

CHAPTER 1

It was a dull morning on November 8th when Kyle stepped out of the car, and yet the daylight seemed to hurt his eyes. He squinted at the whitish-grey sky and thanked the Garda who had given him a lift home.

He stepped onto the gravel path leading up to the house. He had thought, for that brief moment on Saturday night, that he would never see the house again. It was an ugly house on the outside, a big brick and glass thing that was modern when it was built in the early '90s. The rusty-coloured landscape behind it almost camouflaged the house at this time of year. Kyle had always been glad of it, and that morning he hoped that the house with its contents could simply blend into the surrounding nature altogether so that nobody could come looking for them.

As it was, though, he pulled his keys out of his jeans pocket and walked up to the looming front porch. He pushed the door open and was met with the warm, cosy smell of an open fire and freshly made toast. He could hear his sister's voice on the telephone out in the hall, spelling out her name for what sounded like approximately the thirteenth time.

"No, Cassandra DAHLIA French. Yes, that's right, like the flower, followed by the nationality."

Kyle pushed the door closed behind him. He could tell that his arrival had been noticed. The phone call ended soon after.

Kyle had just entered the kitchen when his sister showed up at the other doorway.

"Hi," she said with a worried-looking smile. Kyle nodded and sat down at the end of the long oak table.

"Do you want tea? Coffee?" Cassie asked, stretching the sleeves of her grey, woolly jumper.

"Coffee," Kyle replied, reaching out for the newspaper on the table.

"Toast?"

"No."

"Kyle, you know you need to eat…"

He let out a big sigh. "Fine. Cereal then."

Cassie hurried over to the press to sort out his breakfast.

Kyle turned over the newspaper to see the front page. "Psychic's son survives fatal crash," it said in big letters on the front.

"Why did you get this?" he asked, looking up at his older sister.

Cassie turned around at the fridge and brushed her long fringe off her face. "They gave it to me on the plane."

"When did you get here?" Kyle said, glancing through the article.

"Yesterday afternoon. As soon as I could. It still cost me a fortune."

Cassie put a bowl of cereal and a mug of coffee in front of Kyle and sat down at the table too.

"Where's Ciara?"

"She took Wanda for a walk," Cassie replied.

"That article is a load of bollocks, you know," she continued.

"They only make a big deal out of it because of mum. They wouldn't give a shit otherwise," Kyle said, pushing the paper away from him across the table. "How do they even know?"

"It was in the local papers yesterday," Cassie said. Kyle knew that she was tense around him, as if he was going to blame her for it or something.

"Bastards," Kyle said, dropping his spoon into the cereal. He had no appetite, but he knew that Cassie was right; he had to eat. If he didn't, Cassie would lose it altogether, even though she seemed calm at the moment.

The front door opened and closed, bringing with it a touch of cool air. Ciara appeared at the kitchen door in a grey hoodie. Wanda ran into the kitchen and sat down at Kyle's feet, glancing up at him with her big, bulgy eyes.

"Hi," Ciara said. Kyle could see that she had been crying. She probably hadn't taken the dog for a walk but for a cry instead. Kyle nodded at her and realised, for what felt like the first time, how alike his sisters were. They were both wary around him, ready to catch him if he was to fall or to put him out if he was to go on fire. They had the same expression on their faces. The only differences were the eight years between them and the different manufactured hair colours, Cassie's blonde and Ciara's dark.

Cassie hurried to turn on the kettle and make herself and Ciara a cup of tea.

"So, you got home all right?" Ciara said, sitting down.

"Why not?" Kyle said, pushing the empty cereal bowl away from him.

"So, what's gonna happen next?"

Ciara was pulling her hoodie off over her head and thanked Cassie for the fresh cuppa.

"I've spoken to the funeral home… I think it will be on Friday."

"Friday? What the fuck for?" Kyle glared at his sister.

"It's the soonest they can do it. It will take… a lot of cleaning up," Cassie said, tears forming at the corners of her eyes.

"I don't wanna see them. I don't," Ciara said, glancing at the two of them.

"You won't have to, pet," Cassie said, reaching out to touch her hand.

"Can they not clean up a bit faster?"

"Don't be so harsh, Kyle. They're doing their best."

"Whatever," Kyle breathed into his coffee.

"I spoke to the lawyers too. I'll see them later in the week."

"We won't have to move, will we?" Ciara looked worried.

"No. I'm sure the house is safe. You can stay here. You might need somebody to stay with you though."

"Can't you stay, Cassie?"

"I don't know, Ciara. I can't just up and leave and move back home. I need to have a job… And there's Rob too."

"Yeah, but… I'm 18 next month, it's not like I need a nanny or anything. I'd rather we were all together."

"How do you think we would live?" Kyle said sarcastically.

"Mum and dad had money…"

"Yeah, THEY had money. What about inheritance tax and all that shite? You're a student, I'm a student, and Cassie's hardly gonna be able to give us much from London."

"Kyle…" Cassie tried to stop him.

"Yeah, well, it's just not gonna work, is it? I'll get some shitty job in McDonald's or something just to keep us going, will I? As if that's gonna work."

"Kyle, it will all be fine. We'll get money."

"Sure." He pushed his chair back from the table. He saw tears in Ciara's eyes now too, but he didn't care.

"Where are you going?" Cassie shouted after him.

"To the bathroom, if you must know," he muttered.

Kyle walked to the downstairs bathroom, next to the only

4

downstairs bedroom and his father's study. He walked over to the sink, turned on the cold tap and splashed his face, over and over again, even though it hurt and stung and the coldness of the water made him think his face and hands were going to go numb.

He dried himself off, and then wiped the splashes off the mirror. He put the towel back on the chrome towel warmer and looked in the mirror. His mousey-brown hair with the blond highlights that he had only got done a couple of weeks earlier was now shaved off in two points on the right-hand side of his head. The bald patches were covered in little bandages. The nurse had told him in the morning that the hair would grow back quickly once the cuts were healed, but it looked horrible. He'd have to get his whole head shaved now.

And his face wasn't much better. There was a big, ugly gash right under the hairline on his forehead and two smaller cuts on his right cheek, one of them getting dangerously close to the corner of his eye. "You're lucky to be alive," they'd all said. What exactly was lucky about being 20 and losing both parents in a car crash? More so, he would now have to look after two hysterical sisters as well as the funeral and a whole pile of legal matters that meant nothing to him… What the hell would happen to his father's business, too?

Kyle heard the doorbell outside, followed by a couple of stifled barks from Wanda. That would start now too, now that it was in the papers. People would come over with flowers and other useless things and offer their condolences...

Still, he couldn't hide in the bathroom forever. He unlocked the door and stepped into the hall. He heard another female voice in the kitchen. Iris.

"Oh, you shouldn't have!" Cassie exclaimed just as Kyle walked back into the kitchen.

"It's the least I could do," Iris said, wrapping her arms around the oldest French daughter.

"Thank you so much, Iris." Tears were running down Cassie's cheeks again.

Kyle was annoyed with the buddy-buddy attitude of his sister's. Yes, he knew that Cassie had done some work experience at their father's business during her college years and become friendly with Iris, who was only five years older than her. Still, Iris was only an employee of their father's.

Ciara had spotted him in the doorway.

"Iris brought over some groceries. Isn't that good of her?" Ciara said, encouraging him to say something polite.

Iris had separated herself from Cassie and looked at Kyle. He only nodded. Groceries were the last thing on his mind.

"Look at you, Kyle. You really were lucky." Iris stepped closer to him to inspect the cuts on his face and head, but Kyle turned away. Iris sensed his reluctance and changed the subject.

"Is there anything else I can do for you guys? Anything at all? Do you want to stay somewhere else or call someone to stay here with you?"

"No, thanks, that won't be necessary. We're all adults," Cassie said, wiping the tears from her eyes.

"Are you sure? It's a bad time..."

"We'll be fine," Kyle interrupted. Ciara had started unpacking the groceries – pizzas, lettuce, chocolate chip cookies, a loaf of bread, fresh milk, chicken breasts, pasta, tissues... Bloody tissues, like she was trying to be thoughtful.

"Sure, if there's nothing else you want me to do, I better head back... It's mental at the office... Although I'm sure that's the least of your worries." Iris stuck her hands in the pockets of her smart-looking black jacket.

"Can you bring me into town?" Kyle asked abruptly, much to his sisters' dismay.

"Kyle… What do you want to go into town for?" Cassie asked with a look of horror on her face.

"I've things to do," Kyle said, checking his pockets for his keys.

"Yeah, sure," Iris said, glancing at the two other women as if looking for back-up.

"I think we should stick together," Cassie said, crossing her arms.

"I don't give a fuck what you think," Kyle said so quietly that nobody heard him. "Like I said, I have some things to do." He walked into the hall with Iris right behind him.

He sat down in the passenger seat of Iris's little red Tigra. She reversed out of the driveway and turned the car towards town.

"Where am I taking you?"

"Anywhere in town," Kyle replied. It was too early to ask, they were still a 15-minute drive away.

He sat in silence the whole way into town, and Iris gave up after a couple of attempts. She pulled in to a bus stop on the main street once they got into town and asked if it was OK. Kyle nodded, thanked her and got out.

His hairdresser was just around the corner. It was just after 11 o'clock in the morning, but the streets seemed full of people. They were all looking at him, and Kyle wished that he had worn a hat or sunglasses, maybe both. Wearing sunglasses in November would look odd too.

He had just crossed the street when he heard somebody call his name. He didn't need to turn around because the girl caught up with him. He had hoped to go unnoticed, but no such luck. It was Melanie. Donal had introduced her to Kyle some weeks earlier, hoping that they'd hit it off. It was a bit unnerving, Donal knowing girls who were so much younger than his 28 years. Melanie was only 19, perfect for Kyle and pretty too, but certainly not somebody he wanted to talk to just now.

"Oh Kyle. Oh my god!" Melanie had caught up with him and blocked his way. She was standing in front of him, at least four inches shorter than him, despite her habit of wearing massive heels. Kyle had never felt as self-conscious as he did at that moment, with Mel running her eyes all over his superficial, external injuries.

"I saw it in the paper yesterday, it's so horrible. Are you OK?"

What a stupid question. His parents were dead, what did she think?

"Yeah, yeah. It's grand."

"I couldn't believe it, I was meant to come and see you play on Saturday, but you were gone before I got there... You know Donal only found out Sunday morning? It's, like, nobody called any of them or anything..."

"Yeah. It was all pretty shit."

"Well, the cuts will heal soon. You'll be back to being the hottest boy in town in no time! Not that you're not anyway," Mel corrected herself.

Oh jeez. Girls, Kyle thought, and shook his head; at first he thought he was only doing it in his head but then he realised he actually was shaking his head. Mel looked confused but kept smiling sweetly.

"Yeah, well, I got to go. I've some stuff to do," Kyle said, pointing at a random direction with his thumb.

"Yeah, sure. I think Donal will come and see you in the next couple of days. He felt really bad about the whole thing. Take care of yourself," Mel said, squeezing Kyle's arm.

Kyle picked up his pace and got to the salon in no time. The bell clanged noisily behind him, and everybody's heads jerked up. Luckily, it wasn't busy. Kyle counted one customer having her hair cut and another one having her hair washed. Georgina looked up from the shampoo bottles she had been arranging at the back of the shop.

"Jesus, Kyle, what are you doing here?" she said, rushing over. "My god, you look a state!"

Kyle was painfully aware of all the eyes on him.

"Why are you here?" Georgina asked again.

"I need a haircut."

Georgina looked at him, uncomprehending.

"I need a haircut," Kyle said again, "I want it all shaved off."

"But..."

"Can you please just do it?" Kyle said quietly.

Georgina nodded, her dark curls bouncing around her head. "Yeah. Take a seat."

Kyle sat down in the nearest chair. The place was unusually quiet. There was no chatting between the other two workers and their customers, and the radio seemed quieter than usual. There were no hairdryers on, no water running. Just silence.

"You mean, all of it?" Georgina asked, the trimmer shaking in her hand. Kyle nodded but refused to look into the mirror to face Georgina's worried eyes. He kept his eyes averted while he listened to the buzz of the trimmer and felt tufts of hair fall onto his shoulders. Conversation had resumed around them, although it seemed to be in whispers. Perhaps it was all just in his head.

"Right. Done," Georgina announced and whipped the cape off his shoulders in a one-hand movement.

Kyle stood up without a single glance in the mirror. He had

never wanted to go for the skinhead look, yet here he was.

He walked over to the counter. Georgina shook her head.

"No, I don't want you to pay anything."

"Ah, don't."

"But I only put those highlights on you two weeks ago. It wouldn't be right."

"I don't want your fucking sympathy!" Kyle shouted, slamming his hand on the counter. "How much is it?"

Georgina, taken aback, stepped closer to the counter.

"A tenner."

Kyle pulled a crumpled ten euro note out of his wallet and laid it on the counter.

"Thanks," he said and walked back out onto the street. He caught his reflection in the window of the clothes shop next door and walked straight in. Trying to keep his head down, Kyle walked over to the rack with hats and caps on it and bought a dark-grey woolly cap that reminded him of one he had worn as a teenager on a trip to Norway.

It was a bit easier after that. The hat covered his shaved head with its bandages as well as the cut on his forehead. Judging by his face, he might as well have been in a fistfight at the weekend, except of course for the people who knew him – and in a small town, there were lots of them. His parents had been well known, his father being an estate agent and his mother being a clairvoyant when she felt like it. Psychic she was not, no matter what the papers said.

Kyle dropped into a newsagent's in the outskirts of town and bought a bottle of Coke and a Mars bar. He was not hungry or thirsty, but it was a long walk home and he needed to keep his sugar levels up.

He had not even thought of his mobile for almost two days.

He reached out for it in the inside pocket of his jacket only to find that the battery was dead. Sure, it had been low on Saturday night. The last activity was probably the call to his parents...

He picked up his pace on the side of the road. It wasn't quite lunch time yet, but it would get dark early, and he wasn't exactly dressed for a walk in the dark countryside in his black leather jacket. Let alone that his hands were going to fall off with the cold. Not that he would mind that; maybe the physical pain of frost-bite would take his mind off things...

A couple of miles up the road, the houses got fewer and further apart. It was quiet except for a light wind in the trees and a dog barking some distance away. He didn't normally notice the silence around. He almost always had his earphones on, plugged into his phone. The earphones were still there in his pocket but not much use with the phone dead.

A couple of cars passed him on their way to wherever they were going. The cold air was seriously starting to get to him, and his head was beginning to ache. Kyle pulled the Mars bar out of his pocket and started chewing on it.

About halfway there Kyle started to realise that walking home had not been a good idea. He should have called Cassie, or even a cab. No chance of doing that now. He felt weak, his head was pounding, and the elbow that was not meant to be seriously injured was starting to feel like a knife was stuck into it.

He had just decided to sit down on the stone wall along the road when a silver BMW pulled up beside him.

"Kyle? What are you doing walking around here? It's freezing. Hop in!"

Oh, the neighbours. He hadn't thought of them. Had it been somebody else, Kyle would have thought that they were just after the gossip as well, but Moira McKinley was not like that.

She was possibly the nicest person he had ever met, and she had looked after the French kids when they still needed babysitting.

"Did you walk all the way back from town? And no gloves! Oh, what are you like!" Mrs McKinley yanked up the heating inside the car and Kyle stuck his hands right up to the vents.

"You should have gotten a lift. How did you get to town?"

"Iris gave me a lift," Kyle said, blowing on his fingers. "Iris is…"

"Ah, I know Iris. Michael McGloin's daughter. Your father's very fond of her, you know? Not in a bad way, but she's a great girl is Iris."

Kyle was grateful that Moira did not correct herself for talking about his father in present tense.

"Are you kids OK for everything for tonight?" she asked when they got closer to the house.

Kyle nodded. Moira pulled into the French house's driveway. Kyle put his hand on the door handle but turned back towards Moira.

"The funeral's on Friday. I don't know what time yet…"

"You'll get a lift off me and John, sure. Don't want you driving on a day like that."

"I'll get Cassie to give you a shout," Kyle said, getting out of the car.

For the second time that day, he walked up to the front porch with a sense of foreboding.

"Where the hell have you been?" Cassie stood in the hall with her arms crossed when Kyle came in. "We've been worried sick. And your phone's dead!"

"I know," Kyle said, heading towards the stairs.

"You shouldn't go off on your own like that! You're not fully recovered…"

"Yes, sis," Kyle said in a mocking tone and pulled his cap off.

12

"What the hell…" Cassie shrieked at the sight of his bald head. "You can't go to the funeral looking like that!"

"I could hardly go looking the way I did either," he defended himself and carried on up the steps.

Kyle's room was at the back of the house, looking onto a small forest and a couple of fields with a flock of sheep, normally, and occasionally some horses grazing on it. Ciara had always envied him for having the view of the field with horses in it. He couldn't give a shit about the view, but he didn't want to give up the room.

His room had a dark wooden floor with pale-coloured walls. Duck egg, his mother used to say it was called. The double bed was walnut and a little grown-up for his taste, although very comfortable. The desk beside the door and the wardrobe opposite the bed were of the same set. He hadn't had much of a say in the decor of the room, although he had insisted on framing his signed Slipknot poster and putting it above the bed.

He knew that something was missing as soon as he came in. Of course it was missing; nobody had been worried about it when they left the club on Saturday. Donal probably still had it, and he'd better return it in mint condition.

Kyle plugged his phone in to charge, and as soon as he was able to turn it on, the texts started flowing in. There were voicemails too. What did all these people want? To revel in his loss? To congratulate him on his survival? To offer their condolences? To find out what had really happened? To ask if he needed anything?

He threw his jacket in a corner and lay down on the bed. He hadn't realised how tired he was, not until his head hit the pillow…

CHAPTER 2

He woke up late the following morning. He had gotten up a couple of times since the previous afternoon, to grab something to eat or to just stretch his legs, but he hadn't spoken to anybody. He hadn't seen either of his sisters when he had been downstairs. They must have gone to take care of whatever needed to be done.

This time, Ciara was standing in the doorway and Wanda's black face, going grey with age, was peeking over the edge of the bed.

"Donal's here to see you," Ciara said, tapping her leg to call Wanda away.

"Right."

The pair disappeared from the room, and Kyle sat up on the bed. It was raining outside, and the room felt chilly. Nobody had bothered with the heating, let alone starting a fire. Their mother normally had a fire going during the day; she was old-fashioned like that.

Kyle made his way downstairs and found Donal sitting at the kitchen table with a cup of tea. Kyle sat down where another mug of steaming tea was waiting, along with a bowl of cereal.

"She's good to you, Ciara," Donal said, with a nod towards the sitting room where the low sound of TV could be heard.

"Hmm," Kyle said, getting stuck into the cereal. He realised he hadn't brushed his teeth since the previous morning, and it started to become obvious. The cereal just didn't taste right.

"I'm sorry about what happened, man," Donal said. He looked completely out of place holding a flowery mug and trying to act all correct. He was more at home with a cold pint and having a laugh down the pub.

Kyle said nothing.

"I brought your bass back," Donal said, nodding at the case leaning against the doorway. "I'm sure it's all right. Tony played it Saturday night."

Kyle gave Donal a quizzing look.

"You know we used to play in the same band, so with you gone, he jumped on board. He knew most of the songs anyway, we used to play some of mine together and he obviously knew the covers… Just made sense." Donal shrugged his shoulders.

"He played instead of me?" Kyle could feel an unreasonable anger building up inside of him.

"Yeah. We didn't want to cancel, and he was there. No biggie."

"So, you replaced me, just like that?" Kyle clicked his fingers to make a point.

"It was just one gig," Donal said with a frown.

"Just one gig," Kyle mumbled back sarcastically before another spoonful of cereal.

"Although… We were thinking… Maybe it would be better if you took a break for a while. I mean, with everything that's happened…"

"So, you're kicking me out of the band now?"

"We're not kicking you out," Donal said, tracing the seams of the table with his index finger, "just giving you a break."

"In other words, you're kicking me out." Kyle pushed the bowl away. He had lost even the little appetite that he'd had.

15

"Tony can cover for you for a while."

"Fuck off!" Kyle stood up, his eyes blazing in Donal's direction. "I don't need a break. Tony can piss off!"

Donal looked up at him and started getting up from his seat.

"Fair enough then. I guess I'll see you at rehearsals on Friday." He started walking towards the front door.

"The funeral's on Friday." Kyle reached out to run his fingers through his hair, the way he did when he was upset, only to find that there was nothing there.

"Right. Well, the Friday after then."

The door banged shut behind Donal. Kyle kicked at the guitar case on the floor and moved to put his unfinished tea and cereal in the sink. He badly needed a shower, a shave, a change of clothes. And a toothbrush.

* * *

The rest of the week passed painfully slowly, quietly. They ate the pizzas that Iris had brought, and the girls made an effort to cook chicken curry on Wednesday night. Come Thursday, the panic started to kick in with the funeral arrangements. Kyle kept well out of the way, his only effort being to advise Cassie to get caterers in to look after the food after the funeral.

There was to be no wake, much to the shock of some of the family and friends of Marcus and Maureen French. Ciara and Kyle didn't want to see their parents laid out in their coffins. Ciara wanted to remember them the way they were in life, not in death, and Kyle didn't think he would ever remember them as they were alive, the only image of his parents in his head being of the first few seconds after the crash, and of trying to get out of the car. One of the eye-witnesses in a newspaper article had said that he had been screaming, but he couldn't remember that. All he seemed to remember was a deafening silence, as if he had been the only person alive in the whole world.

Cassie made what seemed a completely unnecessary fuss over what she was going to wear to the funeral as she had, in her haste to get over from London on hearing the news, not thought of packing anything black. Although her long-term boyfriend Rob was coming over Friday morning, Cassie didn't trust him to bring appropriate clothes for her and spent hours around town with Ciara, looking for a black dress.

Cassie drove up to Dublin airport in their mother's little car on Friday morning to collect Rob. Ciara was busying around the kitchen, dining room and sitting room, trying to get everything organised for the caterers. Mrs McKinley came over around 11 to help her, but she ended up sending Ciara upstairs to get dressed instead. Kyle spent the morning moping around, with a nervous Wanda following him wherever he went.

Cassie got back with Rob around half 11. Rob gave Kyle a sympathetic pat on the back. Kyle had never been fond of Rob. He was a bit of an oddball, with long, greasy-looking hair even when it was washed, and he was tall, lanky and ugly. In all honesty, Kyle had expected Cassie to do better.

About 15 minutes later everybody came back downstairs, dressed for the occasion. Rob had changed into a black suit that looked slightly creased after the journey. Cassie was dressed in her new dress and had wrapped herself up in a furry coat. Ciara looked small and young for her 17 years in her black clothes. Kyle felt like a right fool in his black trousers and plain black shirt. It had never occurred to him that he would have to go outside and wear a jacket. He grabbed his leather jacket as an afterthought on the way out the door, stuffing it under his arm on the way to the McKinleys' SUV. Cassie would not approve of his leather jacket, but would hardly make a scene once they got to the church.

The funeral passed by in a blur. Afterwards, Kyle faintly remembered carrying his father's coffin along with one of his uncles, his father's older brother being too fragile to help. It started to rain when the coffins were lowered to their graves. He glanced around at that point, and everybody's chin seemed to be hidden inside a scarf or high collar to keep away the cold. Everything around was black, except the white tissues that women kept pulling out of their handbags. Cassie wept loudly, with Rob trying to comfort her with his arm around her shoulders. Ciara, standing next to Kyle, cried silently and had no tissues.

A lot of people came over and offered their condolences. Kyle didn't know half of them. Many of them were probably his father's business acquaintances. Iris was among them and said she would drop by at the house. Eventually Kyle recognised Donal and a couple of his other mates in the crowd. They wisely kept their distance, because Kyle couldn't see them being able to say anything that wouldn't have been offensive or downright thoughtless.

Back at the house, the caterers had laid out what looked like a smorgasbord. There were sandwiches, casseroles, salads, salmon rolls, cheese, crackers. There was a lot of tea and coffee, and fruit juice for the few kids that were around. People had brought stuff to try to help them; ham, bags of coal for the fire, candles, fish, wine. As if they were going to run out of supplies just because their parents were gone.

Kyle realised halfway through the day that he had never reported back to his college after the weekend. It had never even crossed his mind, and he hadn't bothered checking the messages on his phone. Time seemed to have been moving at a different pace for the last week. Once college did reach his mind though, through a mindless enquiry of one of his aunts, he couldn't shake it off. Studies in creative media didn't seem very important on the grand scale of things. He was halfway through the course and had enjoyed it up until then.

It seemed to be hours before the house was empty of people, including the caterers collecting their bits and pieces. Eventually it was just the three of them in the sitting room. Ciara was curled up in a recliner chair by the window, with her shoes on the floor and her feet stuck under her. For the first time all day, Cassie was alone without Rob and looked miserable on the two-seater. Kyle was sitting in a corner of the three-seater, staring at the fire that somebody, probably Moira from next door, had lit during the day. He glanced up at the clock on the mantelpiece. It was quarter to nine.

"Where's Rob?" he asked. He didn't know why he'd asked, because he didn't really care.

"He's gone to get a Chinese." Cassie didn't bother looking up. Her eyes were red and puffy.

"A Chinese?" Kyle said disbelievingly.

"Yeah. We need to eat."

Kyle didn't agree. He'd had plenty to eat during the day, even if he hadn't tasted most of it.

"Have you taken your meds?" Cassie asked. She rubbed her eyes. He should have warned her not to look in the mirror or she would freak out.

He nodded and got up from the couch. Wanda, who had been dozing off beside the fireplace, tired from all the commotion of the day, got up, stretched, and walked off towards the patio door. Kyle let her have her way and followed her onto the patio.

Without the light, it was pitch black outside. Looking back

towards the sitting room, it was pretty dark there too, except for the fire burning away. It was quiet, too. Some large bird, a pheasant probably, took off in the nearby bushes, causing Wanda to stiffen and let out a low growl. It was still drizzling down. The darkness was momentarily pierced by the lights of a passing car. Then he heard the sound of another engine, pulling up into the driveway. It was his mother's Golf, he could tell by the sound. So could Wanda. Her fan of a tail started wagging enthusiastically, and for a moment Kyle was caught in her fantasy. It was his mother coming back from a shopping trip to Dublin, or maybe from doing tarot cards in town. Not bothering to cook dinner, she would have brought Chinese. She would have got sweet and sour chicken for him, and plenty of prawn crackers for everybody to share. Afterwards, she would pull out a tub of ice cream from the freezer and they'd have dessert although they were all too full to enjoy it. They all loved Chinese food, except dad, who was a more traditional eater and would insist on sticking to a chicken curry with chips.

Wanda was waiting outside the patio door to get back in. Some light was filtering into the sitting room from the dining room, where Rob was standing with two bags bearing the logo of the local Chinese take-away. He put the bags down on the table and waved at Kyle to come in and join them. The girls were already making their way towards the dining room.

Kyle opened the door and saw the visible disappointment on Wanda's short, round face when she saw Rob instead of her mistress. Unlike the dog, who was quickly re-livened by the smell of the food on the table, Kyle felt let down as he made his way into the dining room. Yes, there were plenty of prawn crackers and a sweet and sour chicken with fried rice for him, even a can of Bulmers, but his mother wasn't there, nor his father jokingly giving out to them for unhealthy eating habits. They never would be again, either.

* * *

The following day was quiet. Kyle spent most of the day up in his room watching TV. He didn't want to see people, not that they took the hint. Cassie came up twice, Rob tried once. Ciara left him alone, except bringing him a sandwich halfway through the day. Everybody kept asking if he'd taken his injections, like he would suddenly forget after five years. They were silently blaming him for everything. Well, maybe not Ciara. She wasn't the type to carry a grudge.

Rob cooked the dinner that night. Roast chicken with mash, broccoli and pepper sauce. Kyle hated broccoli but knew that Cassie would give out to him for breaking out of his healthy diet and being rude to Rob, who had only tried his best. The chicken was slightly burned and crispy on top. Kyle missed his mother's succulent roast chicken. It was never had with mash either, but with vegetables and spuds cooked in the tray with the chicken.

After dinner Cassie and Rob suggested that they order a film on Box Office and watch it together. Kyle was getting ready to protest, but Ciara got there first, saying that she was going out to see a friend. Cassie interjected, saying it wasn't a good idea under the circumstances. They should all stay together.

"You're worried about a nervous breakdown in public, aren't you?" Kyle remarked, lifting his feet up onto the couch. Ciara looked shocked first, but then the corners of her mouth turned up slightly.

"I think we've spent too much time together. I just want to get out."

"I'm not taking you into town," Cassie said, raising her glass of white wine. Rob looked on in silence, the outsider that he was.

"I'm getting a lift."

"And how do you plan on getting home?"

"I've got friends to stay with."

"Can I go with you?" Kyle jumped in before Cassie came up with more excuses. "Into town, I mean."

"I don't need a babysitter," Ciara groaned.

"Not that Kyle would be much good at it anyway," Cassie sighed.

"I've no interest in babysitting anyone, I just want a lift."

"Sure. He'll be here at eight." Ciara turned on her heels and left the room.

"He? Has she got a boyfriend?" Cassie turned towards Kyle.

He shrugged. He didn't keep tabs on his little sister's comings and goings, and it wasn't like Cassie hadn't already had boyfriends at her age.

Kyle made his way upstairs, had a shower and got changed. It felt like ages since he had dressed in anything normal, like jeans and a T-shirt. He still hated looking at himself in the mirror, so he didn't. He picked a jacket with a hood instead, though, not wanting people staring at his bandages while he was outside.

Ciara's friend was very punctual. He beeped the horn at eight o'clock on the dot. Ciara ran out to the car, not waiting for Kyle to follow. He sat down in the backseat and was faced with a suspicious look from the driver.

"Yeah, I forgot to say. This is my brother Kyle. He just wants a lift into town. Is that OK?"

"Yeah." The driver turned around in the front seat and offered his hand.

"Ronan."

He was probably just about 18, with short, dark hair. He had one of those faces that one won't remember the day after.

Ciara and Ronan seemed to get on like a house on fire and were chatting happily all the way into town, a bit too happily all things considered. Kyle was glad that Cassie wasn't there. She had started to fancy herself as their new mother, despite being only five years older than Kyle and eight years older than Ciara.

"We're going to the cinema; can I drop you off here?" Ronan said, pulling up at the parking lot behind the cinema.

"Grand," Kyle said, getting out of the car. Ronan carried on into the back of the car park, and Kyle turned his back on his old piece-of-shit of a car and started heading towards Juice. It was their usual spot on a Saturday night, except, of course, the Saturday before.

Although it was early, there was a good crowd inside the pub. Kyle spotted Donal straight away but didn't go over. Donal was not in his good books right now; besides, he seemed to be having a great time chatting up some blonde at the big table at the back. He thought the longhaired fella with him was Tony but wasn't too sure. He had never met Tony properly, and now he didn't want to meet his rival bassist.

He went up to the bar, got his cider and was making his way towards a couple of guys he'd gone to school with when he was stopped by a girly shriek. It was Mel. Again. Was no place safe from her?

"Oh, Kyle, I didn't think we'd see you out so soon," she purred into his ear to block out the music that seemed to be blasting particularly loud that night.

She looked well; there was no doubt about that. She was wearing her trademark sky-high red heels, paired with a matching red mini dress so short that he was relieved she was wearing leggings underneath.

"Yeah, well, I can't be stuck at home forever," he said, pushing

23

his hood off his head. The girl let out an infatuated giggle, as if he'd said something hilarious. She was not the brightest star in the sky.

"Come on, come join us over there. It's Eliza's birthday." She grabbed his arm, the sore one, but he didn't want to cry out in pain and risk being taken for a wimp.

Eliza was a chubby, slightly red-haired girl celebrating her 21st. It didn't surprise Kyle – Melanie came across as the kind of person who only selected friends who were less good-looking than her, so that she could remain the centre of attention at all times.

Kyle sat down on the couch, sandwiched between a girl he wasn't introduced to and the all-too-keen Mel. Across the table sat another girl, presumably beside her boyfriend, whose hand she was holding onto despite him being deep in conversation with the only other male in the party.

"I can't believe you got your hair all shaved off! It looks so weird," Mel said, running her hand across his scalp.

"Going for the rough look, are ya?" the girl on his other side grinned.

"I don't mind a bit of rough tough," Melanie cooed.

"Is it bad? Underneath those things," the other one said with a vague wave towards the bandages on his head.

Kyle shrugged. He seemed to have lost his will to talk.

"Is your hair gonna grow back? I loved those highlights you had," Mel carried on. Kyle started to feel slightly claustrophobic with no way away from the table.

"Yeah. In time." He took a sip of his drink.

A lot of girly chat followed. Kyle couldn't get into a conversation with the other two lads because he couldn't hear what they were talking about. In any case, they didn't seem a bit interested in talking to him.

A couple of drinks later, Mel left the table to go and "powder her nose", and Kyle was left alone with the girl who still had not been introduced to him.

"So, was your mum really a psychic?" she asked, leaning towards him.

"A clairvoyant," Kyle corrected.

"Yeah, same thing." She waved him off and was going to carry on.

"She read tarot cards, that kind of thing," Kyle explained, but his words fell on deaf ears.

"How come she didn't know then?"

Kyle froze in his seat.

"Didn't know what?"

"That it was gonna happen?" The girl seemed insistent in the way people were when they'd had too many drinks. Kyle couldn't even bring himself to look at her.

"It's not how it works," he said through gritted teeth.

"Yeah, but she can tell the future, right?"

"There was no future to tell. Excuse me." Kyle squeezed himself out from behind the table and went up to the bar.

"You not talking to me then?"

Kyle swirled around to face Donal.

"You kicked me out of the band," he reminded him, grabbing his bag of crisps and pint of cider off the bar.

"For one last time," Donal sighed, "we didn't kick you out of the band. I just think you need some time to get your head together."

"Maybe all I need to keep my head together is to do normal things, like play in the band," Kyle retorted.

"Look, Kyle, you're a good bass player, and you're welcome back anytime you want. Just take a break for a while." Donal slammed him on the shoulder in what he must have thought was an encouraging gesture.

"Now, if you want to do something normal," Donal said, lowering his voice and leaning in, "that chick fancies the pants off you, she does. It would be a shame not to nab her."

Kyle didn't need to ask who he meant.

"Come over when you're ready," Donal said with a wink and walked back towards his corner.

Kyle returned to the table, where Mel was eagerly awaiting his return.

"You hungry?" she asked enthusiastically when Kyle ripped open the bag of crisps.

"No," he said, stuffing a handful of cheese and onion crisps into his mouth.

"Ugh, cheese and onion," said the anonymous one who had annoyed Kyle only a few minutes earlier. It hadn't crossed his mind – cheese and onion crisps could stink the place out and were never much good for a fresh breath. Still, they were the only thing available.

For better or worse, the crisps didn't seem to put Mel off.

"If the boy's hungry, he must eat," she said with a flirty look in his direction.

Kyle found himself wolfing down the bag of crisps and trying to drown the aftertaste with his drink. Everything started to seem a bit blurry around him, kind of like an out-of-body experience. He was half-aware of Mel sitting practically in his lap and that he had a great view of her chest, but he didn't care. He stumbled into the toilets and back. He didn't feel right at all, not even when he sat back down. He was distantly aware that Mel was trying to say something into his ear. Next thing he felt a tap on his shoulder, and Donal was handing him a glass of orange juice. Everybody around seemed amused by it. When he had finished his OJ, Donal pulled him up, again by the sore arm, and started to lead him outside.

* * *

When he opened his eyes, Cassie was standing in the doorway with her arms crossed. She was cross. He pulled himself up on the bed. The wall clock was pointing at around 10. The window was open, and chilly air was streaming in. It was a stormy day.

"What happened?" He squinted up at Cassie. The last thing he could remember was being dragged out of the pub.

"You drank too much, that's what happened. Again."

That made sense. His head was sore, and he didn't feel great. That was normal, though, nowadays.

"Your friend Donal called me to come and get you. You remember what happened the week before?" Cassie was seriously pissed off.

"It wasn't the same. I had been eating..."

"Yeah, well, the last time Donal called when you needed a lift, do you remember what happened?" She was downright screaming now. He wasn't listening though. He needed to get up and run to the toilet...

Cassie didn't move from the doorway while Kyle was examining the insides of the toilet. When he returned, feeling even more miserable, she swirled around to head back downstairs.

"I have sausage rolls and tea downstairs for you. Will you be OK?" Despite her sarcasm, there was a note of concern in her voice too.

"Fine," Kyle said, sitting down on his bed. He grabbed the insulin injector out of the drawer of his bedside locker and pulled down his jeans. He'd never understood how some people voluntarily injected drugs into their system. He'd been dealing with this for five years and still didn't like the idea. And he was doing it for health reasons, not trying to kill himself.

Cassie was down in the kitchen when Kyle got there. There was a pile of warm sausage rolls on a plate, a cup of tea and an orange on the table. He didn't feel the least bit hungry, but eating was still the best thing to do.

"Where's your sister?" Cassie asked. She was taking clean dishes out of the dishwasher, drying them as she went along and peering at them suspiciously in case they weren't properly clean.

"Don't know. Has she not come home?"

"She's not in her room. Was she not getting a lift back?"

"I didn't ask." Kyle broke a bit off a sausage roll and handed it to Wanda, who swallowed it in one go.

"She's gonna get fat," Cassie said, nodding at the dog. "You should keep an eye on your sister."

"She's your sister too."

"Well, you went into town with her though, didn't you?"

"She said she might stay over."

"And who with? Was that her boyfriend who picked you up last night?"

Kyle shrugged. Ciara was plenty old enough to look after herself.

"I'm gonna call her. I need to drop Rob off to the airport anyway; I'll pick her up on my way back."

Cassie hung the tea towel carefully back on its hook before walking out of the room.

Kyle was quietly pleased. He would finally have some peace and quiet for a while with nobody in the house.

Yet, when he came back downstairs after having a shower and getting changed and Rob and Cassie had left, he didn't know what to do. The house was too quiet. He brought his iPod downstairs, plugged it into the stereo and yanked up the volume. The house was filled with noise, but there was no more life to it.

He walked into his father's study next to the sitting room. It looked like he had just left it for the weekend, maybe for a holiday. His laptop was sitting on the desk next to a couple of house brochures. A purple tie was loosely rolled up at a corner of the desk. That's probably where he had left it getting home from work the Friday before. Their mother had surprised him that evening. Some acquaintance of hers had given her two tickets to the theatre for Saturday night. They weren't big into that kind of thing, they were more of the type to go for a nice meal in a restaurant, but it had been something different. Kyle couldn't have cared less for going to the theatre and was not the least bit offended that there weren't enough tickets for Ciara and him. He'd had other plans for that Saturday night anyway.

And that was just it. Maybe if he hadn't had other plans, he would either have stayed at home or possibly been persuaded to go with them, if there were still tickets. But there was the gig that night... It was his first live performance with Ulterior Motive. He'd only played with them for three months, and he'd been too nervous to eat that night. Then he'd had too many bracers, considering that he'd not had anything to eat, and his blood sugar had dropped... In fairness to Donal, he had done the right thing calling his parents... He wished he hadn't, though. He really wished he hadn't.

Kyle collapsed onto the high-backed chair behind the desk. He just couldn't help it. Tears started pouring down his face, accompanied by loud sobs. He hadn't cried a drop since the crash, not even at the hospital. It was possible he had cried on the way there, but he couldn't remember. Not crying had made him feel so inhuman, as if he didn't care at all. His sisters had no idea what he had been through. They might have done all the worrying when it came to the funeral and organising everything legally, but he had been there when it happened. They hadn't even asked about it, nobody had. It was as if it didn't matter; after all, he had survived, hadn't he, with only superficial injuries.

It didn't last long, the crying. The tears dried up after a few minutes, but he felt a lot better, sort of lighter.

He walked over to the sitting room and threw more coal into the fire. It was brightening up outside, but it was still stormy. The apple trees in the back garden were bending in the wind, young as they were. There were more memories right there, planted with the trees. He had helped his mother pick those trees in the garden centre and then plant them in the garden. Cassie had been the age when doing anything with her parents would have been seriously uncool, and Ciara had been too young. She had appreciated the help, although probably not the mess that he had made of his clothes. It had been worth it in the years that had followed. She had made lovely apple tart out of those apples – well, of the ones that weren't too worm-eaten. She had never been a great gardener.

The front door opened up, and Wanda trotted to the hall to welcome the arrival. Soon Ciara showed up in the doorway.

"Can you turn that down?" she mouthed over the music. She had never shared his love for loud music. Kyle did as he was asked. She looked tired, although a happier kind of tired than she had been for the past week. Her make-up was smudged and her top was crumpled.

"I'm starving, do you want something?" she asked, wobbling her way into the kitchen in shoes that must have been uncomfortable to begin with. Why did women put themselves through all that pain?

"No, thanks." Kyle sat down on the recliner and started mindlessly leafing through a TV guide. It was a week old.

"Has Cassie gone to drop Rob off?" Ciara asked, carrying a massive sandwich into the room.

"Yeah."

"She's taking all this really bad, isn't she? She called me this morning and was screaming down the phone. It's like we're reporting to her now, huh?" Ciara's mouth was full of sandwich, and it was hard to make out what she was saying. "I mean, mum was never like that."

"She's not our mum," Kyle pointed out, walking over to the fireplace and chucking the TV magazine in.

"Do you think she's gonna stay?" Ciara asked, eyeing him from behind her sandwich.

"I guess she has to, for a while. Sort everything out."

"I meant for good." Ciara licked her fingers clean of left-over coleslaw.

"She can't do that. She's got a job, and Rob."

"That rhymes," Ciara said with a flicker of her eyebrows.

"You're in a good mood today," Kyle pointed out.

She sighed. "I guess it will come and go, won't it? I was miserable all day yesterday, until..." She seemed to bite her tongue to shut herself up.

"Until Ronan called you?" Kyle didn't know where that came from. Although it was obvious really...

"Yeah. Until Ronan called," Ciara admitted with a blush. "Please don't say anything to Cassie, will you? She'd just make a big deal out of it, and I know she had boyfriends when she was my age."

Kyle wanted to point out that they'd had parents then, but that would have been unkind. They'd had parents whenever Ciara had started seeing Ronan – maybe they had even known about him.

"And I'm sure you've had girlfriends too," Ciara said with a teasing smirk.

"No, I haven't," Kyle spoke up.

"Is that right? Because Cassie said that last night, when she came to pick you up from the pub, there was some slapper glued to your side."

"Some slapper?"

"Her words, not mine," Ciara said, taking a sip of her tea.

"She's not my girlfriend," Kyle corrected hastily. Had she really been there? Oh fuck...

"Well then, it must be a fitting description of her," Ciara replied cheerfully.

"Whatever," Kyle said, trying to hide his awkwardness by looking intently at the blazing fire.

"Unless it's the other way around. I know you never bring them home, but..."

"Hey!" Ciara shrieked when a cushion hit her and sent tea down her shiny top. She wasn't slow to respond. She put her cup down and grabbed another cushion, which swiftly went flying towards Kyle. Soon the room was full of flying cushions, giggles and barks with Wanda trying to catch the cushions that were well above her head.

That's when Cassie walked in.

"What are you doing?"

Feeling guilty, Kyle and Ciara dropped down their cushions.

"What am I going to do with you? You're acting like two little kids." Cassie slumped down onto the two-seater.

"I think we deserve a bit of fun," Ciara said defensively.

"It seems you've had a good bit of it recently," Cassie said, looking from Ciara to Kyle and back. "Where were you last night?" she asked her younger sister.

"Just out in the cinema."

"You didn't come home though. Were you drinking?"

"I had one or two, yeah," Ciara said with a blush.

"Oh, leave her be," Kyle butted in.

"Yeah? And who are you to say? If it wasn't for Donal, you'd probably be lying in a ditch somewhere, and we'd be looking to arrange another funeral."

"Don't be so morbid, Cassie," Ciara said with a note of pleading in her voice.

"Go on and blame me," Kyle said, ignoring Ciara's worried looks.

"If it wasn't for you having all that drink..."

"Cassie, please..."

"...and you haven't even shed a tear for their sakes. I have worked my ass off to keep everything going in the past week, with no help from you at all."

"You really think you've had the hardest time of us all, don't you?" Kyle said sarcastically. Ciara had sat down, glancing back and forth between her brother and sister.

"I do! It's like babysitting two little kids, it's like I'm your mother."

"You're not our mum," Ciara said in a voice so low it was almost a whisper.

"You think that's the hardest part of it all?" Kyle kept starting at his older sister. Cassie didn't reply; she just kept glaring right back at him.

"I saw mum and dad die."

Kyle's words were followed by a deathly silence.

"I thought you were unconscious," Ciara finally said.

Kyle shook his head.

"They said you were screaming," Ciara said, now a little louder.

"Unconscious people can't scream," Kyle pointed out. Actually, he didn't have a clue if that was true.

"Was it…" Cassie bit her lip before carrying on. "Was it because you were in pain or because you knew they were…" She wasn't able to say it. She was looking at Kyle but couldn't look up into his face.

"I can't remember." Kyle leaned back in his chair, pulled up his feet and turned to look out the window.

He didn't remember. He didn't remember everything that had happened, but his sisters hadn't even known he'd seen it.

CHAPTER 3

He had a restless night that night. Cassie had told them later in the evening that they would have to go to see the solicitor in the morning, all of them. He hadn't thought it had affected his nerves, but he had been wrong.

He dreamt that he was sitting in the backseat of a car. He didn't know who was driving, either there was nobody there or he just couldn't see their faces. The road was wet and slippery, and there was sharp bend after sharp bend, and at every bend, very close to the road, was a big rock. It seemed to come closer at each turn, and the car wasn't slowing down.

He woke up drenched in sweat. He flicked on the light on the bedside table because he didn't like the look of his room in the dark anymore.

The wall clock pointed at half five.

Was this going to start happening all the time now? Nightmares, not being able to sleep, waking up in the early hours of the morning. Maybe he was going to be haunted. What if they were going to come back to blame him for what had happened?

Kyle got up abruptly and felt the chill night air on his skin. He needed to have a cold shower. He didn't believe in ghosts.

* * *

Kyle felt out of place at the solicitors. He hadn't realised that he should have dressed smartly for it. The two girls were all dolled up as if going out on a date, whereas he was wearing torn jeans and a shapeless jumper. To his utter surprise, Cassie hadn't said a word about his appearance.

Mr O'Connor was in his forties and dressed in a suit, as solicitors supposedly always did; Kyle wasn't sure, since he'd never met one before. He shook hands with them all and expressed his sympathy.

Most of what he said went past Kyle's understanding. It was all legal jargon. Cassie asked a lot of questions, but then, she understood what he was talking about since legal bullshit was part of her job too. The wills included all their full names, much to their embarrassment.

"...to my eldest daughter, Cassandra Dahlia French..."

"...to Ciara Louisa Jewel French..."

"...to my son, Kyle Parker Abraham French."

Kyle realised that everybody's eyes were on him. He slowly retraced the last words he had heard but not registered. The house. The solicitor had been talking about the house.

"The house at Oakhill. He's leaving it to you, Kyle," Mr O'Connor said, nodding at him with a slight smile.

They had to sign some papers after that. It was all more jargon that made no sense to him. He heard the solicitor saying that it would "take some time to get everything sorted out".

On the way out, Cassie shook her head with an odd smile.

"That's so like dad."

Ciara and Kyle looked at her, bemused.

"Leaving the house to Kyle. So traditional. Leave the house to the oldest son."

"I don't want the house," Kyle remarked. He remembered his thoughts on that Monday morning, only one week ago. He thought the house was ugly. It didn't even have that warm and fuzzy feeling inside anymore.

"Well, you're getting it, whether you want it or not," Cassie said, sitting down in the car.

"I think dad was right. What would you do with the house, I mean, you live in London. And I'd be lost with it. I'm too young to have a house." Ciara was sitting in the back, leaning her elbow on the armrest and her chin on her palm.

"You'll change your mind in the years to come," Cassie said, carefully reversing the car out of the space.

* * *

Kyle woke up again in the middle of the night, sweat pouring down his face and his eyes darting to and fro in the room. He had flicked the light on as soon as he woke up, but there was a chill in the room that he didn't like, especially as he was still roasting. He didn't have a clue what he had been dreaming of.

He tried to lie down again, pulling the duvet down to waist level. He left the light on but couldn't get back to sleep. His thoughts were running wild, unusually so for four o'clock in the morning. It crossed his mind that he still had not contacted his college to tell them what had happened. They probably knew, since the incident had been all over the papers. The local paper had even found a picture of him from a couple of years back, horrid as it was.

His thoughts turned to the newspaper articles that he had so painstakingly tried to avoid. Nothing had ever come out of the couple of attempts of trying to make their mother an actual psychic. There was no truth in the claims. She had always been interested in all things spiritual – making her a very odd match for their father, whose feet were firmly on the ground – and had enjoyed reading tarot cards and had ventured into a bit of palm reading and dream interpreting as well. It didn't mean that she would have known something was going to happen.

Kyle turned over onto his other side and stared at the curtained window for a while. What was it that Mel's friend had said in the pub? Should she not have known something was going to happen? Could he tell for sure that she hadn't? Surely if she had, she would have stopped it from happening; she would have tried to tell him not to go out that night or would have packed a bag full of snacks before he did. Or she might have driven the car, although she hated driving at night.

Kyle sat up in bed suddenly. She had always kept a diary of her dreams and other things worth noting. It was probably in their room. None of them had set a foot in their parents' bedroom for fear of disturbing it. That's what he would do. Not now, though. The idea of their room in the dark of the night was too ghastly.

* * *

Cassie dropped him off at the front door of the hospital the following morning. She said that she was going to drop by at their father's office and have a chat with Iris about something.

Kyle dragged himself in, not looking forward to his appointment at all. When he announced his arrival, he was told that there was a queue and he would be waiting about 20 minutes.

Kyle walked out of the waiting area and found a quiet alcove to make a call to his college. He didn't get to speak to the right person, which was to be expected as it was in the middle of the day. He left a message. He didn't leave a number to be contacted on, not that it made much difference. If they wanted to call him back, they would have the number in their records.

He sat down in the waiting room with a number of other people. Although most of them didn't seem to notice him, a couple of them gave him curious glances. He sincerely wished that he would get rid of the ugly bandages; they were an eye-sore.

He was still holding on to his mobile. Although it was on silent, he saw the screen flash to announce the arrival of a text. He had cleared the unread messages and missed calls a few days earlier, not bothering to read any of them properly. He didn't recognise the number this one had come from, though.

"Hi Kyle. Donal told me about ur condition. I didnt no. Hope ur ok. xxxx Mel"

Oh God. Where had she gotten his number from? She would never leave him alone now. He'd be best off ignoring this one, at least for a while.

"Kyle French," a voice announced. Everybody's head seemed to perk up at that, and Kyle was unusually self-conscious walking towards the nurse.

The nurse was good-humouredly chatting away while taking off the bandages, cleaning the cuts and – to Kyle's disappointment – putting new bandages on them.

"I see you decided to get everything shaved off then. Just as well, it will all grow back the same then. It's starting to come back a bit already, a bit of stubble.

"Are they giving you any trouble then? Itchiness or anything?" the nurse carried on while inspecting the couple of stitches on top of his head.

Kyle shook his head, which was not the best idea under the circumstances.

"Good, good. You don't need to worry about the stitches; they'll dissolve in their own time, no need to take them out."

She started re-dressing the bigger cut on his head.

"I'm just going to put on smaller bandages this time. They're healing well, just keep them clean and you should have no problems. You shouldn't need to come back again. How's that elbow of yours?"

"Grand," Kyle said, trying not to wince as she twitched it to test it out. It HAD been fine up until then.

"OK. You should be good to go. If you have any issues, please don't hesitate to drop by anytime."

Kyle absent-mindedly thanked the nurse. He made his way into the gents' to have a look at the new bandages. They were smaller, but still just as ugly. However, the gash on his forehead was getting better and the other cuts on his face were no longer red. He rather looked like a cat had scratched his face or – he hoped – he'd been intimate with a hot bird. He grinned at the thought of that.

When he re-emerged in the waiting room, he spotted Cassie further down the corridor, talking to a doctor and the nurse who had looked after him. On seeing him, Cassie quickly turned away from them and wiped her eyes when approaching him.

"You OK?" she asked when they turned back towards the front door. Kyle nodded.

"I see you got smaller bandages. They're healing OK then?"

Kyle nodded again, not feeling like talking. He never did nowadays.

They were fast approaching the front doors when Cassie started slowing down.

"You know, Kyle, they think you should see a therapist."

"What?" He stopped and turned around to face her.

"You know, to help you cope with what you saw," Cassie said quietly. "We could all go, as a family, and then maybe do some private sessions too… I think we can get help with the costs."

"We're not a family," Kyle retorted, pushed his hands into his pockets and started walking again.

He made his way outside well before Cassie, who had remained standing in the corridor, stunned by Kyle's harsh words.

A man was walking up towards the door. There was nothing unusual about him, he was dressed in civilian clothes, he was dark-haired and in his forties, he barely looked at Kyle, and yet all colour drained from Kyle's face when he saw him. He froze on the spot. The all-too-familiar cold sweat grabbed him, and he felt dizzy.

"Are you OK? Is it your blood sugar? Do you want something to eat?" Cassie had arrived at his side.

Kyle was so stunned he couldn't speak.

"Come on, sit down for a moment," Cassie said, pulling him towards a bench beside the door.

Kyle did as he was told. He leaned forward for a moment, but he knew it was nothing to do with his blood sugar or his barely-there injuries.

"I know him."

"Who?" Cassie looked confused.

"He pulled me out of the car."

Kyle started to shiver all over, as if he were horribly cold, but it was quite warm in the sunshine outside and he was wearing a warm jacket.

"Who did?" Cassie was looking around.

"He just passed me there."

"Oh."

"He's an ambulance driver."

"He wasn't in uniform."

"I guess he doesn't live in it," Kyle said, his head finally starting to clear up. The image had been all too clear. He remembered it now. The ambulance driver had pulled the driver's side back door open – how, he didn't have a clue, because from what he had seen afterwards, it was badly warped. He had spoken to Kyle, tried to calm him down for he had been crying and he had been screaming. He had told him to focus on his face and he would help him out. Now, in hindsight, it was clear he had not wanted Kyle looking at his dead parents. He had thought that he hadn't seen the carnage yet and had wanted to spare him. He had pulled him out. Kyle couldn't understand now how he could ever have forgotten his face at all. It wasn't that his face was so memorable, but it was one of the most significant faces he was ever going to see in his whole life.

"You sure you're all right?" Cassie said, with a hand on his shoulder. Her face was full of concern.

"I'm fine." Kyle got up and started walking towards the car. Cassie walked close to him, as if ready to catch him if he started feeling dizzy again.

They got home after picking up some supplies from the supermarket. Cassie had promised to make shepherd's pie. She must have felt sorry for him.

Ciara had stayed home that day and had the kettle boiled when they got home.

"Somebody called for you, Kyle," she said, her head buried in the press full of mugs, except that it wasn't because most of them were in the dishwasher. She found three, mismatched but not broken. Kyle had never understood why his mother had wanted to hold on to mugs that had no handles or that were so chipped that one's lip would split every time one took a sip.

"An Angus McIntosh. Is he Scottish?"

Kyle nodded. "Half. He grew up here. What did he want?" His conscience was knocking at his temple, wanting to get in.

"He asked you to call him back. I think he wants to see you before you make any rash decisions."

Too late, Kyle thought. What's done is done.

Ciara put three chocolate chips muffins on a plate. Moira

McKinley had dropped in with them the previous day, a tray full of them.

"Who is he?" Cassie said, emerging from the hall with the shopping bags.

"He's my lecturer," Kyle said, grabbing a muffin and carefully separating the paper form from it.

"Oh. So, you've decided when to go back then," Cassie said self-assuredly, handing a box of eggs to Ciara.

"I'm not." Kyle tore a piece of the muffin and stuffed it into his mouth.

"You're not what?" Cassie said, carrying on unpacking the shopping.

"I'm not going back," Kyle specified. Ciara put the cups of tea down on the dining table, and it was just as well she did because she would have dropped them otherwise.

"YOU WHAT?" Cassie shouted, slamming a milk carton on the worktop.

"You heard me," Kyle muttered and stuffed another piece of muffin into his mouth.

"You are going back," Cassie insisted.

Ciara pretended she wasn't there, carrying on with the unpacking that Cassie had forgotten about.

"They were paying for it, were relying on you to complete your studies and be something." Cassie had her hands on her hips. It was worse than the crossed arms.

"They're not paying for it now, are they?" Kyle looked up. When he'd been a teenager, a girl he had been seeing for a while had said that he had puppy-dog eyes that no woman would ever be able to refuse. They had worked on her just fine, he remembered with a sense of victory that made the corners of his mouth twitch a little, but they would not work on his sister.

"No, YOU will. You will get your inheritance and pay for it yourself. What are you gonna do? Become a bum? Or do you think you will grow up to be a rock star?" Cassie sneered at him.

"I thought I'd get a job," he announced proudly. Not straight away, of course, but after a while. He didn't need to tell her that.

"Oh yeah? Get a job when there are thousands unemployed around the country! Good luck with that!"

Cassie turned around to stare out of the window.

"Come on, sit down," Ciara said, pulling out a chair that was a safe distance from Kyle. Cassie let out a big sigh and sat down. She took her mug and squeezed it between her two hands with such strength that Kyle wondered if she hoped it was his skull she was crushing.

"What about you, Ciara? When are you going back to college?"

Ciara blushed slightly.

"I'm not quite sure. I spoke to them last week. They said I can take as long as I need. I might go back after Christmas. Or maybe," she bit her lip nervously, glancing at Cassie before continuing, "I might take a year off and start anew next September. I mean, I was only about two months into it."

Cassie nodded. That annoyed Kyle. It was OK for Ciara to give up on college and take a year off, but not for him.

"I suppose that would make sense. What would you do for the year though?"

"I don't know. I guess I could try to find a job too."

"See. She has less qualifications than I do," Kyle pointed out.

"Yeah, and a whole lot more common sense. You're halfway through your studies." Cassie eyed Kyle from behind her mug. "Nobody's asking you to go back next week."

"And what about you?" Kyle asked. "When are you going back?"

He knew he sounded like he wanted to get rid of Cassie. He

did. She was really getting to him, acting as if she was his mother and in charge of him.

"I'm going back on Sunday."

"So soon?" Ciara sounded panicked.

Cassie nodded. "There's some stuff I have to do at work. I'll be back soon, I promise." She reached out to squeeze Ciara's hand. "And you must promise me to stay out of trouble. Aunt Lizzie will look after you anyway."

Kyle couldn't help the snort that escaped from his lips.

"What's so funny about that?" Cassie inquired.

"Nothing."

Aunt Lizzie was the last person to look after anybody. She was the only relative nearby who could call over. Their father had two brothers and three sisters, but one of their aunts had died of cancer a couple of years earlier. The brothers and the third sister lived down in Cork where their father was from, and their mother was an only child. Their two grannies were too old to be of much help, especially with one of them down south as well and the other one in a retirement home and never having learned to drive.

But Lizzie… She always forgot things, and she always had. She left behind gloves, wallets, keys, umbrellas, hats. She forgot to pick up milk on the way home from work, and the one time she had looked after them when they were small, she had forgotten to pick Cassie up from school despite remembering to collect the two younger ones from theirs. She was a mess.

"I didn't say she would move in with you, just that she will call you and drop in every now and then. She's worried about you too, and she lost a brother."

That much was true. Aunt Lizzie was two years older than their father had been, and they were the closest in the family.

That's how they had moved up from Cork originally, together.

"I like Auntie Lizzie. She always brings those little oat biscuits when she comes. They're lovely."

"When she remembers to bring them." Kyle's comment brought a stifled giggle out of Ciara.

"Well, she won't forget to visit you, I'm sure, biscuits or not," Cassie concluded, slamming her empty teacup into the sink.

* * *

It was Friday before Kyle got a chance to go looking for the diary. For some reason, he did not want to do it when the girls were around. He didn't want to talk to them about it. After all, nothing important was going to be found inside. He just wanted to see it for his own peace of mind.

Cassie and Ciara went into town on Friday afternoon to run some errands – those never seemed to run out, it was like they were forever arranging name changes on accounts here and there – and do the shopping. Kyle announced that he didn't want to go, and nobody questioned him.

He stood at the top of the stairs until he saw the Golf pull out of the driveway. It was the best spot in the house for keeping an eye on the driveway. There was a huge, tall strip of glass covering the entire front porch and staircase, making the hall and staircase bright and airy.

When he was sure that his sisters were gone, he walked over to the door leading into their parents' bedroom. It had been closed for the past two weeks, which it normally had never been. The room had remained untouched, and nobody had even mentioned what was going to be done to the room or its contents.

He pushed the door open. There were butterflies in his stomach. He had been in that room many, many times before, although less often in the last few years.

He was met with a waft of stale air, yet there was a familiar scent in it as well. He took a deep breath and stepped into the room.

Everything looked as usual. Everything was in its place. The room was not the most colourful place in the world, with a pale-coloured, fairly new carpet and cream-coloured walls. The furniture was white, and the only splashes of colour in the room were on items that were easily changed. His mother had liked to change the look of the room by changing cushions, throws and curtains, whatever was easily replaceable. The current colours were dark purple and chocolate brown.

Kyle walked over to the bed, covered with a purple satin throw. A couple of cushions were thrown over it, but the comfortable-looking pillows with their white covers had been left on show.

He let his hand run down the smooth surface of the bed. It looked like it always did, whenever he had looked into the bedroom in the last few weeks. And yet, everything was totally different.

He rubbed his eyes to stop the forming tears. He stepped over to the big window at the head of the bed and opened it to let some fresh air in. Although this window was onto the front of the house, it still had lovely views of the surrounding countryside.

Afraid of sitting on the bed, he sat down on the floor beside his mother's bedside locker. She had always slept on the right-hand side of the bed.

There was a layer of dust on the locker itself. There wasn't much on it, just a lamp with a purple shade on it – she had liked buying new shades too – a paperback copy of *Emma* – she had liked her classics – and a pair of reading glasses. They were always scattered around the house, and they were always the kind one could buy in a pound shop for a few quid. She had refused to get prescription glasses, saying that they were for old people. She had never got old. She never made it past 45.

He pulled open the only drawer. A pack of tissues, some hand cream, painkillers, and – to his disgust – a pack of condoms. At least it was only a five-pack, so they must not have been crazed sex maniacs.

He pushed the drawer closed and walked over to the wardrobe. It was a huge, built-in thing that went from floor to ceiling. Cassie had always wanted one of those things as a teenager, but their parents had refused, knowing that she would not live in the house forever.

He opened all the doors first. It was hard to believe that anybody could share a wardrobe with another person, but they had. The wardrobe was packed to the brim with their stuff – suits, skirts, dresses, shirts, waistcoats, jeans. There were boots, sandals, runners and shoes on the floor. Mainly it was his father's clothes on the left and his mother's on the right. There were hats and handbags on the top shelf. A quick inspection of the contents quickly proved that there was nothing but clothes, footwear and accessories in the wardrobe.

Kyle walked past the door of the en suite and glanced inside. There was nothing there, no storage except the unit under the sink and the shelves around the mirror. There was, however, something beside the sink itself.

He walked over and carefully touched the object. He turned it over to get a proper look. It was eye shadow. It was purple, just like everything in the bedroom and the towels hanging over the towel heater.

He remembered her wearing it that night. On the way out the

door, she had asked Ciara if it looked OK with her new purple cardigan. Ciara had laughingly approved and commended her mother on her great sense of style. Kyle remembered seeing it on her too, in the light of the hall before they had left. She had looked at him enquiringly, asked if he had enough money for a taxi home in case he couldn't get a lift or a place to stay and then handed him a 20 euro note. Then she had grabbed her handbag, he had taken his bass, and they had walked over to the car where his dad had been waiting for them.

It was all a bad idea. Very bad indeed. He looked in the round mirror above the sink – it matched the shape of the window next to it – and he hated what he saw. He didn't normally mind his looks, having been blessed with his mother's blue eyes and his father's smile, complete with a dimple to the left of his mouth. He hadn't smiled much recently, so it was like all the evidence of his father had washed away. His eyes were still there, but they were constantly puffy and surrounded by dark circles, not to mention the scratch that reached his right eye. He didn't like the look of his shaved head either. How long would it take for the hair to grow back?

He turned away from the mirror, feeling foolish about being vain when there was so much to worry about.

Kyle returned to the bedroom and looked at the chest of drawers under the small mirror, where the slanted ceiling met the wall. There were several drawers in it, but his search returned nothing useful. Evidently, they had both kept their socks and underwear in those drawers, along with some of his mother's jewellery, her tarot cards, phone chargers, a digital camera and some old receipts.

The only remaining place in the bedroom was the TV stand. There was a shelf on it, but there were only some magazines on it. The two drawers produced a couple of video tapes – now that was old-fashioned – and a pack of batteries, presumably for the remote control.

He felt deflated. If it was not in the bedroom, where on earth could it be? She never took it out of the house, so it couldn't have been in her handbag that night. Besides, the bag had been too small; he remembered it well for the 20 euro he had been given. Where were their belongings after the crash? Surely, they were entitled to get them back; there had been money and cards on them, keys, mobile phones… The usual.

Kyle closed the bedroom window and left the room. Wherever the diary was, it wasn't in there.

CHAPTER 4

C assie left on Sunday afternoon. She drove to the airport in their mother's blue Golf with Ciara and Kyle in tow. They followed her all the way up to the check-in area, where Cassie reluctantly handed over the car keys to Kyle.

"The two of you will take care of each other, right?" she said, looking over from Kyle to Ciara and back.

"We'll be fine," Ciara said, unconvincingly, with tears in her eyes, before reaching out to hug her sister.

"And you're the man of the house now," Cassie said with a pat on Kyle's upper arm.

He nodded. As much as Cassie had been annoying him over the last couple of days, he was going to miss her. He wasn't sure how he and Ciara would get on without her. He suddenly felt very young and inexperienced.

"Remember that you can call me or Aunt Lizzie whenever you need. Just don't hesitate. I'll be over soon anyway."

It was a relief from the lump in his throat to see Cassie disappear in through the gates to the security checks.

They got back to the car in the short-term car park. Kyle sat down in the driver's seat and felt panic grip his throat.

He had not driven since that night. He had sat in the car as a passenger, but being in control of the car was a different story altogether.

He started fiddling with the seat and mirrors to cover his nerves while trying to convince himself that he would be fine driving home. The roads were good and wide, it was daylight, if a little dull, and most importantly, there was no black ice.

"You OK?" Ciara said with a hint of a nervous giggle in her voice.

He really had not wanted it to show.

"Fine." He was exceedingly glad that he had kept his hood on. It was originally intended to cover the bald head he so hated, but it was now proving a good cover from Ciara's worried eyes.

"It's just… You've been fiddling with the seat and mirrors for ages."

"Well, Cassie's an entirely different shape to me and she drives in a weird position," Kyle retorted.

"Right," Ciara said, turning to look out the window.

Right. Kyle checked his mirrors, not for their angles but for actual traffic. His hands and legs were shaking, and he couldn't for the world of him imagine how he was ever going to reverse out of the space. It was quiet in the car park. There was nobody in sight, just stationary cars.

He turned the engine on. The sound of it was fairly soothing, as was the quiet chatter on the radio, although he had no idea what they were talking about.

He put his foot on the clutch and reached out for the gears. Reverse. He checked the mirrors again, and again, and once more for the sake of it. He released the handbrake. He tapped on the clutch, or so he thought, but the car started moving backwards at an alarming speed. Ciara winced, but he took no notice. He was halfway out of the space now and couldn't stop there.

The car was finally perpendicular to the parking space. He

was facing the exit. With a deep sigh, he changed the gear into first.

Once they got out of the car park with its narrow, one-way lanes and exits, he relaxed a little. When they got out of the buzzing area of the airport, he could finally breathe normally, and the sweat and shakes that had kicked in finally started to ease off.

"Are you sure you're all right?" Ciara asked.

"I'm fine."

"Just for a moment I thought you might… you know…" Ciara was looking seriously concerned.

"Really, I'm fine. I've had my injections, and I have been eating."

He felt he'd had too much to eat, since Cassie had insisted on cooking a roast chicken before she left. It had been much too early for such a heavy meal.

"I know. It was just the way you looked… You look better now."

"Thanks," Kyle said with a sudden, unexpected grin.

"Speaking of eating, what are we going to eat this evening?" Ciara reached over to flick through the radio stations.

"I thought you were looking after it," Kyle said, glancing at her from the corner of his eye. There wasn't a hope he was going to take his eyes off the road.

"No. I thought you were," Ciara said.

"We'll figure it out when we get hungry," Kyle concluded in a determined manner, although he didn't feel in the least confident about the whole cooking business.

They drove on in silence for a few minutes.

"You know Cassie wants us all to go to therapy," Ciara said then.

Kyle snorted at that. So she had decided to talk to Ciara too,

53

then. She was trying to use Ciara to talk him round, thinking that they were closer, especially now that they were living together.

"She wants us all to go. Although I don't know how that will work, with her in London."

"It won't work."

"Well, we could get a therapist here, and she could get one over there... Sure we don't all have to see the same guy."

"I'm not going to see anyone," Kyle said through gritted teeth.

"Do you not think you should?" Ciara was trying her best puppy-eyes look on him, but it didn't work on him either.

"What is he gonna say? 'So, your parents died, how do you feel about that?'"

"Don't be mean."

"Any amount of talking about it is not going to bring them back," Kyle said.

That seemed to shut her up. She knew he had a point.

* * *

The following day, he drove over to his college. He had not felt that nervous about driving this time round. He just needed to keep at it, especially as with Cassie gone, he was now the only driver in the household.

He parked the car at a good distance from the buildings, wanting to avoid the panic he had experienced in the parking lot the day before.

He pulled his hood up again when he entered the building, not wanting to be spotted by anybody he knew. He saw a good few familiar faces on his way to the office, but he kept his head down. Even without the hood, they probably wouldn't have recognised him, what with the shaved head and the grungy look he had recently acquired.

Angus McIntosh's office was in a block of a few offices. There was a young woman sitting at a desk, kind of like a receptionist. Kyle had never seen her before and had no idea what her job was.

"You're here to see Angus, aren't you?" she said with a bright smile in his direction. He dropped the hood and nodded.

"You can go on; I believe he's expecting you."

Kyle had been to Angus's office before, so he knew the way in. He knocked and entered when he got a reply.

"Ah, Kyle. I was waiting for you. Have a seat." Angus pointed at a seat opposite him at his desk.

Angus McIntosh was in his late twenties or possibly early thirties. He had long, curly, blond hair that had always made Kyle think of '80s glam rock bands, but he also had a ridiculously pretty face, in a 19th century nobleman kind of way, which made him a big hit with the female students. It was not unheard of that some girls had picked his shorter courses only for the eye candy, not because they were interested in the subject.

"I'm really sorry about what happened," Angus said, pushing away a pile of papers he had been studying.

Kyle nodded in response.

"And I was even sorrier to hear about your decision." Angus crossed his hands on his chest and looked directly at Kyle. "Are you sure you won't re-consider?"

Kyle shook his head. "It's all different now."

Angus let out a big sigh. "I understand. It is a big change, and I wouldn't wish this on anybody, and least of all you. But don't you think it might be better to have something familiar to hold on to?"

"I have. I have my sisters. And the house," Kyle said, suddenly remembering that he was to be a house owner.

"But what about your future?"

"I haven't really thought about it," Kyle muttered, looking out the window that gave onto the corridor.

"That's fair enough. Look, nobody wants to push you into anything at the moment. You can obviously take as long as you need. You can catch up."

Kyle tried to force a smile onto his face. It was a pathetic effort.

"Personally, I think it would be a real shame if you were to give up. You were doing so well, and you have potential for much more if you make an effort," Angus said with a grin, hinting at Kyle's sporadic laziness and occasionally wandering mind – and eye.

Kyle didn't know what to say. He knew that Angus was right, whatever he was saying.

"Your class mates will miss you. And what about your project?"

"They'll be fine without me," Kyle said. He wasn't convinced. George was pretty good but rarely spoke his mind, and Kate and Mary were less than reliable.

"As far as I had gathered, you were the brains behind the project." Angus looked at him with raised eyebrows.

"The brains have done their work. It just needs to be put together now," Kyle said.

"Right. Do you want to tell them, or will I?" Angus said, scribbling something on a piece of paper.

"You do," Kyle said hastily. He really didn't want to see any of his class mates.

"OK then. I certainly wish you will think about it again though. You could return after Christmas if you wanted, take some time off."

Kyle said he would reconsider. He wasn't going to, but he didn't want to say that out loud.

They shook hands, and he left the office feeling guilty. Angus was, despite his charms not working on him, his favourite lecturer, and he hated the thought of disappointing him.

He was walking past the canteen entrance when somebody called him. He had forgotten to try and sneak out unnoticed, and he had forgotten to put his hood back up.

"Oh Kyle, I'm so sorry." The words were muffled straight into his ear while a pair of arms wrapped themselves around his neck.

"You look a mess. The hair suits you though," Kate said, standing back to look at him. Her eyes were positively beaming up at him.

Kate was the last person he had wanted to see. She had a cute face, but she was a little plump for his liking. That had not stopped a little accident happening towards the end of the previous term. It had been at a house party, and they'd both had a bit to drink, which had unavoidably led to a slobbery kiss. Kyle had felt awkward about it ever since, but Kate seemed to have no such inhibitions, clearly thinking that she still had a chance. She hadn't. Besides being curvy in the wrong places, she was really short. He always seemed to do that, meet girls who were way shorter than he was, despite only being 5'10" himself.

She also didn't seem to notice that he had not spoken yet.

"So, how are you?"

"I'm OK," Kyle said, fidgeting with the car keys hanging from his thumb.

"I was so shocked when I heard about it. So, are you back then?"

Kate moved out of somebody's way and stepped closer to him. She was suffocating him. She didn't seem to know the term "personal space" at all.

"No, I'm not."

"When are you coming back? We seriously need help with the project, it's really stuck…"

"I don't know."

Kyle looked towards Kate. His response seemed inadequate.

"It's not really high on my list of priorities just now."

"Sure," Kate said, forcing a smile that didn't reach her eyes.

"I got to go," Kyle said, pointing at the door behind him. "Ciara's cooking dinner."

"Ciara?" Kate enquired with a frown.

"My sister," Kyle explained. Surely, he had mentioned Ciara before.

"Right." Kate nodded. "It was good to see you. Look after yourself."

"You too," Kyle said, turning around.

"I hope you'll be back soon," Kate shouted after him.

Kyle rushed back to the car before he saw anybody else. He sat down inside and took a deep breath. He wanted a moment before starting the drive back home.

He was staring straight out the windscreen when he spotted George. He didn't want to speak to George. George was Nigerian, or from some other African country where people had dark skin. They would probably have some strange custom when it came to condolences, and he didn't want to find out what it was.

He ducked, throwing himself across the passenger seat. It was while he did that that he thought of something. He had not checked the car. Maybe the diary was in the car.

He reached out to open the glove box. There was nothing in it but CDs. He went through them; some spiritual stuff, some country, a blank CD.

Kyle glanced at the contents of both doors, but there was

nothing in them except a pair of gloves and a pack of cleansing wipes. She had always kept the car tidy.

He got up, slowly and carefully, checking that George was safely out of sight. He started the engine and stuck the unlabelled CD inside the stereo. If there was data on it, it wouldn't play, and if there was music or other sound on it, it was hardly a diary.

There were trumpets.

* * *

He got home and pulled into the driveway. When he was getting out, he thought he should have a look in the boot as well.

This turned out to be another dead end. There was a jack, and that was it.

He went in and walked into the kitchen, following the smell of food.

"What were you doing in the boot?" Ciara asked, clearly amused.

Kyle gave her a worried look.

"Oh, there was a noise. I thought there was something loose in the boot. It was the jack. What's for dinner?"

Ciara flushed. "Oh, just some spuds. And mince…"

Kyle frowned on hearing that.

"Spuds and mince?" He walked over to the hob and found that this was the truth. The potatoes were boiling away and the mince was frying in the pan. "So, what's the plan?"

"I don't know." Ciara was embarrassed. "Maybe I should sort out a sauce."

"Can you make a sauce?" Kyle asked in surprise. He had thought Ciara was useless in the kitchen.

"Well, no. There's bound to be something in the press."

Ciara walked over to the dry food press and pulled out a sachet of curry sauce ingredients.

"I'm not eating curry with mince," Kyle said, shaking his head.

"Me neither."

"Could we make burgers?"

"No," Ciara said in disgust, "the mince needs to be raw for that."

"Shepherd's pie?"

"I don't know what goes into that. Cassie made it out of one of those sachets." Ciara started to sound defeated.

"I really don't want another take-away," she carried on.

Neither did Kyle.

They ended up eating potatoes with mince and ketchup.

CHAPTER 5

The week passed by quietly. Mostly they spent their time moping around, trying to watch TV or look for jobs. They cared for Wanda as if their lives depended on it. They tried to cook meals but ended up eating lasagne that they found in the freezer, fried eggs with chips and lots of sandwiches. Aunt Lizzie phoned them, Iris gave them a call, Cassie rang, and they even spoke to their granny from their father's side. Although everybody's intentions were good, they ended up causing more heartache.

On Friday afternoon, they headed into town to do their shopping. Kyle expected it to be a complete disaster, budget-wise and utility-wise. They ended up doing all right though. They bought pasta, chicken, salmon, broccoli, biscuits, oranges, cereal, bacon, milk... He glanced at the trolleys of the other shoppers – mainly women, he noted – and to his relief noted that they were buying much the same stuff. They mustn't be completely off track then.

When Kyle started wheeling the trolley out of the market and into the parking lot, Ciara surprised him by saying that she had to run and get something. He said nothing but kept pushing the awkward trolley towards the car. Friday afternoon was a painfully busy time for shopping. They would want to bear that in mind for the next time.

He loaded the bags into the boot of the car and returned the trolley. He had just sat down in the car when Ciara returned with a brown paper bag and a beaming smile.

"What's in the bag then?" Kyle asked.

"You'll see," Ciara said with an even bigger smile.

They got home and started unpacking the bags. Ciara kept moving everything that Kyle put into the fridge or the presses, saying that they all had their own place. Kyle didn't get it. As long as what needed to be kept cold was in the fridge, he was happy. He didn't care if the chicken breasts were in the vegetable compartment, but clearly women were different. They must be born with some housekeeping gene.

He left Ciara to put away the last items and flicked the kettle on.

"You wanna know what's in the bag then?" Ciara asked.

Kyle leaned back against the worktop. It would want to be something good, the big deal she was making.

Ciara took the bag and pulled a large book out of it.

"It's a cookery book." She sounded triumphant.

Kyle stared at the book in astonishment.

"Look, it's got these easy recipes. We can learn to cook proper food."

"Right," Kyle said, unsure of the appropriate response.

"Look, we can't keep eating frozen food and take-aways forever," Ciara said, exasperated.

"Fair enough," Kyle said, turning to make the tea.

"Have a look at it, will you? It's really simple stuff, like salmon with pasta, pancakes, colcannon, chicken wrapped in bacon…"

"Cool." Kyle couldn't get excited about the prospect of having to learn how to cook. Their mother had been a great cook, and their father had been able to put a decent meal together too, but he had never had to lift a finger.

"Use for those home ec classes then, huh?" Ciara said enthusiastically, taking the offered mug of tea. Then she sat down at the table and looked enquiringly up at Kyle.

"What are you doing tonight then?"

"Nothing," Kyle said with a shrug, "what's it to you?"

Ciara's cheeks flushed at that.

"It's just... Ronan is coming over."

"So, is he your boyfriend then?" Kyle said with a cheeky smile at his sister. Her flush deepened.

"He is. I was just hoping that you could stay out of the way."

"You've some plans for him then, huh?" Kyle couldn't help teasing her. At the same time though, he was a little worried. Was she just taking advantage of the new situation? Should he act all grown up? At the end of the day, she wasn't quite 18 yet, and she would hardly have brought him over if their parents were around... On the other hand, he had been no angel at her age and hadn't exactly changed his ways since. Besides, if she was allowed to shag her boyfriend in the house, it opened up a whole world of possibilities for him too.

Ciara hadn't responded. She just looked mortified at having to ask him.

"Right," he said. "That's fine. I'll stay out of the way."

"Really?" Ciara said incredulously.

"On one condition," Kyle said, bending down to look at her close-up.

"What's that?"

"You cook me a nice meal tonight," he said smugly.

"Aaargh," Ciara protested.

Kyle raised his eyebrows.

"Right, you got it."

"Great," Kyle said, strolling out towards the sitting room.

* * *

She did cook him a nice meal. It was simple enough, and she made the most of the stuff they had bought, including the cookery book. It was salmon in some kind of cream sauce with pasta, and it was delicious.

Soon after the meal she sent him upstairs with a bottle of Coke and a pack of biscuits. It was like being grounded, not that their parents had ever believed in that method.

He sat down on the bed and flicked through the TV channels for a while. For a Friday night, there wasn't much on. The films were all crap or he had already seen them – or both – and the so-called entertainment was too boring to earn its title. He ended up going through the music channels over and over again, constantly looking for a good song to come on.

He eventually tired of it and looked over at his bass guitar, lying in the corner of the room in its case. He turned off the TV and collected the guitar. He had not played for three weeks. He hadn't been to rehearsals either, and for all he knew, Tony was still standing in for him.

He absent-mindedly plucked at the strings for a while, then moved on to do a couple of songs he knew. Then he played a few of the songs they had meant to play at the gig that night – a couple of covers, some of Donal's own songs. He enjoyed the practice but sorely missed the accompaniment of a guitar and drums, even Donal's rough vocals.

He put the bass back where it belonged and lay down on the bed. He started wondering about Ciara and her boyfriend. She had never, ever mentioned a Ronan before, not until two weeks earlier when he was picking her up. Had they been going out for long? Had mum known about it? Unless Ciara was a complete slut, and he didn't want to think that of his own sister, they must have been together for a while. They were obviously sleeping together or she wouldn't have minded him being around, not if they were innocently watching a film or something. They were probably at it like rabbits by now…

He shook the mental image out of his head. It was disturbing, and it was made all the more disturbing by the fact that he had hardly thought about sex in the last three weeks. It was unheard of. He normally had a one-track mind with only one destination. It was natural for someone his age. Besides, women would never get better-looking as they got older; they were at their best in their late teens and early twenties.

He should make a move on Mel, now that he could invite her over if he wanted. She was desperate to get into his pants; she'd made that quite clear. He should have taken advantage of that long ago. She was hot, and he didn't know why he wasn't more excited by the idea. She mightn't have much of a brain, but he was not looking for a relationship, not by a long mile. She would be easy enough to shake off afterwards, or he could just keep her at arm's length…

His thoughts returned to Ciara downstairs. He didn't know Ronan at all. For all he knew, the man could be a junkie, a psycho or a pervert.

He got up and walked to the door. He sneaked to the top of the stairs and listened out for sounds from downstairs.

He could hear voices. He couldn't make out the words, but the voices sounded calm and equal. There was no shouting going on. Obviously, they were not shagging each other's brains out either though. Was there a small chance that Ronan was a decent kind of fellow?

He returned to his room and quietly closed the door behind

him.

* * *

He woke up tangled up inside the bed throw, fully clothed. The TV was still on, and Sky Sports News was showing its usual Saturday morning headlines and predictions of the weekend's events. Kyle had little interest in sports, but he found it his duty as a man to at least have a general idea of what was going on.

He struggled his way out of the throw that he must have wrapped around himself during the night. He squinted at the TV screen and made out that it was 8.53am. He felt ragged and stiff. Definitely time for a shower.

He made his way down to the kitchen some 20 minutes later. To his utter surprise, he found Ciara and Ronan sitting at the kitchen table, giggling over two cups of steaming tea, their noses almost touching each other. With a pang of some odd feeling he couldn't put a name on, Kyle thought it was good to see Ciara look happy again. Her face had a lovely, healthy glow, and her eyes were gleaming brightly with a smile.

The two of them quickly withdrew from each other when he entered the room.

"Morning," Ronan said with a polite smile, reserved for those odd moments when he had to look innocent in front of a girl's older brother.

"Morning," Kyle said, reaching out for the kettle to refill it.

"I just boiled it, there should be some left," Ciara said over her shoulder.

Kyle was just starting to look for a cup – this was getting harder and harder by the day – when the doorbell rang.

They all looked at each other. There was an environment of guilt in the kitchen, as if they had broken in and been caught red-handed.

Kyle stretched his neck to see out the window.

"Shit!" he hissed, catching sight of a car in the driveway. "It's Aunt Lizzie."

"Shit!" Ciara repeated. She shoved Ronan's mug into his hands. "You need to go upstairs. Stay in my room."

Ronan looked flabbergasted but obediently made his way up the stairs. When he was well out of sight, Ciara went to open the door.

"Oh, Aunt Lizzie," she shrieked upon opening the door, as if she hadn't known.

"Ciara, darling."

Judging by the silence that followed, Aunt Lizzie had reached out to hug Ciara.

"Do you have somebody else over? I thought I saw somebody on the stairs," Lizzie's voice then said.

"Oh no… Ah, that was just me, running around the place," Ciara's voice replied nervously.

A moment later, a group of people strolled into the kitchen. Lizzie had brought her two kids, Dawn and Donald. Kyle immediately started to feel awkward and was relieved when his cousins made their way straight into the sitting room, where they turned on the telly. None of them had ever been close to Lizzie's children. They always acted like they were all high and mighty, somehow better and smarter than everybody else. Kyle suspected nobody liked them much.

"Kyle, how are you my dear?" Aunt Lizzie said. She made a move to hug him too, but he moved away. Instead, she reached out to touch his head where the scars were. He had stopped wearing bandages on them a few days earlier; they had been a nuisance and not much good anyway.

"I see you got rid of your bandages. And your hair is growing back. That is wonderful." Aunt Lizzie had her hands on her hips, in the fashion that Cassie so much liked to imitate.

"Have you had breakfast yet? I brought fry-up ingredients," Aunt Lizzie said, starting to pull items out of a plastic bag that she had left on the kitchen counter.

"That would be lovely," Ciara said, giving Kyle the eyes behind their aunt's back. Lizzie started pulling out pots and pans out of the press.

"Oh, would you believe it!" she breathed after she had started throwing things into a saucepan. "I forgot to bring eggs." She looked round at Kyle and Ciara in deep disappointment.

"We've got some," Ciara said and went to take the box of eggs out of the fridge.

"Thank you, pet."

Aunt Lizzie resumed her cooking and talking. Kyle suspected that she kept talking to hide her awkwardness and sorrow. She always did talk a lot anyway.

"So, how are you two coping?" she asked.

"We're all right, I guess." That was Ciara. "It's weird, especially since Cassie left. She was so good with everything."

"I have a feeling Cassie will be back," Aunt Lizzie said with a reassuring smile.

"Are you psychic too?" Kyle retorted. He didn't particularly want Cassie back, bossing them around.

Ciara gave him a warning look before turning towards their aunt.

"Don't mind him. Kyle's been really snappy since then. Must be the head injury."

Aunt Lizzie turned from the frying pan to give Kyle a gentle smile.

"You've got enough reasons to be mad at the world. No, I'm

not psychic. Just call it female intuition." Her smile widened again before she turned back towards the frying pan.

"Ciara, will you be a good girl and make tea and toast please?"

Aunt Lizzie must have thought that they had the appetite of elephants. There was way too much of everything, but she insisted that they eat up. Still there was a huge pile of sausages, rashers, mushrooms and beans left. She told them to just put it all in a tub and heat it up another day.

"That's the best way to cook meals, I'm telling you," Aunt Lizzie said with a wink in Ciara's direction.

She reached out for the empty plates and went to put them in the dishwasher.

"Oh my god!"

Kyle and Ciara exchanged a guilty look.

"Why haven't you done the dishes?" Aunt Lizzie looked at them in disbelief.

"We didn't know how to," Ciara mumbled.

Aunt Lizzie let out a big sigh and brought her hands to her hips again.

"Come here, my dear. Now, where are the dishwasher tablets?"

Ciara got up and fetched the box from the press under the sink.

"Now, what you need to do with these is put them in the cutlery rack. Like this. Make sure everything in here is dishwasher safe. No wooden objects. This is all fine here. Make sure that these can move freely. Then you close the door, turn the power on, and you press this, this and this."

Aunt Lizzie looked at Ciara triumphantly, hands on hips again, as the familiar purr of the dishwasher droned out.

"Thanks," Ciara said with flushed cheeks.

"And then, when you hear a beep and these two lights come

on, it's finished. Just open it up and leave it for a moment before you empty it."

Kyle still didn't have a clue how the thing worked, but as long as Ciara did, it was all good. He focused on emptying his third cup of tea that morning. It was much too strong and going cold, and he felt like he couldn't possibly fit another drop into his stomach, but he kept going.

"Right. We better get a move on. I promised the kids we would go into town today and have lunch in McDonald's afterwards."

Aunt Lizzie wiped her hands on a tea towel and shouted into the sitting room: "Dawn! Donald!

"You look after yourselves now. You let me know if you need anything at all. I'll give you a ring during the week."

Aunt Lizzie herded her teenage children out of the house.

Kyle leaned back in the chair. He felt about five pounds heavier than he had getting up that morning.

"I can't believe this," Ciara said from the countertop. "Look."

Kyle turned around to look at her. She was holding up two €50 notes.

"She really shouldn't have," Ciara said.

She was right. She shouldn't have. Aunt Lizzie was divorced and had two children to look after too. She didn't have money to throw away. On the other hand, they needed the money...

Ciara sighed and put the money back on the countertop.

"I better get Ronan. He must be bored out of his mind."

Kyle remained sitting at the kitchen table, wondering if €50 notes were just going to keep falling from the skies or if they were going to have to find another way.

CHAPTER 6

On Sunday, Ciara announced that she wanted to have "a few friends" over for her birthday on Saturday, despite her actual birthday being two days earlier.

Kyle's first reaction was no. He didn't like the idea of having the house full of people. It didn't seem right somehow.

Then he thought, why not? It was Ciara's 18th, and she deserved a bit of happiness. So did he, as a matter of fact. She had explicitly said that he could ask some of his friends over too. It might be the best thing that had happened to them in almost a month.

Cassie would not agree, of course, but Cassie was in London and would never have to know.

* * *

Ciara's birthday was on a Thursday. Kyle was broke and had no idea what to buy her, so he went for the easy option and got her a voucher for a clothes store. Girls always needed clothes, didn't they?

Everybody called that day. Lizzie phoned, their grandmother from Cork rang up, Cassie called from London when Kyle was in the middle of cooking the meal that Ciara had persuaded him was his duty to make on her birthday. It wasn't anything fancy; just spaghetti bolognese, but it was well advanced for him and she should be happy he had even made an effort.

71

She was pleased. She declared the meal delicious and was over the moon with the voucher. She also loved the new jacket that Cassie had sent from London.

And yet, when they were having a cup of coffee after their meal, there was a cloud hanging over their heads.

* * *

Kyle was not particularly excited about Saturday night when it came. Ciara had been slaving away to make the house presentable, preparing finger food and making room for drinks in the fridge. She had dragged Kyle into the preparations, and he had reluctantly vacuumed the whole house – no small task, that – and brushed Wanda, although he saw no relevance in that to the party.

By nine o'clock though, the house was spotless and smelled of dozens of candles that Ciara had smattered over the house – vanilla, chocolate and coffee, if his senses were to be relied on. She had decided to keep other lighting to a minimum. Kyle was slightly concerned that his sister might be a pyromaniac as she had spent ages lighting all the candles, tea lights and even the fire.

Ronan arrived early with a couple of friends that were introduced to Kyle but whose names he forgot as soon as he had heard them. A little while later, what seemed a bus load of Ciara's friends arrived. He knew some of them a little, but he wasn't interested in company. A couple of them tried to make conversation with him but soon gave up, getting tired of their monologues. One or two of Ciara's friends were fairly good-looking too, but they had an agreement that each other's friends were off limits.

When Kyle got tired and slightly embarrassed of sitting in the recliner with a bottle of beer, just staring into the fire, he made his way into the kitchen, where most of the gang were hanging about. He grabbed a handful of crisps off a plate and was trying to decide who to try and make conversation with when the doorbell rang. Kyle went to answer it and was relieved to see his band mates.

"All right, mate?" Donal said with a pat on his shoulder. He stepped in carrying a massive pack of beer and was followed by John with his girlfriend, Sam and another few women. There was a stunning-looking, tall, dark-haired woman that Kyle had not seen before – he would have remembered – and a much shorter brunette who paled by comparison to the taller one. That was Mel. She'd brought her nosy friend along too, the one who had asked him annoying questions about his mother.

"Hello gorgeous," Mel flirted, walking up to him with a huge smile on her face. She was dressed in a tiny, golden, glittery dress, full of those little irritating things that fall off and leave a glittery trail behind. What were they called? Sequels? Sequettes? Sequins?

She was also dressed in ridiculous heels that were apparently very uncomfortable to walk in, as she dragged her feet on the floor. Kyle was certain that she dug a trail into the laminate floor behind her as she made her way towards him.

That aside, she looked rather sexy, and what's better, she was as keen on him as ever. She kissed his cheek so close to his mouth that it would have been inappropriate under any other circumstances. He could taste the fruity lip stuff that she must have applied only moments earlier.

Donal had made his way into the kitchen and slammed the beers onto the counter. He hugged Ciara and kissed her on the cheek – nothing inappropriate about that either, Kyle made sure to check. To his surprise, Donal handed Ciara a little parcel that turned out to contain a personalised key ring with Ciara's name on it. It wasn't much, but Kyle was stunned by Donal's thoughtfulness. He had not thought it was a quality he possessed.

Mel had never met Ciara, but she ran over – as well as she could – and surprised Ciara with a warm hug. Kyle left the girls to it. They seemed to be getting on like a house on fire, which sort of surprised him. He had thought Mel a lot shallower than Ciara.

Ciara looked well, too, in her electric blue dress. He supposed that none of the guys around would have dared to make a move on her in his presence, but even if they had, she would have turned them down. She seemed to have eyes for nobody but Ronan.

Kyle had remained at the archway between the hall and kitchen, quite content taking in the atmosphere from the outside. A moment later Donal came over.

"You look a little more human nowadays," he said, lifting his bottle up towards Kyle's head. "Your hair's growing back."

"Hmm," Kyle agreed and took a gulp of his beer.

"You know man, you've really got to do something about her tonight," Donal said with a sidelong glance towards Mel. "I'm telling you, if you don't make a move on her tonight, she's going to force herself on you. She's dying for it." Donal gave him an encouraging grin.

"I will. I will," Kyle said, brushing a hand across his face. He said it more to convince himself than Donal. Mel was an attractive girl, but he just couldn't seem to get his act together.

"You better. It could get embarrassing for you otherwise," Donal said with a cocked eyebrow before heading off towards the bathroom.

Kyle swigged down the rest of his bottle. Dutch courage. He

didn't normally need it; well, he had not normally needed it, but since the accident it seemed he was just not able to get into gear at all when it came to chatting girls up. Maybe the hit to his head had damaged the part of his brain that controlled flirting?

He glanced at Ciara. He was sure that she was still drinking her first glass of wine. Not that he could blame her – if he was to drink wine, it would take him about six hours to get through one glass. He hated the stuff. That was hardly her reason for drinking it. She probably liked it, but if anybody was to get drunk that night, it should be her; it was her 18th birthday. Maybe she was worried about what he would think and was taking it slowly.

Kyle had no intention of remaining sober enough to worry about his sister. He walked into the kitchen and got Sam to hand him a new beer. He took another handful of crisps and munched on, launching into conversation with John and one of Ronan's mates, who evidently was also into decent music.

Melanie was standing in the dining room, chatting to her annoying friend. Although Kyle was standing sideways to them, he was conscious of Mel's eyes on him. He normally liked girls checking him out, especially if he knew for sure that they fancied him – it was a flattering thing being adored like that – but he wasn't sure about this. He knew he had lost weight in the last few weeks. He still wasn't downright skinny, but if he didn't start eating and exercising, he was going to be a bit of a beanstalk. Maybe Mel had realised that his body was not what she had hoped for?

He had gone through another couple of beers by the time Donal came over and handed him a glass of orange juice.

"We don't want another repeat of your previous performances," he said with a cheeky grin and disappeared. Evidently the hottie that had arrived in his gang was there with Donal. Kyle didn't understand what women saw in him. Except for being tall and the singer in an only barely locally known rock band, he was very average-looking. Yet, he always found gorgeous women to hang out with, and this one was hotter than any he had seen before.

"What's that?"

Kyle turned around to see Mel at his side. She seemed to be giggling at his drink.

"This is OJ."

That inspired another fit of giggles.

"You won't get drunk on that."

"Actually, it's for the blood sugar," he said quietly, looking down at his feet. He hated talking about this.

"Drinking alcohol lowers the sugar levels. Orange juice brings the levels back up, as well as helping him to sober up," Ciara said from the other side of the table, where she was arranging more chocolate biscuits onto a plate.

"Oh," Mel said, looking foolish. "I'm sorry. I didn't realise…"

"It's OK," Kyle said with a feeble smile. "It's only diabetes. It never killed anybody."

As he said that, he felt all blood drain from his face – possibly from elsewhere in his body too. Ciara's eyes and his met in shocked horror at his words. Nobody else had noticed. Two people had died as a cause of his diabetes, and only recently.

"Sure. Well, if you need anybody to keep an eye on your sugar levels, just let me know," Mel said with a look up into his eyes. She left her hand on his arm before walking away. Kyle met Ciara's eyes again. She looked back at him with frustrated, angry and wondering eyes.

The doorbell went off again. Kyle went to open and was

amazed to see Iris.

"I'm sorry I came over so late… I just have something for Ciara. And I was wondering if I could get your… your father's laptop. There are some documents on it that we need at the office." She blurted all this out in a nervous outburst. She peeked in over his shoulder, evidently having heard the sounds of the party.

At that moment Donal showed up behind Kyle.

"Who's your girlfriend then?" he said with a wink towards Iris.

Kyle was stunned beyond words. Iris was ten years older than he, and apart from having a slim figure, she was not much to look at at all. She had a long, rather horsey face and not a very cool dress sense. She was wearing a baby-pink jacket.

"This is Iris. From dad's office. Donal."

The pair of them shook hands.

"Where's Ciara? I'd like to hand this to her," Iris said, stepping in.

"I know where she is. I'll take you to her," Donal said, taking Iris by the shoulders and pushing her into the hall. He winked again, this time at Kyle.

Kyle made his way into the study. Dust was gathering on the desk and shelves. The air was stale too.

The laptop was still on the desk, where it had been left that Friday night. Kyle picked up the case off the floor and was about to put the laptop inside when a thought struck him.

He had not checked the study for his mother's diary.

She was not much of a wiz with computers but had occasionally used the laptop to go online. It was a possibility.

There were three drawers on the side of the desk. The first one did not have much in it – printing paper, paper clips, some house brochures, ordinary things like that.

The second drawer was more successful. The diary was sitting on a pile of random papers, as if waiting to be found. He picked it up with shaky hands. There could be something in there.

"What are you doing, lover?"

This was Mel, cooing at him from the doorway.

Kyle dropped the diary back into the drawer.

"You're not very sociable at all, are you?"

She stepped in and started walking towards him with a confident shake of her hips.

"I was just getting the laptop. Iris came to collect it."

He hastily returned to arranging the laptop and its cable into the case.

"You must really enjoy playing hard to get," Mel whispered. She had gotten very close to him. She was standing at the short end of the desk, her rounded toes only inches from his feet. Before he had time to react, she had lifted her finger to his lips, tracing them delicately. Her eyes were fixed on his, and he found himself unable to look away.

"It's a good thing I am not shy," she said barely audibly, leaning in towards him. Her lips touched his, only for a second before she pulled away. She met his eyes bravely before leaning in for another, more daring kiss. She didn't hesitate this time but went straight in, tongues and all. She was an extremely skilled kisser, and the by-products of her kissing were very enjoyable too. She had one hand caressing his neck and another one under his shirt. She had partly climbed on to the desk, leaving her left buttock deliciously uncovered. He might have been feeling self-conscious recently, but his body had no such restraints. His hand found her round buttock easy enough.

There was a throat-clearing sound in the doorway.

Kyle jumped back, pulling the laptop inside its case with him, the strap being wrapped around his arm – the one that hadn't been busy with Mel's backside.

"Everything good to go?" Iris asked with an enquiring frown at Kyle. She seemed to purposely ignore Mel.

"Ahhm... Yeah." Kyle disentangled the strap from his arm. The laptop mightn't be, but he certainly was.

Iris walked over and grabbed the case off him with more force than was required.

"Thank you, Kyle. You enjoy your party," she said with a sweet smile and a rather bitchy look towards Mel.

"Is she always that nice?" Mel said, with a criticising look following Iris out of the door.

"No, no, she's all right," Kyle said, dumbfounded. She must have seen everything. He had turned on the light when entering the room, so it was better lit than the rest of the house. She had probably seen his hand on Mel's backside...

"Anyway," Mel said with a rather lusty look up at him, "where were we?"

"I... I gotta go," Kyle said, pulling away from her and following the sight of Iris's pink coat into the hall.

She must have seen everything, and it was mortifying. He didn't know why. She wasn't his mother, not even his sister, and yet he felt like Iris finding out that he had sexual feelings for a woman was disconcerting.

He made his way to the kitchen doorway, straightening his shirt and trying to forget that he was still wildly turned on by the events of only a moment ago.

"What did you say to her?" Donal said, nodding at the door that had just banged shut behind Iris.

Kyle opened his mouth but was unable to think of anything witty to say.

"I know she has the face of a horse, but underneath those

clothes, she has some figure," Donal carried on, not minding Kyle's silence. "You shouldn't overlook her just because of her age." He waved his beer bottle in a meaningful movement before returning to the kitchen.

Kyle spotted his sister at the kitchen sink. She looked upset. He walked over, grabbing what he believed was his beer off the table.

"Kyle, are you having a good time?" Ciara asked. She tried to wipe her eyes.

"I'm OK," he said, pushing his free hand into his pocket, "are you all right?"

Ciara bit her lip, holding back the tears. "Yeah." That came out in a deep, strangled breath, almost like a sob.

"Look what she brought," Ciara said, pushing a parcel towards him on the countertop.

Kyle gingerly lifted the paper wrapping.

"It's the pocket camcorder I'd wanted for ages. She says," Ciara sobbed again, "she says that dad had that in the office for a few weeks before..." Ciara stopped talking, presumably to stop herself from crying.

Kyle said nothing. It was like a present from beyond the grave. It was sort of eerie, even if there was nothing supernatural or odd about it. He had just bought it well in advance, he was like that... He had always been organised.

"It's a great present," he said eventually, pushing the parcel back towards Ciara. She touched it gently, almost as if it had been their father and a last chance to touch him. She had never had that chance. Cassie was the only one who had seen them since their deaths. He had had that chance, but he had done nothing about it. Those few moments he had spent in the car afterwards were a blur. He must have lost consciousness, but he couldn't tell for sure. Maybe he had just been screaming his head off. It could have been seconds or half an hour. All that time his parents had been in the front seat, within touching distance, and he had not reached out and touched them. He had never even tried to find out if he could have done…

"You OK, pet?" That was Ronan. He appeared from what seemed like nowhere and wrapped a protective arm around Ciara's belly and waist, nuzzling his head at her neck. Kyle immediately felt like an outsider, as if he had been trying to chat up somebody else's girlfriend and been shut out on the boyfriend's arrival.

He turned away, towards the table. He grabbed a couple of chocolate biscuits and headed to the hall. He sat down on the staircase. He could hear Wanda's peaceful snoring from her bed beneath the staircase.

He took a bite of one of the biscuits, followed by a sip of the beer. Chocolate biscuits and beer were a horrible combination, but he didn't mind. He carried on, slowly munching away on the biscuits. He wasn't as slow with the beer though. He felt like the most miserable person on earth. He wanted to cry too. It was OK for Ciara, who still acted perfectly sober. It was all right for her to cry. She had a big birthday only a few weeks after her parents had died, of course she was allowed to cry. He was meant to be the older, strong one who looked after her, and being a man didn't spell out big, public outbursts of tears. It sucked.

"You're like a little snail, aren't you?"

Mel had appeared at the bottom of the steps. She was holding on to the round decoration at the bottom of the handrail. There was something seductive about the way she was touching it.

"Is that so?" he said with a tired smile, mouth half-full of

81

biscuits.

"You come out for a sneak peek at the world and then pull right back into your shell," she explained, putting her other hand on the decoration too. It was like she was massaging it.

That wasn't a compliment. He was a snail. Probably as slow as one too.

"This is a gorgeous house," she said with a look up towards the top floor and the high ceiling.

"It's mine now. Or will be," he said, pushing the last piece of biscuit into his mouth.

"Really? Lucky you." Melanie let go of the decoration, much to his disappointment, which didn't last long.

"These things are killing me," she said, putting a hand on his shoulder for support to take her shoes off. Her breasts were practically pushed into his face, not that he minded that. They were like a pair of small punching bags. Not that they were small, and not that he wanted to punch them either. Balls. He wasn't making any sense even in his own head.

Mel let out a relieved sigh and straightened up, shiny shoes dangling from one hand.

"Come on," she said, offering a hand, "you haven't even shown me your room yet. I assume it's upstairs?"

She pulled him up by his hand and started leading him up the stairs.

CHAPTER 7

He woke up the next morning, freezing. He tried to pull the duvet tighter around him but couldn't find it. It just wasn't there.

He sat up, too cold and annoyed to get back to sleep. He realised that he was naked, totally naked. His clothes were scattered over the floor, not that that was anything unusual.

The duvet was piled up on the other side of the bed. He stretched his neck a little and saw Mel's head just peeking out. Shit. Oh shit. Double shit.

He couldn't tell by her head if she was naked too, but there was a high possibility that she was. She was so tightly wrapped up that he could not loosen the duvet to check. He didn't want to wake her up, even if he was curious to see…

He jumped up before more dirty thoughts could enter his head. The cold air of the room put a stop to them. He grabbed a pile of clothes and made for the toilet.

When he re-entered the room a few minutes later, Mel had not budged. He sneaked across the room to the door and made his way downstairs.

The kitchen was a mess. There were empty bottles, cans and glasses everywhere, and some were not even empty. There were spills on the countertop. He was afraid to check if there were spills on the carpet in the sitting room. There was an ashtray on the kitchen table, despite Ciara's insistence that smoking should only happen outside. The air was cold but stale. Kyle opened the window in the kitchen, the smell of alcohol all around making him feel sick. Too tired to even think about lighting a fire, he went to turn on the oil heating. So what if the oil decided to run out just now?

He flicked on the kettle and pulled a couple of sausage rolls out of the fridge. He was half-way through his second roll when the phone rang. The landline, it was.

"Morning," Cassie's voice said when he answered.

"Cassie," he said in a sleepy voice, unable to fake enthusiasm. It was not quite ten o'clock yet. He heard steps upstairs on the landing. Please don't let it be Mel, please don't let it be Mel...

"You had a good night then," Cassie said sarcastically.

"What?"

"Oh, cut it out, Kyle. I know all about it. Iris told me about it." That little bitch.

"I sent her round last night."

Kyle repeated his latest curse in his mind.

"It was her 18th," Kyle said in defence.

"The two of you certainly seem to be moving on quickly." Cassie had a real edge to her voice. It wasn't like they had broken the law or anything. "It's not even a full month yet."

A day short. They would have to go to the graveyard for that... One month.

"So, she came around to check up on us?" Kyle said, not knowing he was going to say it until he had.

"Looks like it was needed. Who's this Ronan then?"

"He's all right. It's been going on for months." He was possibly lying. He didn't know. He hardly knew Ronan at all.

"She never told me about him."

I can understand why, Kyle thought. Nothing good would ever have come out of telling Cassie anything.

"And you, well you don't exactly act like the responsible older brother, do you?"

Kyle groaned at that. What did she want?

"You could at least save it for the bedroom!"

"Oh, piss off," he hissed.

"Oh, I will. Good luck cleaning up the mess." She hung up on that.

Kyle put the phone down and turned to face Ciara and Ronan at the bottom of the steps.

"It was Cassie," he said, making his way back into the kitchen.

"What did she want?" Ciara said, re-boiling the kettle and starting to make tea for herself and Ronan.

Kyle swallowed the last piece of his sausage roll.

"She knows."

Ciara and Ronan exchanged a frightened look at that.

"Knows what?" Ciara asked.

"About the party."

"Oh," Ciara sounded relieved at that, strangely enough. "How?"

"She had a spy."

"What?" Ciara exclaimed. Ronan's eyes grew wide at that.

"Iris." It made sense now. It was an odd time for her to call over, on a Saturday night at what must have been around 11 o'clock. Surely collecting the laptop would have made more sense during the week when she was working?

"You're kidding me! Who does she think she is? We're both grown-ups." Ciara was fuming. She did not lose her temper often, but when she did, she was not nice to be around.

"She's probably just worried," Ronan said, wrapping a calming arm around her shoulders. First it looked like Ciara was going to push him away, but she relaxed into the embrace and pursed her lips to try and fake a smile.

Footsteps sounded from the staircase, and Kyle turned around to face Mel. It was as awkward a moment as he could imagine.

She was wrapped up in his bathrobe that he rarely used, preferring to get dressed straight away in the mornings. She was also wearing a pair of his socks.

"I hope you don't mind. It was just so cold, and my dress wasn't going to be much help."

A quick glance at her chest proved that she had not bothered to put the dress on at all. The realisation that she might not be wearing anything at all underneath his bathrobe made his throat choke up, as if somebody was squeezing it with their hands.

"It's fine," he mumbled, pulling out a chair to sit down on. He felt like he needed to sit down. He didn't get the chance, though, because Mel thought him all gentlemanly and sat down on the chair instead.

"Who is The Who? You've a poster inside your wardrobe door. Is it something to be embarrassed about?" There was a teasing edge to her voice.

"You don't know The Who?" Kyle said disbelievingly and pulled out a chair for himself.

"I don't," Mel said, with a look at Ciara and Ronan for support. "Should I?"

The other two did not seem to join in on her ignorance.

"Yeah. They're only one of the most influential bands ever."

"Oh." Mel looked stunned but not a bit embarrassed.

"Your dad would probably have listened to them," Ronan said helpfully. "Mine still does."

"Right. Fair enough." Mel shrugged, as if her ignorance was understandable.

"Do you want a cup of tea?" Ciara asked Mel, who nodded eagerly. "Anything to eat?"

"Oh no thanks, I'm not much of a breakfast eater," Mel said with a satisfied smile, as if that was something to brag about.

Ciara and Ronan started chatting quietly between themselves, and Kyle realised that he would have to try and make conversation with Mel. He had no idea what to say, not without the help of some liquid encouragement – stronger than tea. Plus, he had no idea what had happened after they had made their way upstairs the night before… Although it was quite clear what must have happened.

"You were lovely," Mel whispered, looking straight up at him with a beaming, appreciative smile.

Lovely? What the hell had he done to her to deserve that? It was acceptable to be great, fantastic, wild or amazing. Not lovely.

"Here." Ciara saved him by handing Mel a steaming cup of tea. She accepted it gratefully and did not seem to expect a reply from him after that. The girls fell into a lively conversation. Kyle drifted out altogether, staring out the window.

"What's that?" Ciara's alarmed question brought him back to focus.

"There's someone upstairs," Ronan said with a bemused look towards the stairs.

Ciara and Kyle exchanged an enquiring look and shook their heads.

There were footsteps on the stairs, then a bit of conversation. A man and a woman.

For a moment, Kyle had a ridiculous thought that they were his parents' ghosts. It was so stupid that he should have laughed at it, but it didn't seem a bit hilarious.

Then Donal showed in the doorway with his lady friend.

"Good morning," Donal said with a huge, wide grin on his face. What was there not to smile about? He had spent the night with an absolutely gorgeous, long-legged brunette.

"I didn't know you were staying," Ciara said accusingly.

"I hope you don't mind. It was late."

"It's grand," Kyle confirmed. Judging by the look on Ciara's face, she was not in agreement.

"Where did you stay?"

"In one of the rooms upstairs. A double, just above from here," Donal said, pointing up at the ceiling.

It was like all colour drained from Ciara's face at that. She stared at Donal for a moment, unblinking, before getting up and heading up the stairs.

"What's wrong?" Donal asked with a frown.

Kyle felt a lump in his throat too. It was hard to speak. He would have to go after Ciara, even if he didn't know what he was going to say.

He pushed his chair away from the table and got up.

"It's mum and dad's room."

He didn't wait for everybody's reaction. He headed out to the hall and up the stairs.

Ciara was sitting on the floor near the end of the bed. Her arms were wrapped around her knees, her chin resting on her hands. She was crying.

"It's ruined," she said, without even looking to see who had entered the room.

Kyle moved a bit closer. The bed was made, although not as tidily as it had been. Apart from that, there was nothing to prove that anybody had been in the room.

"It's ruined," Ciara said again.

Kyle stopped beside her, standing there awkwardly. She seemed more upset than was reasonable.

"They've ruined everything," she said with a loud sob.

"Maybe it's for the best," Kyle said, trying to reach out to put a hand on her shoulder but pulling it back when she swung around at him.

"How could it possibly be for the best?" Her eyes were blazing.

"I mean, we couldn't leave it like this forever. We are going to have to clear it out."

"No, we're not," Ciara said, but there was a note of resignation in her voice.

"We are. Besides, there was no way they could have known. It could have been a spare room for all they knew." That was true. Donal had only barely been in the house before.

"But it's so disrespectful. What would they think?"

Kyle assumed that by 'them' she meant their parents.

"They didn't mean it that way," Kyle said, hoping to bring the conversation back to Donal rather than to their parents.

"I don't want to clear it out. I just want to remember this room as it was. I want to remember them."

Kyle felt his eyes sting at the held-back tears.

"We won't need to destroy everything. We will leave something to remember them by."

Ciara stayed sitting on the floor, looking straight ahead now, as if he wasn't around at all.

"I'm gonna open the window," Kyle said. He walked up to the big window and pushed it open. A faint whiff of fresh air reached his nose.

"Their smell is going to be gone," Ciara exclaimed with a new sense of loss.

"It will happen, sooner or later," Kyle said. He moved closer to Ciara again. "Besides, we can hold on to mum's perfume and dad's aftershave."

"It's not the same. I wanted their scent to remain on the bedclothes. I remember it from when I was a child and used to run to sleep in their bedroom. Especially on Saturday and Sunday mornings." A brief smile touched her lips at that memory.

It reached Kyle's lips too. He remembered that as well. They had both done that as children, run to their parents' bedroom in the mornings just to take in the warmth and cosiness. Usually it had just been their mother in the bed at that time, their father being an early riser. At that stage, Cassie had been too old for things like that and thought their behaviour childish.

It made him sad, realising that their smell was going to be gone for good one day. Even if they kept all their clothes, the scent would vanish eventually and become only a memory, just like everything else about them. Sometimes he thought he couldn't even remember their voices anymore. There were photos of course, but it wasn't the same. Although he had not hugged either of his parents in years, the thought of not being able to do so was too painful to bear, especially when he felt like he needed it. Eventually he would forget what it had felt like to be near his mum or what kind of a presence his father had. They were just going to be names, mere mentions in conversation that were glazed over and didn't mean much to anybody.

He glanced at the closed wardrobe with heart-rending longing. Then he reached out his hand towards Ciara.

"Come on. Let's get these sheets off." He spoke in a calm, determined but sympathetic voice. Somebody had to be strong. It might be him today but Ciara tomorrow.

She looked at him for a moment, then took his hand and got up. She wiped her eyes and tightened her ponytail. She nodded.

They pulled the sheets off the bed in complete silence. They were getting ready to leave the room when Ciara touched Kyle's arm to stop him.

"I don't want to see him. Can you make sure he leaves?"

Kyle nodded, and they walked downstairs. Kyle handed his half of the pile of sheets to Ciara.

"You take these to the utility."

Ciara scurried on, not even looking towards the kitchen.

Donal gave him a worried look when he entered the kitchen.

"Is everything OK?"

Kyle nodded, reaching up to brush his hand to his hair. It felt weird now, stubble a few millimetres long.

"Yeah. She's fine."

"I'm sorry mate. I had no idea." Donal looked troubled – something Kyle was not used to seeing. He was normally Mr Confidence.

"It's grand. She wants you to go, though."

Donal looked at his woman – who, for all Kyle knew, could have been mute for she had not spoken a word that he had heard – and then back towards Kyle.

"Of course. Do you want a ride back into town?" Donal asked of Mel.

"Thanks. I'll just go and get changed."

The girl got up, smiled encouragingly at Kyle and ran up the steps.

"Look, we're playing a gig next Saturday if you wanna come. Free drinks and all."

"I'm not in the band," Kyle said through gritted teeth. He didn't want to get into this again.

"Temporarily," Donal reminded him. "I'll take care of the drinks."

Kyle nodded.

Mel reappeared in her silly little dress a matter of minutes later.

"Right. Let's get going then," Donal said, taking the brunette by the arm and guiding her into the front porch.

"I'll text you," Mel said, surprising Kyle with a long, slow kiss that he thought was a bit much in the morning, in front of so many people and after the earlier incident.

When the three of them had left the house, Ciara walked in from the sitting room where she had been hiding. She walked straight over to Ronan, who protectively wrapped his arms around her. Kyle felt like he was shut out again.

"I'll just go… put new sheets on the bed," he announced, pointing a thumb at the utility, but the pair of them did not seem the least interested in what he was doing or not doing.

He did get some fresh sheets from the utility. On his way upstairs, though, he called into his father's study. He pulled the diary out of the drawer. He didn't open it; he just took it upstairs with him and pushed it to the back of his wardrobe.

He went to his parents' bedroom. He left the pile of sheets on the bed. He never put the sheets on.

Instead, he sat down on the floor and cried.

CHAPTER 8

They went to the graveyard the day after. It was a miserable day, cold, windy and wet. As soon as they sat down in the car, Kyle turned up the heating on full blast and set the windscreen wipers to work.

They were driving a couple of minutes before Ciara started a conversation.

"That Mel seems to be really into you." She said that enquiringly, as if poking for more information.

"I don't know. I guess."

"Well, she talked about you all night, and when she wasn't talking about you, her eyes were constantly on you. I think she was mentally undressing you, in preparation like."

There was a smug, cheeky smile on Ciara's face.

"I think that's all she is interested in," Kyle said, slowing down to allow more room for a car they were meeting on the narrow road.

"Whoa there! That's not the Kyle French I've known all my life."

"What do you mean?" Kyle glanced at his sister.

"If that was all a woman was interested in, that used to suit you just fine."

"It does," Kyle said, but he sounded unconvincing, even to himself.

"Do you actually want to get into a relationship with her?"

"God no. She's about as bright as a tea light in a cellar."

Ciara looked confused by his made-up simile, and so was he. Anyway.

"As if that should bother you."

"It doesn't. She's fine for what I need right now."

Ciara was about to say something else, but they had just arrived at the graveyard, and Kyle butted in before she had a chance.

"We're here."

He pulled up near the stone wall that lined the entire graveyard. It seemed to be a quiet morning. Then, who would want to be at a graveyard on such a miserable Monday morning?

"Are we going to have to do this every month then?" Kyle wondered out loud as they were walking towards their parents' grave.

"At least," Ciara said with great conviction.

"Have you been here since the funeral?" Kyle suddenly felt guilty. He hadn't been near the place.

"Yeah, a couple of times. Just to pay my respects and... contemplate everything. Have you not?" Ciara gave him an accusing look.

He thought it best not to answer. His sisters had that in common – they could make one feel the size of an ant if things weren't done the way they wanted to. Control freaks, they were.

The grave was near a big oak tree by a stone wall. The tree was on the other side of the wall, but it still gave some shelter from the weather. The grave itself was a miserable, bald mound of earth. It had been so cold since the funeral that there was no hope of anything growing on it. Instead, there was a large pile of plants and bouquets scattered over it. Some of them seemed a little worse for wear due to frosty nights, but a couple of them looked pretty fresh. Kyle had never liked the stone that the girls had picked. He had been asked for his opinion, but he had not cared at the time.

"I think Aunt Lizzie has been here recently," Ciara said, clearing some of the flowers out of the way, making a sheltered gap for their lantern. Kyle didn't think it was ever going to work. The fire would never catch in the wind and the rain.

He stood back and let Ciara do the work. After she had, surprisingly successfully, lit the candle with a lighter – he didn't understand why she had one, she didn't smoke; well, didn't used to anyway – she stood back and started crying.

Kyle just felt numb. He had only come because it was expected of him. The place meant nothing to him. His parents were not there, they were not lying in their coffins under that patch of soil. They were not there or he would have known it, felt it. They were nowhere where he could feel them anymore. The closest he could get to them was in their room, in the house, sometimes in his dreams. He wasn't sure if he believed in souls, but they certainly did not wander around graveyards, expecting people to come and pay respect to their loved ones.

That was why he didn't even reach out to comfort Ciara. If the grave made her feel better, then fine. It didn't touch him.

He saw movement from the corner of his eye. There were a couple of people approaching a grave on his right. An elderly couple, in their fifties maybe, was walking up to a grave. He knew they were whispering to each other, and when the man noticed Kyle looking at them, he lifted his hat in respectful acknowledgement. Poor orphaned sods, they probably thought. That's what everybody thought. That's all they were now, poor, pitiable young people whose parents had died.

"We should go," Kyle said, touching Ciara's arm. She was

wiping her nose with a tissue and looked annoyed at the intrusion.

"Why?"

"I just want to go." He didn't want people looking at him, or her. He just wanted to get away, back to the safety of the house where people wouldn't see them or feel sorry for them.

"You go. I'll be in the car in a bit." Ciara was determined.

Kyle nodded. He turned around and walked out of the graveyard without another look at the pitying couple.

He sat down in the car, found a rock station on the radio and turned it up, drowning his foul mood in some Nirvana.

* * *

When he got downstairs the following morning, after a restless night with no dreams that he could remember, Ciara was sitting at the kitchen table and hurried to stick a plate into the microwave when he appeared.

"I made you breakfast. Your favourite," she said with a charming smile over her shoulder.

"What's that?" Kyle sat down on the opposite side of the table, yawning widely.

"Pancakes and bacon with maple syrup."

She put a cup of coffee in front of him.

"And what have I done to deserve it?" Kyle asked with a grin. He didn't remember the last time she had made him breakfast, except maybe giving him a bowl of cereal.

"I need to talk to you about something," she said. Her face looked serious when she slid the plate of wonderful-smelling pancakes and bacon across the table along with a bottle of syrup.

"Right."

He picked up the knife and fork and got stuck in. There was silence. He swallowed his second bite and glanced at Ciara.

"Shoot," he encouraged her.

"Well… The thing is…" Ciara tugged at her jumper sleeves nervously. Although there was a fire already roaring in the sitting room, the heat had not yet reached the kitchen or the radiators.

"It's just that I'm… I'm pregnant."

Kyle stopped chewing on his mouthful and looked at Ciara. She had pulled one foot up on the chair and was now holding her knee as if for support. She wasn't looking at him.

"Right," he eventually said, for lack of a better response.

"Ronan knows. He's fine about it. He's known for some time. I'm about two months gone. I knew before… before it happened. I want to keep it." This all came out in a great blurb, as if she had practised it.

"Did they know?" The question was out before he realised it had formed in his head, let alone on his lips.

Ciara shook her head. "No. I had only just found out… Two days before. I was going to tell mum, but I was worried… Why haven't you freaked out?"

He wasn't sure. He should have freaked out. It was his duty as her older brother. He just didn't have the energy in him.

"You're going to be an uncle," Ciara said with an attempt at a smile.

"Does Cassie know?" Kyle tried to return to his breakfast, but it didn't taste the same anymore.

"No," Ciara replied in a small voice, "do I have to tell her?" It was a hopeless question even if she tried to sound hopeful.

"I'm sure she will find out. Especially if you're going to keep the baby." Kyle took a sip of coffee. He hoped that there had been something strong in it, whiskey or something.

"She's going to go mad." Ciara started gnawing on a fingernail.

She looked at him pleadingly. "You won't tell her, will you? I promise I will, I just need to find the right time."

Kyle nodded although he wasn't really listening. "Ronan. What is he going to do? Does he have a job?"

"He works as a delivery man. It's a decent job. Tough but he likes it. He can support me." There was something childish and innocent about the way she said it. As if it would be that easy. Kyle suddenly felt a hundred years old. He had aged at triple speed since the accident. Maybe not physically – hopefully not – but mentally. That's how it seemed to him, although he was certain that some people, such as Cassie, would not agree.

"Are you gonna live together?"

"I don't know. I suppose." Ciara bit her lip. There clearly was a lot that she didn't know yet.

He ran out of questions. His thoughts were flying about like a disturbed swarm of bees.

"I'll leave you to it. I know it's a lot to take in." Ciara got up from her chair and went upstairs, taking each step at a time, holding the handrail, just in case.

It was a lot to take in. Kyle sat at the table long after his breakfast was finished.

* * *

Ciara went out that night. She was going to see Ronan and said that it would be good to give Kyle a chance to think things over on his own.

He made himself dinner – fried eggs and bacon – and fed Wanda. He wandered into the sitting room and flicked the TV on.

The house was disturbingly quiet. He was uncomfortably aware of all the empty rooms around him and of how quiet it was. Wanda was happily asleep on her cushion beside the fire, and apart from her content snoring, the only sound was from the TV.

He was struck by the thought that that was how the house was going to be in the future. With Cassie in London and Ciara moving in with Ronan – that was bound to happen – he would be left in the house on his own. What would he do with six bedrooms and two reception rooms? At the best he would keep Wanda, but one man and a small dog did not need that much space. It would cost a fortune to keep the house going too. Although he could try to invest his inheritance wisely. He would probably turn into one of those crazy people who never left the house and get a whole army of dogs to keep him company.

It was frightening. It scared the life out of him, being left on his own. He had never lived alone before and was not used to spending so much time alone. He had always liked a certain amount of solitude, but now even an evening on his own seemed too much.

He felt so uncomfortable downstairs that he turned the TV off and made his way upstairs. Wanda followed him, and he lifted the dog on to his bed. With legs that were too short in comparison to her back, joined by the stiffness of her eight years, Wanda was not able to jump onto the bed.

He sat on the bed for a minute, scratching the dog's ears. Then he glanced at the wardrobe on the opposite wall.

He got up and pulled the diary from its slot at the back of the wardrobe. He returned to the bed and sat down.

He left the book on the bed for a moment, staring at it. Wanda reached her head out, sniffing at the diary enthusiastically. Kyle envied her for that. She was able to get a scent of it, a sure comfort in her longing for the lady of the house. Their mother had spent the most time with the dog, at least in the recent years when Kyle and his sisters had gotten a little older and busier.

Kyle picked up the diary and opened it randomly. He browsed through to November 6th. There was nothing unusual about it. The date wasn't circled, and there were no odd comments on the page. There were two appointments on it, a hairdresser's appointment at quarter to twelve and the play at eight o'clock. Nothing else.

He checked the monthly planner too, and the same thing. He quickly flicked through the rest of the diary, but there was nothing that stood out at a quick glance. The only dates that were marked were their birthdays; Ciara, Cassie, Kyle, Marcus. Their names were written beside the big number that showed the date.

He sighed and shoved the diary into the drawer beside his bed. He didn't know what he had expected. She was not psychic.

* * *

He woke up on the bed the following morning, fully dressed and with Wanda curled up beside him. When his mind cleared enough to figure what was going on, he saw Ciara in the doorway.

"Auntie Lizzie's here," she said. She looked well rested and had gotten changed since last night. Had she come home for the night? He had heard nothing.

"Right. Right," he responded. Kyle sat up on the bed. "I'll be down in a minute."

"I need to feed Wanda," Ciara explained. The dog was wagging her fluffy tail on the bed upon hearing her name. Kyle reached out and picked her up, placing the dog carefully on the floor. She happily followed Ciara out of the room.

Kyle got downstairs a few minutes later. Ciara and Aunt Lizzie were sitting at the table with cups of coffee and a plate of biscuits.

"There you are," his aunt said with a smile when he appeared. "Oh dear boy, have you slept in your clothes?" To Kyle's embarrassment, she got up and came up to him and started to inspect him.

"Does he do that often?" she asked of Ciara.

"Sometimes," Ciara replied at the same time as he said: "No I don't."

Lizzie clicked her tongue. "You need a woman to look after you. You promise you will look after him, Ciara?"

Aaargh, how infuriating that was! He was well able to look after himself. He just didn't feel like it.

"Well, your head and face have healed well. How is your arm?"

"It's fine," Kyle responded and headed to the safety of a chair, slumping down on it before she could inspect him any further. His arm was fine. There had been no problems with it after the first few days.

"Good. You need some breakfast. You're fading away while your sister looks to be getting plumper. No harm in that Ciara, you always were too skinny. What would you like?"

"Just some cereal. And coffee." Kyle picked up the newspaper that his aunt must have brought with her and started browsing.

"Everybody would like to see you down in Cork for Christmas. Are you coming?"

That was the first time Kyle had even thought about Christmas. It seemed irrelevant.

"I don't think so. The journey is too much." Ciara looked flushed when she said it.

"But you can't spend it alone, the two of you." Lizzie looked at the two of them while putting down Kyle's breakfast in front of him.

"I might go over to Ronan's." Ciara's face reddened visibly at that.

"Who's Ronan?" Lizzie asked. She sat back down at the table. "Is he your boyfriend?"

Ciara nodded. She was too embarrassed to look at her aunt.

"Ronan who? Is he a decent fella?" She looked at Kyle at this point.

He nodded.

"Ronan Gallagher. You'd love him. He has a job and everything."

"He's not older than you, is he?" Lizzie's brow had turned into a frown.

"Only a year."

Lizzie abandoned this line of enquiry and turned towards Kyle. "And have you got somebody to spend Christmas with? A girlfriend, perhaps?"

Kyle shook his head. He had no plans to even try and swing that one.

"He could have," Ciara said, happy to have escaped the attention. She shut up at Kyle's murderous look.

"No. I'll be fine."

"I think you should both come to Cork. At least you'd have some family. Is Cassie coming over?"

"I don't know," Ciara replied.

"Ah, I'll find out. I must call her anyway. Poor girl, back to work so soon."

Aunt Lizzie got up and started unpacking a bag of groceries that was on the countertop.

"How are you getting on with the dishwasher?"

"Oh great. I've had it on a couple of times since you were here last," Ciara said proudly.

"Good, good. Oh, I meant to bring you some briquettes for

the fire, but I must have forgotten. I've plenty at home."

"We're fine," Kyle said. There was a whole big pile of coal in the shed, some briquettes and lots and lots of timber that he had helped his father chop up during the summer.

There was a silence for a while as Lizzie kept piling things up into the presses and fridge.

"I really think you should come down to Cork for Christmas. You need the support."

Ciara exchanged an amused look with Kyle behind their aunt's back.

"We'll think about it. It's still over two weeks away."

"Fine. Oh, is that the time? I must get going. I'm meant to drop the car in for service at 12. Will you be OK for everything now? Just let me know if there's anything I can do." Aunt Lizzie kissed Ciara on the forehead and squeezed Kyle's shoulder before running out the door.

"Can we go into town later? Around two. I have an appointment," Ciara asked when their aunt had left.

Kyle was about to ask what kind of appointment, but then he decided he didn't want to know. It was probably some weird baby stuff.

"Sure," he said, burying his head deeper into the newspaper.

* * *

Kyle parked the car in the parking lot behind the supermarket. Ciara trotted off as soon as he had turned off the engine, and he was left to gather up the coins for the parking and to fend for himself until she was done with whatever it was.

He was walking around town for a while, trying to hide from the cold inside his hoodie. He was so unprepared; he hadn't brought gloves, and the hood was the only thing he had to cover his head. He was frozen and wanted to go in somewhere to keep warm.

He eventually came across GG's, Georgina's hair salon. He looked in for a moment, then turned on his heel and crossed the street. He dropped into the coffee shop and got two cappuccinos.

He was met at the door with the steamy heat of a hairdresser's as well as the sweet smell of different hair products he had come to associate with the place. While the other girls nodded hello to him, Georgina didn't even notice him, being deep in conversation with a woman whose head was stuck inside one of those things that are used to dry one's hair, the big UFO-like things. She was dressed in the colours of the salon, bright pink and black. Kyle had always thought it an odd choice of colours for a unisex salon.

Eventually Georgina turned around and looked straight at him.

"Oh, Kyle! How are you?" She started walking over towards him. "I hope you haven't come in for a haircut. I really can't fit you in today. And I'm not going to shave off all your lovely hair again." She stopped in front of him, looking him up and down. "You're going to have to sort yourself out. You look more and more like Kurt Cobain every day, except the hair."

"Kurt Cobain's a legend," Kyle said, insulted, although he wasn't sure if he was insulted on his own behalf or Kurt's.

"He's also dead," Georgina said with a wide smile. Her white teeth glistened as she did so. She was a very attractive woman; she had gorgeous, dark skin, wild black hair and big, brown eyes. Kyle was certain that she had never regarded him as a male at all, being five years or so her junior.

"This is for you," he said, handing out the paper cup.

"Oh, lovely. You shouldn't have. It's perfect. I have a few minutes just now. Sit down."

Kyle sat down on the couch in the waiting area, and Georgina sat down on the armrest. She stretched out her legs. They looked extraordinarily skinny in the tight, black jeans she was wearing, but gorgeous. She was skinny overall, despite having a great appetite and not a particularly healthy lifestyle. She was always munching on junk food when Kyle called in, and she had confessed to hating the gym.

"So, how are you?" she said again, taking a sip of her coffee.

"I'm OK."

"Everybody's talking about you. Not just you either, but your sisters too. The topic of the week. Or maybe year at this stage."

Kyle's mouth twitched in what was not even supposed to be a smile.

"Show me how your hair is." She reached out to pull the hood down from his head and leaned towards him to inspect the cuts.

"They're healing all right," she said, with a finger tracing the bigger cut.

Her touch sent pleasurable shivers down his spine and made him tingle in all the right places, except at the wrong time and place. Shit.

"There's no hair growing there yet though. I would say there never will be either. It often happens." Georgina pulled in even closer to look at the other cut. Kyle swallowed hard, trying to focus on her words rather than on her touch and her scent, never mind her boobs almost nesting on his shoulder.

"It's nothing to worry about really. Once your hair grows longer, there will be plenty to cover the bald patches with."

"Don't say that!" Kyle cried in alarm.

"Say what?" Georgina said, pulling back to the armrest with a puzzled look on her face.

"The b word."

"Bald? Jeez, Kyle, you're not going bald. It's just the scar tissue that may not have hair growth. You're only 20 for God's sake."

Ouch. How painfully she reminded him of that.

"Don't worry, you'll still have your looks for years to come." She said that with a teasing smile.

"Look, I need to be getting back to work. I don't know how it's so busy today, it's a bloody Wednesday. Are you going out at the weekend?"

Kyle nodded.

"Juice?" she enquired further.

He nodded again. "The band's playing."

"You're not back in, are you?"

He shook his head.

"You're not much of a talker talker nowadays, are you?" Georgina said with a laugh. "Sure you're better off with the timeout. People would probably think you a right jerk if you went back too soon."

She didn't say it, but Kyle knew it was there. People would think that he was out for a repeat performance.

"Whatever you do, get rid of that grungy look before then. It's totally not in fashion. Girls don't like it." She ran her hand across his head when getting up. "I will see you on Saturday then."

Kyle stared at her as she walked over to the customer with the hair-dye. She really was quite something, and it wasn't that she was 25 and ran her own, successful business. She had a lot of other assets that interested him a lot more.

* * *

Ciara called him about twenty minutes later, cheerful and full of life. They met up at the car, and she was all smiles.

"What's so great today?" Kyle asked as they left the car park.

"I got a job!" she exclaimed, making him jump in his seat and almost stall the car.

"You what?"

"I had an interview at Kieran's, and I got it!" She was doing that annoying screaming that girls did when they were excited.

"You mean the fast food place?"

Kieran's was an institution in town. Cheap and delicious chips and burgers.

"Where else?"

"But there are no jobs out there. How did you manage that?"

"Kieran is Ronan's uncle. I thought you knew that? He put a good word in for me. It's only flexi hours, part-time like."

"And do they know about… eh, the baby?" It was odd to say it. It seemed to make it very real.

"Sure. It's not a permanent job anyway, it's only as long as they need me."

"So, when do you start? And how the hell are you gonna get to work?"

"Well, that's the catch. You might have to chauffeur me." She gave him a charming smile.

"I don't remember agreeing to that."

"Well, you didn't. But it's only so often and Ronan can help too. I knew I should have learned to drive a long time ago."

That would have been impossible. She was only 18 now. He said nothing.

"Look. Let's go home and celebrate. I'm making your favourite – spicy chicken and wedges. And," she said triumphantly and lifted up a bag, "I got some cheesecake."

Kyle groaned. Cheesecake was his favourite. If that was how she treated Ronan, he was one lucky guy.

* * *

After a successful and filling dinner, the two of them were

lazing around the kitchen table, quietly chatting about this and that. Kyle told Ciara how Georgina thought that he looked more and more like the Nirvana frontman every passing day – he left out the bit that he thought Georgina looked more and more like Halle Berry every day – much to her amusement. To his horror though, she agreed with Georgina.

"It's true. Your clothes are at least five years old, don't fit you and they look scruffy and dirty. The shaved head and cuts don't exactly help. Plus, you need to shave."

Kyle self-consciously touched his chin and realised that her last comment was true. "Kurt never had a shaved head though," he said, hoping that this was right. Not that he had ever seen.

"Well, it goes well with your look."

"I have nothing to wear anymore," Kyle grunted.

"Me neither."

"I can't afford to buy new clothes."

"I know. But I'm going to have to soon. I'm not going to fit into these much longer."

"Do you think we should…" Kyle started carefully. Ciara nodded.

"Do you know how?"

"We were shown once in home ec," Ciara said with an embarrassed smile.

"Right." Kyle got up and led the way into the utility room.

The place was a disaster. They had outgrown the laundry basket in the tall boy cabinet long ago, and there were clothes thrown onto the floor of the press. The door would no longer close, and clothes were falling onto the floor and thrown on the countertop.

"Oh shit," Kyle said quietly, taking in the sight in front of him. His mother had always kept the utility area so clean. Everything was washed, dried and ironed systematically and returned to their wardrobes. He had somehow been fooled into thinking that laundry took care of itself. Evidently it didn't.

"Oh my god. I must have stopped even coming in here to throw stuff in," Ciara said.

Kyle certainly had. He had clothes all over his bathroom floor, some under the bed and some stuck back inside the wardrobe in the hope that they might magically be clean again the next time he took them out.

"Right. What will we start with?" Ciara said, getting stuck into the pile at the foot of the press.

"Blacks?" Kyle missed his black clothes, having never been one for colours. Besides, most of his underwear and socks were black, and all that he had left were full of holes.

"Sounds good to me."

Ciara picked up an armful of black clothes off the floor, opened the washing machine and threw them in.

"Give me a few more. There's more room."

Kyle handed her another pile of black stuff. The washing machine ended up so full that they could barely close the door.

"Now what?"

In hindsight, he didn't understand why he had never learned to do his own laundry. What had he expected? That he would move from home straight into the arms and care of a girlfriend or wife? As if.

"Well, this is the stuff that goes in… Here, I think," Ciara said, biting her lip.

"Sure, that can't do any harm," Kyle said. Ciara took that as encouragement and poured purple liquid into the little drawer.

"I already plugged it in. It's kind of like the dishwasher really, I think. I need to pick a programme… It's set to 40; that should be fine. Main wash sounds good, doesn't it?" Ciara looked at Kyle, who nodded to confirm his acceptance.

"And then I press this button in..."

They stood staring at the machine for a few seconds. Then they heard some gurgling sounds and saw water building up inside. They high-fived and grinned stupidly at each other.

* * *

It took them the rest of that evening and the following day to sort out the laundry, including all the clothes that had not made their way into the utility. They did one load after another, throwing them into the tumble dryer as soon as they were done. Ciara did any ironing that was required while Kyle folded everything and paired up socks. They ran up and down the stairs with the clean clothes, re-filling their wardrobes and talking about how they had forgotten how many clothes they actually had. Kyle felt excited; it was almost like Christmas, having all those clothes to choose from when he got up in the morning. It was almost like having a reason to live again.

CHAPTER 9

Saturday came. Kyle drove into town to make his way into Juice. The band was not meant to be on until midnight – the bar's cunning plan to hold onto people rather than let them go into nightclubs – but he wanted to catch up with them before their duties took over. He was – he had to admit to himself – very curious to see if Tony was any good on the bass.

It was still early and quiet when he got in. He spotted Donal, Sam and John at the bar. Tony was hanging out at the bar a bit further away, long, sleek, dark ponytail tidy as hell.

The lads greeted him with pats on the back, and he was soon handed a cold pint of cider. Conversation flowed, even though he found it hard to take his eyes off Donal's new girlfriend who had shown up. Even in flat shoes, she was a good bit taller than Kyle, and although she was dressed in jeans and a plain white tank top, he still thought that she was probably the most gorgeous woman he had ever seen. She still did not seem to speak, at least to him, but that didn't bother him.

After a while, somebody tapped him on the shoulder. He turned around and faced Mel. She, on the other hand, was a good bit shorter than he, despite another pair of dangerously high shoes. She was dressed in such a tight, knee-length skirt that he wondered how she was able to walk.

"Hello," she said with that fake-coy smile.

Kyle greeted her with just a fake smile – not coy.

"So, you're still not playing tonight?" There was a note of disappointment in her voice.

Kyle shook his head. Mel looked at Tony as if judging.

"Well, I'm sure he's nowhere near as good as you," she said with a flattering head-tilt towards him. Then she carried on: "You should come over and say hello. The girls are dying to meet you."

Kyle looked over at the group of five or so girls nearer the door. He recognised Eliza and the annoying one that seemed to follow Mel everywhere. He had no interest in meeting any of them and could not imagine why they were so interested in him.

"I'll come over later," he said with a smile.

"Cool. Have a good time." Mel turned to go back to her crowd and let her hand rest on his arm when passing.

Kyle looked at her for a while as she was walking away. She was having trouble walking, but whether that was because of the heels or the tightness of her skirt, he could not tell. Whatever it was, it made her wiggle her bottom in an enticing way.

He threw himself deep into a conversation with John and Sam, Donal being too busy with his lady friend – not that he could be blamed for it. He was most stunned when he saw Georgina walk into the pub. It wasn't that she was there, because she had said that she would be, but she looked amazing. There was something wrong with him. He had gone from having no sexual interest whatsoever to wanting every woman that he laid his eyes on. Not right. He shook his head like a wet dog but could not help the imbecilic grin that conquered his face when she came over to him.

"Hello Kyle. You look well. I see you have ditched the Cobain look."

Kyle chuckled. "Yeah. You said it wasn't working. Who do I look like now then?"

He enjoyed the sudden change in him that she seemed to have brought on.

"Umm…" She was looking him up and down with a glint in her eyes. "Can I get back to you on that?" She giggled at that. That was unusual. She was normally not a girly girl who giggled. That was what surprised him about her attire too; she was dressed in a pale-coloured dress that clung to precisely the right spots. He felt the same tingling all over him that had caught him short at her salon the other day.

"You're not here on your own, are you?" he asked, half-hoping that she was and that he could ask her to join them.

"No, no. The girls will be here in a few. It's actually our Christmas party, from the salon. They just had to go and get cash and fags and things. I said I'd go on ahead and grab a table."

Dammit. He had hoped she was going to say "grab a man".

"So, you're here to see your old band then?"

Kyle nodded. "It's still my band."

"Oh, right. I heard what happened. You're better off taking a break."

Georgina accepted the drink that the bartender had finally gotten ready.

"That's a serious drink," Kyle said with a nod at the cocktail.

Georgina tilted her head and gave a laugh. "It's a serious occasion."

"So, it's just the girls then, is it?" How desperate. She probably had a six-foot-something of a dark-skinned boyfriend, a Will Smith-lookalike.

"Just us, yes. We're all girls at the salon and most of us are single. No boyfriends allowed tonight." She winked.

He was trying to figure out a way to find out if she had one, but he ran out of time. A group of slightly familiar-looking girls came in the door.

"Oh, there they are. I better go and join them. Well, you have a good night then, Kyle. I might talk to you later." She gave him one final, dazzling smile and headed back towards the girls.

He might have enjoyed the sight of Mel walking away from him – for mixed reasons – but watching Georgina was a painfully pleasurable sensation. He wished she wasn't going, but at the same time enjoyed watching her so much that it was perverted.

"Somebody did not enjoy that." Donal's voice came from behind his shoulder. Kyle twitched his neck to glance at him and then turned back to stare at Georgina.

"I enjoyed that very much," he said in a dreamy voice.

"Oh, I know you did. I think someone else does too," Donal said with a nod towards Mel. She looked petrified, her head turned towards Georgina's crowd but her eyes averted in his direction. She had clearly seen the exchange between him and Georgina. She was jealous.

A twisted feeling of pleasure boiled up inside him. He had thought he had lost it, but obviously not.

"Careful there, man." Donal patted him on the shoulder and turned back towards the bar to order another round. Kyle accepted the new pint that he consequently handed over.

Ciara and Ronan showed up soon afterwards. They came over to have a quick chat with him but soon found a quiet corner for the pair of them. It was odd seeing them together, slightly disturbing with Ronan's hands all over Kyle's little sister. It was made all the odder by the little new person that was supposedly growing inside of her, also Ronan's doing. Kyle detested Ronan a little but knew that Ciara was happy with him and that he treated her well. It was best not to meddle, even though someone should have before the damage had been done.

Mel came over a little later too, trying to act distant but too keen to give up that easily. She was joined by Eliza, who seemed totally in awe of Sam. Sam normally did not get an awful lot of female attention, and therefore Eliza's longing looks went ignored, much to Kyle's amusement. Sam wouldn't have minded. He wasn't picky, nor could he afford to be.

Mel didn't mention Georgina, although she kept glancing in her direction. Much to Kyle's disappointment, Georgina seemed to have forgotten about his presence after her staff had arrived. He tried absentmindedly to flirt with Mel, although his thoughts were elsewhere. He was getting tipsy.

After Mel left, Kyle made a point of mentioning to Sam that Eliza had been eyeing him up. The drummer would not have any of it and would not go over and talk to the girl despite everybody's – except Tony's – encouragement.

Their rowdy laughter and conversation was interrupted by the arrival of Ronan. He tapped Kyle on the shoulder and gestured for him to join him away from the group.

"Your sister thinks you should go easy on the drink," he said without further ado.

"Does she now?" Kyle said with a snigger. That was not like Ciara.

"Yes, she does. She thinks you've had enough, and so do I to be honest with you."

"And who are you to say?" Kyle glared at Ronan.

He ignored his question. "She just doesn't want a repeat performance of what has happened twice now. I don't think she cares whether it's the drink or your diabetes, she just wants you to stay out of trouble."

"I'm fine. If I need help, I'll ask for it." Kyle started to turn away from him.

"That's just it. I don't think you will."

He turned around to face Ronan again. He had his arms crossed in front of him. He looked adamant.

"I have not asked for your opinion, Ronan," Kyle retorted, emphasising his name in a sarcastic tone.

"I'm just saying to be careful with the drink," he repeated.

"Piss off!" Kyle shouted, taking a step towards the little wanker.

"I won't fight you," Ronan responded, not moving his arms from his chest.

"Will you not now?" Kyle's nose was inches away from Ronan's face.

"Wahey. Easy tiger." Donal's hand was on his shoulder, firmly pulling him away from Ronan.

"Get off me," Kyle snapped, pushing Donal away from him. He glanced around at the astounded faces around him, then slammed his pint glass on the bar and grabbed his jacket off the stool. He started heading towards the door but took an unexpected – at least to himself – halt at Mel's table.

"Come on," he said, reaching for her hand.

She looked up at him in surprise. "What?"

"Come on. We're going."

"But it's still early. The band…" She glanced around at her friends.

"Take it or leave it." He pulled his hand away but kept his eyes on her.

"OK then." Mel grabbed her coat from the pile on the couch and hastily said goodbye to her friends.

"Are you OK?" she asked when they had made their way out

of the pub.

"Sound," he said, zipping up his leather jacket to keep the chilly December air out. "Where do you live?"

"It's just about five minutes away. That way." Her gloved hand was pointing at a direction away from town centre.

They started walking, first in silence. Kyle eventually made a point of asking her how her week had been. To his amazement – and boredom – she started talking about her week in great detail, including everything that had happened at work. Most of it made no sense to him. She was working as a beauty therapist, for God's sake.

After a couple of blocks, he didn't know what got into him. Maybe he just wanted to shut her up or it was just all the sexual tension that had been building up. He took Mel's hand, pulled her aside and pushed her against the wall of a house and kissed her as if his life depended on it. He took her by surprise, and she was startled for an instant, but then she threw herself wholeheartedly into the kiss and looked at him admiringly when he finally pulled away.

"You're hot tonight," she said with a giggle.

"Yes, I am," he said, pushing his lips against her neck for a lingering moment. He was. He felt powerful, sexy and in control. He hadn't felt like that in a long time, and he had forgotten what that felt like.

"Come on then," he said, taking her hand and pulling her back towards the direction they were going. She seemed wobbly on her feet, and he wasn't sure if that was because of her shoes, skirt, the drink or him.

They came up to a three-storey townhouse a couple of minutes later. Mel let them in to the dark house and started walking up towards the stairs. He held her back by her hand, swinging her back round towards him.

"Is there anybody home?" he whispered.

"No. Everybody's out."

"All right then."

Kyle dragged her into the sitting room and gently pushed her onto the couch.

That was probably the only gentle thing that he did to her for the rest of the night, gentleness being replaced by a passion that had not had a chance to flourish in a while.

* * *

He woke up in Mel's bedroom the following morning. The sun was shining in through light curtains. He sat up and looked around to find that Mel was nowhere to be seen, and there was nowhere to hide in the room. It was tiny, with only enough room for a single bed. The little floor space that was left was taken up by a desk, two small shelves and a huge wardrobe. There was girly stuff everywhere; bottles of nail varnish, lipsticks, handbags, jewellery, clothes and shoes. It was like being thrown into the very being of a woman, except that he had no idea what most of the things were for.

He realised that what had woken him up was a knock and a whisper from the door.

"Mel," the whisper came again, a little louder. "Mel, I'm coming in."

The door opened before Kyle's sleepy brain had the chance to react. A dark-haired young woman appeared in the doorway, peering in from behind the door. He had never seen her before.

"Oh my god. I'm so sorry. I am so sorry," she said. Her eyes had widened at the sight of him. No wonder. She had just realised that there was what appeared to be a naked man in her friend's bed, even if she could only see his chest and head.

She was turning away from the room when a voice sounded from the hall: "I see you have met."

This was met with a stunned silence.

"Rose, this is Kyle, Kyle, Rose." Mel had appeared at the door with a tray.

"Yeah. I just wanted to talk to you about… something. It can wait." Rose had blushed all the way up to her ears.

"No, it's OK. Hold on." Mel carried the tray in and laid it down on the bed next to Kyle. She smiled at him. "I brought you some breakfast. Is tea and toast OK? I figured you need to keep your blood sugar levels… I don't know, right or something."

"It's grand," Kyle muttered. He was ravenous.

"I'll be back in a jiffy," Mel said and turned towards the door.

Through the closed door, Kyle could hear the girls chattering. He could not make out what they were saying for they were speaking quietly, but a certain amount of laughter was involved. He bit into a slice of toast with great appetite.

Mel returned to the room a couple of minutes later. She was wrapped up in a bright pink, fluffy dressing gown. She sat on the bed and reached out for another slice of toast.

"I don't eat toast very often. This is white too, really bad." She bit into the slice with a suspicious look on her face.

"You'll have to beat her back with a stick now," she said after she swallowed her bite. Kyle looked at her enquiringly, not having a clue what she was talking about.

"Rose. She has a thing about naked men," she said. She reached out to rub his short hair teasingly.

"Is that so," Kyle said, disinterested. She had certainly not seemed too excited. He had thought that he had started to re-gain the weight that he had lost immediately after the accident. Perhaps that wasn't a good thing. He was not doing much exercise recently, never having been a huge fan anyway.

"Couldn't blame her." Mel tucked her feet under the duvet. They were freezing cold against his thighs, but he didn't want to seem a wimp and didn't flinch.

"So, any chance of a repeat of last night?" Mel asked. She was batting her eyelids at him, the remaining piece of toast suggestively at her slightly open lips and the bathrobe halfway down her right shoulder, revealing just the right amount of her breasts.

"Let me have my breakfast first," he said. He pulled his gaze away from her, hard as it proved to be.

* * *

Mel was an unusual woman, he had found out. She hadn't been a bit bothered about letting him see her naked in the daylight of her room. Most women would either have covered the windows with something dark or demanded that he was blindfolded – not that he would have had a problem with that either – but not Mel. She was completely comfortable being seen. Kyle, on the other hand, had felt shy at first, not that he would have let her see that.

He stepped out of the car at his house – his future house anyway – and walked in. It wasn't until he got in that he remembered that Ciara was cross with him.

She was in the kitchen making a cup of tea and didn't even say hello when he came in. Wanda let out an excited bark and came over wagging her fluffy tail.

"Good morning," Kyle said testily. No response.

"Good night last night?" he carried on. He walked over to the fridge. It was a couple of hours since breakfast, and he was starving. He found some bacon and started working away at a grilled bacon sandwich.

"You obviously did," Ciara said sarcastically.

"I sure did."

"What the fuck were you thinking, picking a fight with Ronan?"

"He's not exactly bigger than me. I could have taken him." He knew that would annoy her. He wanted to annoy her.

"He's my boyfriend!" Her eyes were blazing.

"Indeed he is. He should not let that get into his head."

"You're such a jackass!"

"Thank you." Kyle stuck the prepared sandwich inside the grill and proceeded to make himself a cup of tea.

"What the fuck is wrong with you?"

"There is nothing wrong with me."

"Well, obviously not. You think it's OK to shag everyone again, as if nothing happened."

"I didn't think one woman could be multiplied to make up everyone."

Ciara was beyond words, at least for a moment, she was that angry.

"I think I preferred you when you were depressed. You were a real pain in the backside, but at least it was only mine and Cassie's backsides."

"I don't think I'd like to go there again."

"Well, you better leave Ronan alone. I love him."

"Good for you."

"Well, you know what, it is. It's very, very good. You should try it some time." Ciara grabbed her mug and headed towards the stairs.

"And maybe you should just leave my affairs to me." He lifted the lid of the grill and pulled out his delicious-smelling sandwich.

* * *

He spent the afternoon on the couch, dozing off and flicking through music channels, Sunday afternoon being a disastrous day for real TV. Besides, he hadn't felt like watching anything in weeks, and he was too tired.

He was half asleep when Ciara returned to the room and snatched the remote from him.

"Hey!" he exclaimed, rising onto his elbow.

"I'm watching Gossip Girl," she announced and sat down in the recliner.

"At... half three on Sunday afternoon?" he asked with a frown, after a look at the clock above the fireplace.

"I recorded it," she snorted and flicked it on.

He grunted and fell back onto the couch and to his half-asleep state. He woke up when Ciara dumped the remote back on him.

"You're taking me to work tomorrow morning. 11 o'clock."

"Am I now?" Kyle said. He sat up and rubbed his eyes. He felt stiff all over, and he had a feeling it wasn't all just because he had slept on the couch. It was that bloody woman.

"You are. Unless you want us to stay poor forever."

"You could just walk. Or get Ronan to bring you over."

"If he ever wants to come near the house again." She was looming over him, but that didn't make her much taller.

"Afraid of me, is he?" Kyle asked with a wry smile.

"Not a bit," she said with a laugh, "he's just annoyed."

Kyle stood up. "He should just keep his nose out of other people's business."

"It is his business!"

"I'm not a bit of his business." Kyle was pushing himself closer to Ciara.

"Are you going to hit me?" She sounded half-serious, but he

still wanted to laugh at her comment. He didn't.

"I don't hit women." He sounded cocky even in his own ears, as if he was in the habit of hitting men.

"You've hit me before."

"No, I haven't," he replied, but he was taken aback by that.

"Yes, you have. I was three."

That would have made him five or six at the time. He couldn't remember it at all. In any case, she had hardly been a woman at the time.

"That must have been some hit," he said, looking up and down at his sister.

"What's that supposed to mean?" she enquired.

"Look at what it's done to your head," he said, walking past her with a knock on his own head. She was still boiling with rage.

"You know, I still much preferred you when you were depressed and didn't speak!" she shouted after him.

He suppressed a smile and a further comment as he opened the fridge. He would have been happy with some version of himself in between. He hadn't missed talking to people. It generally just brought on all kinds of issues and awkward situations.

* * *

As promised, he drove Ciara to work the following morning. They were on relatively peaceful terms, although they didn't speak much. He dropped her off outside the shop. It wasn't due to open for another hour, but apparently, staff came in the hour early to get everything organised ahead of lunch time.

He parked the car with the intention of going around a few shops while Ciara got through her first day. He walked into a department store, thinking that he was going to look for some decent DVD box set for her.

He walked in through all the shelves of electricals – TVs, Blu-

Ray players, stereos, phones, iPods, all those things that they could not afford. He walked past the shelves of CDs, afraid to even check what was out for fear that he would end up spending his budget reserved for Christmas presents on himself.

There were tons and tons of DVD box sets. There was everything from Sex and the City to Lost, Friends to House and Ugly Betty to Scrubs. He didn't have any idea what she was watching nowadays or what she liked. Something girly, she was definitely a girly girl. Maybe she wouldn't have time to watch anything at all once the baby came? Of course, that was months ahead. Or was it? Had she ever said when she was due?

He pushed the worrying thought to the back of his mind and tried to focus on the task at hand. He had just spotted Gossip Girl when his eyes veered away from the good-looking people on the cover to a teenage boy at the CD shelves. He was about 16, and he was laughingly pointing at a CD cover to an older man. It was obviously his dad; they kind of looked alike and they both laughed at the same thing. Then the suspected father lifted up another CD that they were inspecting for a while.

Kyle was frozen on the spot. He was still clutching the box set in his hand, but it was all forgotten about. His eyes were welling up. He had always used to do that with his dad. They'd go Christmas shopping together, trying to sort out the womenfolk of the household, thinking that it was best to put their heads together to figure it out rather than alone. It was the only time they ever went shopping together, but it had always been a great time, something they looked forward to every year. It hit him that he would never do that again.

He let go of the DVDs. He was aware that they fell; he didn't know where and didn't care as he half-ran out of the store and back into the car park. He stopped at the corner between the department store and an empty shop unit, burying his head in the cold stone. The tears came down in big, loud sobs. He was shaking, he was shivering from the cold and he felt miserable. He had no father, he had no mother. He had nobody to go Christmas shopping with and hardly anybody left to buy for. There was going to be no turkey, no homemade mince pies, no Irish coffee and no piles of presents under the tree. There was going to be no tree. It was just going to be him and Ciara, feeling miserable.

"Are you OK, young man?" It was an elderly woman's voice that came from behind him.

He tried to nod, but it was hardly a distinguishable movement from all his shaking and shivering.

"Yeah, I'm fine," he muttered.

"Are you quite sure?" It sounded like she was taking a step closer.

"Yeah, thanks." He waved dismissively over his shoulder.

"If you are sure." Her footsteps descended down the footpath.

Kyle pulled himself away from the wall. His face felt numb, and he knew it wasn't the cold. It was the crying. He used his gloves to wipe away the tears from his cheeks while trying to avoid being seen by the people leaving the nearby cafe. He felt terrible. He felt weak and somehow lifeless, as if something had suddenly been pulled out of him, even if that had happened weeks earlier. He was grateful for the hood on his top. He pulled it over his head and proceeded to go into the cafe. He didn't want to be seen, but he desperately needed some sustenance, preferably something that would warm him up, and since he was going to have to drive home, going to the pub was not an option.

CHAPTER 10

The week went by quietly. Ciara seemed quite pleased with her new job and more or less forgot about her quarrel with Kyle. She was working at the till and learning all the different meal options. She liked her workmates too. All in all, it all sounded boring to Kyle, but at least it was extra money for them.

He dropped her into work on Friday evening for five o'clock. While he was at Kieran's, he went in and got himself a burger and chips. He started the rather slow drive home, making his way out of the rush-hour town centre as quick as he could.

He pulled into the driveway about 20 minutes later. The lights were on in the hall, he noticed when he was walking towards the door. They must have left them on when they were leaving.

He opened the door, walked in and saw two suitcases in the hall, along with a massive bag that probably still qualified as a handbag.

"There you are. I was wondering what happened to the two of you." Cassie appeared from the sitting room.

"What are you doing here?" Kyle asked in astonishment.

"No need to sound that excited," Cassie replied. "Where's Ciara?"

"I've just dropped her into work."

"To where?" Cassie's eyes reached the size of saucers.

"Work. She got a job at Kieran's."

"Oh my god. She's going to hate that."

"She says she likes it," Kyle said with a shrug.

"When did she start there?"

"On Monday."

"She'll get to hate it yet so. Poor girl. She never told me." Cassie threw her gloves on top of the handbag. "So, what have you been up to?"

"Do you mind? My food's gonna go cold." Kyle pointed towards the kitchen.

"Umm, food. I've had nothing since breakfast." Cassie sat down next to him and reached out for some of his chips as soon as he pulled them out of the bag.

"There's macaroni cheese in the fridge," he pointed out, hoping that that would take her mind off his chips. His mouth watered at the sight and smell of them. He was ravenous, and Kieran's chips were among the best things he knew.

"All right, all right, I get the hint." Cassie let out a deep sigh and got up. She threw the tub in the microwave.

"So, what are you doing here?" Kyle managed to mumble with his mouth full of burger.

"I'm moving back," his sister announced with a huge smile on her face.

"Moving back? What about your job? And Rob?"

"I have a job. I'm starting in dad's office after Christmas. As for Rob, he's already started looking over here."

"You're gonna work in the office?" Kyle was so astounded that the chips he had held in his fingers fell back onto the paper bag.

"Yeah. He did want one of us to take over."

"But you know nothing about property."

"Iris and James are going to show me the ropes, and I can learn on the side. I will start as a receptionist anyway, you know, just someone who's always at the office to answer the phone and that type of thing."

Kyle stuffed the re-picked-up chips into his mouth, his eyes wide with disbelief. Cassie was not a property type of person.

"I think people will be glad to know that someone in the family is taking over. I will get some business cards done for myself with the company logo on it. Cassandra French, real estate agent. Doesn't that sound cool?"

That was a remarkable change of tone from the last time he had seen her. She had been a wreck and had totally not considered what the future might bring.

"How long have you known about this?"

"Oh, Iris and I had it all pretty much agreed before I went back. I still had to go and pack of course, and I had to have a proper chat with Rob."

"And he's OK with all this?"

"He's happy to go wherever I'm going," Cassie said. She sat down and started eating her macaroni cheese off a plate. A plate. Kyle would never have bothered with a plate if he was microwaving something in a tub.

They carried on chatting while eating their meals. Cassie wanted to know what had been going on since she left, and Kyle was just trying to get his head around the new situation. Ciara had no way of not telling her now. It was going to be a nightmare all over again.

"I tell you what. If you bring my stuff up to my room, I'll make you a cup of tea."

Kyle didn't think that a fair deal at all. He would much rather have made his own cup of tea and left the suitcases where they were, but he didn't want to start arguing first thing. Besides, they looked too heavy for Cassie.

That turned out to be the case. He grabbed the two suitcases with the good intention of taking them both up at the same time, and he did, despite having to stop about six times on the way up to rest. The luggage weighed a ton – each.

He felt like he had run a marathon when he made his way back downstairs – a marathon on a full stomach.

"What took you so long?" Cassie said with a cheeky grin when he hauled himself up on his chair and accepted the offered cup of tea.

"Very funny," he muttered in response.

"It's so bloody cold in here. I just turned the heating on."

"The oil is low," Kyle pointed out. He worried about that every so often, the oil running out and them not being able to order any more.

"And let me guess: you can't afford to get more?" Cassie asked with raised eyebrows.

"You got it."

She sighed. "Right. I'll get some ordered on Monday so."

"And how can you afford it?"

"I got a good bit of money when I left work. Christmas bonus, my normal bonus, holidays I haven't taken, that kind of thing. I'll be all right until I start earning money after Christmas. Actually, I am going in for a little while on Monday, just to see what the story is. I look forward to working with Iris, she's so lovely."

Kyle felt an unpleasant twinge. His last memory of Iris was not exactly cheerful. Well, it was in a way, but he had not wanted her to catch him with his hands on Mel's buttocks.

* * *

He woke up in deep confusion. He was lying in his bed on his back. He was unable to move. It wasn't that he was in pain; it

129

was just that his brain was not able to send the signal to move his limbs. It was like he was paralysed.

He remembered having a dream about being in the hospital. He had been sitting on a hospital bed, just like he had that time.

He had been sitting on the bed in the early hours of the morning. His head, face and arm were sore and he was cold. He felt extremely drunk and totally sober at the same time. For hours, he had kept asking any member of the hospital staff if he could see his parents, and they all either declined or just avoided the question. He had kept at it, kept and kept at it, until eventually a plump, kind-faced nurse had given in.

"Believe me love, you don't want to see them," she had said.

He had asked why he wouldn't.

"You want to remember them the way they were." He could still hear those words exactly as she said them, sympathetically but resolutely, making sure he would not ask again. They had been going around in his head for days afterwards, but when he first heard them, he had just stared at her. She had not looked at him but just busied herself with the chart or something and eventually asked him what he wanted for breakfast. He hadn't wanted any, but they had brought some anyway.

Eventually the penny had dropped, and the realisation had brought along a new wave of shock, which had kept him in the hospital for another 24 hours. It wasn't literally shock, but they had kept saying that he was not ready to go home.

He slowly came out of his paralysis and sat up on the bed. It was only early, but he could no longer sleep. He went to have a shower, got dressed and headed downstairs.

He had expected a cold and deserted kitchen, but instead, he was met with a mouth-watering smell of pancakes and the sound of a roaring fire in the sitting room. He had also forgotten in his confused state that Cassie was back.

She was standing at the cooker turning over pancakes. She was all dressed up in a tartan skirt and a green jumper.

"Good morning." She turned around and looked at him with a bright smile. "I am making your favourite, although I was not expecting you for," she paused to look at the clock on the wall, "at least another two hours."

It was ten past eight.

"I couldn't sleep," he said, sitting down at the table.

"Me neither. I was too excited. It's so good to be back."

Kyle gave her back a weird look. What the hell was she on?

"Does Ciara know you're here?"

"Not yet. I was gone to bed when she came home. I heard her though. She was talking to Wanda and she started barking when Ciara let her out. Such a racket!"

"So, when are you going to tell her?"

"When she gets up." Cassie smiled again.

She had barely finished her line when they heard a door open upstairs. Then they heard the bathroom door close, a few moments later the sounds of sloshing water and then footsteps on the stairs. Cassie gave Kyle a conspiratorial smile to keep quiet.

Ciara stepped into the kitchen in her pyjamas and dressing gown. She looked at the figure at the hob.

"Am I still asleep?" she asked. She continued with a big yawn.

"Nope," Kyle replied. Cassie's smile widened further.

"Cassie, is that really you?"

"It's me!" Cassie spread out her arms in a dramatic gesture.

"Oh my god! It's so good to see you!" Ciara ran straight into her sister's arms.

"What are you doing here?" Ciara asked once they let go of

each other.

"I'm moving back."

"Oh, that's brilliant! I'm so excited!"

Kyle was touched by how young and naive Ciara looked right then. She did not look like a woman who was about to become a mother in the next few months.

"I'm making breakfast. It's nearly ready. Kyle, will you make some coffee?"

Kyle groaned but did not disagree. That was how it was going to be now, again – his sisters bossing him around and him not bothering to stand up for himself, except occasionally when it would all get out of hand and they would all want to kill each other – or him, anyway.

With the coffee ready, Cassie put three plates of pancakes and bacon with maple syrup on to the table. Kyle remained mostly quiet while Ciara and Cassie had practically the same conversation as he had had with Cassie the evening before.

When their plates were empty and their stomachs full, Cassie sat back in her chair and looked from Ciara to Kyle and back with a triumphant smile on her face. Kyle was immediately worried.

"I think we should decorate today."

Ciara and Kyle looked at her with mixed feelings.

"I mean, for Christmas. Put the decorations up."

There was still a stunned silence.

"Are you sure that's... you know, correct?" Ciara asked in a small voice.

"I'm sure it is. They can't take everything from us, can they? But we don't need to write Christmas cards."

"Phew, what a relief," Kyle said mockingly.

"Enough of that," Cassie said, but to his surprise, she did not sound annoyed. "What do you think?"

"I need to get changed," Ciara pointed out. Cassie nodded.

"No such issues with you then," she said with a look at Kyle. "You look like you could be in a nineties boyband."

He was dressed in old clothes – a pair of grey combats and a black turtleneck jumper. He was just trying to feel comfy.

"And what would you know about nineties boybands?" he enquired.

"Oh, a lot. Late nineties, I was a teenager and I was quite into them. Particularly 5ive. Do you remember them?" Cassie looked at Ciara.

"Not really. Just the name really."

"Yeah. They used to spell it with a number five and then 'ive', the five replacing the f."

"Right." Kyle was about to fall back asleep again.

"It's not a bad thing to look like you're in a boyband. Girls like boybands."

"They don't anymore," Ciara pointed out, "boybands are out of fashion."

"If you were in a boyband," Cassie carried on, ignoring Ciara's valid point, "which one would you be? Let me think." She leaned closer to have a look at Kyle, as if she had never seen him before.

"You know, I think you would just be The One That Nobody Ever Remembers Is In The Band," she said with a laugh.

"That's a great compliment," Kyle said and got up to put his dishes – and not anybody else's – in the dishwasher. "Just as well I'm not in a boyband then."

"Are you back in the band?" Cassie asked.

"Not yet," he said. "But I will be."

* * *

They all met up at the upstairs landing about half an hour

later, Cassie having walked the dog, Ciara having changed into something more appropriate and Kyle having spent most of his time looking for the ladder in the shed and then dragging it up the stairs – on his own, of course.

Now he was balancing on the ladder while trying to open the hatch into the attic. It was stuck, as usual. Eventually, after enough pushing and shoving, it gave in and slid onto the attic floor.

"All right?" Cassie asked as Kyle looked uncomfortable on the top step of the ladder. He was not a fan of heights.

"Yeah. Here." He started handing stuff down – bags of tinsel, wreaths, lights, stars. Next came the leg for the tree. It was a heavy bastard.

"Here, I'll take it," Ciara offered, reaching up for it, which pulled her top up to reveal her stomach. Kyle quickly moved to hand the leg to Cassie instead. Once she had reached for it, he gave a meaningful look at Ciara's belly. She quickly pulled her top back down and blushed. He didn't think anything was showing yet, but then, women were better at that kind of stuff.

He handed down the tree and the reindeer-shaped light frame that was normally up on the front lawn.

"Right," Cassie said, beaming at the two of them. "Should we get started?"

Kyle carefully descended the ladder, knowing – unfortunately – that he was not done with it yet. All the empty boxes and bags would have to be put back up in the attic once the decorations were up.

"You'll sort this one out, won't you?" Cassie looked at him with a nod towards the reindeer. "We'll start on the house."

It didn't sound like he had much of a choice. The girls started dragging bags downstairs, and he was left with the awkward box of lights.

* * *

It took him the best part of an hour, several blown light bulbs, a lot of cursing and a pair of frozen hands to get the bloody reindeer up and working on the lawn. He walked over to the sitting room to warm his hands by the fire. They were so cold he could probably have stuck them inside the fire without feeling a thing.

The two girls were sitting in the room with half-empty cups of tea.

"Where is mine then?" Kyle asked with an expectant look at them.

"Oh. We just thought we'd have a cuppa while we were waiting for you to finish. You know, before we start on the tree."

"And it never crossed your mind that I might want one?" Kyle exclaimed. Let alone that he just might have wanted help with the damned animal.

"I'll go make you one now," Ciara said and leapt up from the recliner. She had guessed that a fight would have ensued otherwise.

Starting to feel his hands again, Kyle went to sit down on the couch.

"I think we should go down to Cork for Christmas," Cassie announced and finally looked up from her mug.

"I won't be able to."

Cassie and Kyle both turned to look at Ciara, who was standing in the kitchen doorway, looking at them across the dining room.

"There's no point. I'm working Christmas Eve and again on St Stephen's night. There's no point to go just for the night."

"You can't stay here on your own either," Cassie replied.

"I don't need to be on my own. I've Ronan and his family. It wouldn't be fair on you."

"I think we should be together. Can you not get the time off?"

"I'm only on flexi hours to help out when they're busy. It wouldn't be fair."

Cassie looked unhappy.

"I guess we'll just have to do our best then," she sighed, burying her head in her hands.

"Sure. We can have a Christmas to ourselves." Ciara returned to the room and handed Kyle his tea.

"What is the point? None of us can even cook a turkey."

"We could have a go," Ciara said but was cut short by Cassie's angered look.

"And what the fuck do you think we should do then?" Her eyes gave Kyle a piercing look.

"We should fuck Christmas and just pretend it's not there. What the hell are we gonna do here on our own? It's not going to be Christmas without them."

"Not with that spirit it's not! We're still a family."

"We're not a family!" Kyle was squeezing the mug so hard he thought it was going to break. "There's five of us in this family, except that there isn't any more. I don't want a Christmas this year. Full stop. No, exclamation mark."

"Well, I don't know about you Kyle, but I will…"

"What is it with the two of you?" Ciara had stood up from her chair. "Why do you always have to fight? Can't you just get along for God's sake!"

"It's because she always thinks we should do as she wants," Kyle said at the same time as Cassie said, "Because he never does as he's told!"

They exchanged annoyed looks.

"There's three of us in this… household. It's not a dictatorship."

Ciara looked at Cassie, who, much to Kyle's amusement and triumph, looked ashamed and blushed. "But we really don't need any rebels either. Can't we just discuss things like normal people?"

Kyle felt embarrassed and hid his face behind the mug, taking an unusually big swig of tea.

"Right. I'll try to. He just really gets on my nerves recently."

Ciara shot a warning look at Cassie. "None of that. You both get on my nerves, but I try not to shout at you."

She fails miserably at that, Kyle thought quietly. They had been tearing each other's hair out only the other day, only she had not been very successful at that, him not having much to grab onto.

"Now, will we put up that tree or not?" Ciara pointed at the boxed tree that was lying next to the door.

CHAPTER 11

Kyle got up late on Sunday morning after a restless night. He wasn't sure what had kept him awake exactly, apart from a loud, howling wind and hammering rain, but he had kept waking up only to fall straight back into an uneasy sleep.

Cassie had taken Wanda for a walk when he got downstairs, and Ciara was sitting in the kitchen with a glass of orange juice, reading what looked like a women's magazine.

Kyle made himself a cup of coffee and some toast and sat down at the end of the table, staring across the table through the dining room and sitting room and out the back door. It was a miserable day with rain falling sideways.

Ciara pushed her magazine away and looked at Kyle. She was staring at him for a long time. He lowered his slice of toast and looked back at her questioningly.

"What's wrong?" He was annoyed. He had looked at himself in the mirror before he came downstairs and had looked his usual self, dark circles under the eyes aside.

"I need to tell Cassie," she breathed. Kyle thought that his heart missed a beat at that. There was going to be war…

"Right. What do you want me to do, though?" He took a big gulp of his coffee. It burned his mouth, black and fresh as it was.

"I think it would be better if you weren't here… You know

what she's like."

"And where am I meant to go?"

Ciara shrugged.

"It's the last Sunday before Christmas. The shops will be open. You can go anywhere, really. It's just for a couple of hours. You know, until it all blows over." She looked at him pleadingly.

Kyle sighed. "I guess. Now?"

"You can finish your breakfast," Ciara said with a smile. "Thanks, Kyle."

Cassie appeared about ten minutes later with a thoroughly wet and muddy Wanda, who immediately made her way to the rug next to the fireplace. By that time, Kyle had already grabbed a couple of chocolate bars from the kitchen press and was dangling the car keys from his hand when Cassie re-emerged downstairs, having changed into dry clothes.

"Where are you going?" she asked with a quizzical look at him.

"I'm just going for a drive," he responded, immediately slipping into defence mode.

Cassie shrugged on her way into the kitchen.

"Oh," she said turning around, "will you get some tomatoes on the way back? I need them for dinner, and the ones we have have gone soft. Thanks."

Tomatoes. Urgh. They were the furthest thing from his mind, and he could have sworn he was going to forget them.

He reversed the car out of the garage and started off towards town. He had no idea where he was going. He didn't want to go shopping. It was going to be a disaster again, and in any case, he had already got most presents. Online shopping was a blessing.

For some reason, he found himself on a familiar street of three-storey townhouses. He pulled up beside a white-washed house with a simple front garden – gravel on either side of the stone

139

path – and sat in the car for a minute or two. Then he smiled to himself and got out of the car, walking quickly up the path before he could change his mind.

The door was opened within a matter of seconds after he pressed the doorbell.

"Hey! What are you doing here?" Mel shrieked when she saw him in the doorway.

"I was just… in the area." He grinned at the cliché.

"Oh. Lovely. Come on in," she said waving him off towards the hall.

It was weird to see her dressed like she was, in a big, bulky jumper and a pair of tracksuit bottoms and particularly without her trademark heels. She was a good seven inches shorter than him in her slippers. He thought that she looked better, with her hair tied back and without a trace of make-up, than she normally did. Sort of fresher and more natural, like God intended or something.

"Do you want a cup of tea or anything?"

She seemed oddly nervous.

"Is anybody home?" he asked, glancing around towards the sitting room and kitchen.

"No, they're all at work. Last Sunday before Christmas, you know," she said with a smile.

"In that case I don't. How about…?" he said with an upwards glance towards the stairs.

Her eyes lit up and a cheeky smile reached her lips. She reached out a hand towards him and partially dragged him up the stairs.

* * *

His phone rang about an hour later. It was Ciara.

"I think I need you to come home," she said the moment he picked up the phone. She didn't even ask where he was.

"What's going on?" he asked, trying to pull his thoughts away from the hand that was caressing his stomach.

"It didn't go down too well. She's like an anti-Christ. I think it would help if you were here."

"Right," he sighed. "I'll be there in about 20 minutes."

"Thanks Kyle."

"Who's that?" Mel asked when he put his phone down on the pile of clothes on the floor. Her hand was slowly making its way further down. Not exactly ideal, considering that he had 20 minutes to spare.

"It's my sister. I need to go home." He reached out to pick his shirt off the floor.

"I'm sure she can wait. I have a few plans for the afternoon... I mean, since you're here."

Kyle looked at her over his shoulders while buttoning his shirt. It was a crying shame. There were a thousand promises on that face, let alone on her fingertips...

"No. I'm sorry. I have to go."

He got up and pulled the rest of his clothes on without looking at her. She looked heart-broken. Why did women have to be such drama queens? Make a big deal out of everything. And she had no idea how he felt... Bullshit.

"Can I see you during the week?" Mel asked when he threw his jacket on.

"Yeah. Sure." He pulled the car keys out, his mind already elsewhere.

"Cool. It was great to see you," she said when he walked out the door.

"You too," he said with a smile.

On his way back to the car he started thinking how rude he must have seemed. He should have kissed her. He really should have kissed her. She would be offended by him not kissing her. She would pore over that for hours now, possibly with her friends. Oh gosh, the friends. What exactly did girls talk about with their friends? How much detail did they go into?

He cringed when he sat down in the car. Focus. Home to face the war.

It was surprisingly quiet in the house when he got back. Wanda ran to the door with her tail wagging. The two girls sat at the kitchen table, not looking at each other. Kyle took the remaining bar of chocolate out of his pocket and sat down opposite to Ciara.

"What's up?"

He took a bite of the Mars bar, sending little bits of chocolate falling on the table.

"Cassie's not happy about the news," Ciara said. She kept her eyes on the table and stretched her sleeves to what seemed like impossible lengths.

"You mean you knew about this?" Cassie said with a disgusted look at Kyle.

"Only a few days…"

"He was here. And he took it much better anyway."

"How did you really think I could have taken this well? You're barely 18 and just about know this fella… How could it possibly be good news?" Cassie stared at her sister with blazing eyes.

"Ronan is a nice person, and I love him. Of course it's good news."

"What do you think mum and dad would have said? This would never have happened if they were around. They wouldn't have let it happen."

"It DID happen when they were around! They would have been happy to have a grandchild."

"Oh Jesus. I should have stayed here to keep an eye on you.

That was meant to be your job." Cassie's eyes focused on Kyle.

"He's hardly much good at that. He can't keep it in his pants either."

"Don't speak like that, Ciara! At least he hasn't gotten anybody pregnant!"

"Not that we know. It's between me and Ronan anyway. He's happy about it. He'll support me."

"And where are you gonna live? You don't even know anything about kids. You've never held a bloody baby!"

"No, but a normal baby," Ciara said with a triumphant look at her sister. "You're just jealous because I'm going to be a mother before you!"

"That's a load of bullshit! I don't want children for many years yet! I'm only 25!"

Ciara stuck her tongue out at Cassie. Kyle had to hold back the laughter.

"I'll have nothing to do with the kid. I don't care. I just won't." Cassie made a dismissive motion with her hand.

"Good! You wouldn't be much of a role model anyway!"

They just carried on like that. Kyle sat there listening to their argument and wondering why he was there in the first place. They were going to be at each other's throats soon. Maybe they needed some distraction. Possibly he could get them to gang up on him instead... He was going to be in so much trouble, but...

He loosened the top button on his shirt and straightened the collar a bit, as if to scratch his neck. The girls were so engrossed in calling each other names that they didn't notice. He did it again, this time clearing his throat at the same time.

"What the hell's wrong with you, too?" Cassie said, turning towards him, presumably about to tell him to stay out of it. Then her eyes shifted to the dark spot on his neck, exactly like he'd intended. "What the hell is that?"

"You dirty little sod!" Ciara exclaimed.

"Where did that come from?" Cassie said with a furious look in her eyes.

"You've been to see Mel, haven't you?"

"You talk about her as if she was a prostitute," Kyle pointed out.

"Well, she's not far from it. Except I think she actually does it for free, because she likes you for some strange reason." Ciara looked disgusted.

"You haven't got her pregnant as well, have you?" Cassie butted in.

Kyle gave her an annoyed frown in response.

"That's the last thing we'd need. You're obviously not even going out with her, are you?"

"Nope."

"I told you. He's a male slut, is our Kyle." Ciara sat back in her chair with crossed arms and stared at him.

"And what is wrong with what I'm doing? It's not like you have never screwed anybody just for the sake of it."

"I fucking haven't!" Ciara shouted.

"She isn't just a piece of meat." That was Cassie.

"I didn't say she was."

"The way you talk about her, that's how it seems to me," Ciara retorted.

"Maybe she's happy with that."

"I'm telling you, she's not," Ciara said quietly.

"And you don't need to come in here and brag about it," Cassie said, with a wave towards the bite on his neck.

"I'm not bragging about it."

"I bet you asked her for that," Ciara added.

"It was her own idea. Handy though, huh? Got you talking."

"Is that what this is about? To get us talking?" Cassie looked at him in disbelief.

"You no longer want to kill each other, do you?" He got up and got a can of Coke from the fridge before sitting back down again.

"Damn right we don't. I think we'd rather kill you now," Cassie said.

Kyle leaned back with a grin. "Such was the plan."

"You're weird," Ciara said shaking her head.

"Maybe you could actually have a sensible, adult conversation now. She's not changing her mind, you know?" He started getting up again and nodded towards Cassie.

"I know," she sighed, leaning her chin in her hand.

He pushed his chair back under the table and started walking towards the sitting room, conscious of their eyes on his back.

CHAPTER 12

He listened to the girls leave for work the following morning. It all seemed acquiescent enough downstairs. He didn't hear any shouting, slamming doors or such. It wasn't until they were gone that he realised that he was going to be stuck at home all day, until they got back. He had no car, so he either needed a lift or to attempt that walk again if he wanted to get into town. He didn't feel like either. He'd had a bad night's sleep and got up from bed with a heavy head. It was a bit like being hungover even though he knew that he wasn't.

Wanda wagged her tail at him enthusiastically from her spot in the sun, conveniently in the middle of the kitchen floor. He didn't have the heart to tell her to move, so he made his breakfast carefully stepping around the dog.

It was, amazingly enough, a sunny day. It seemed kind of pointless to have all the Christmas lights on on such a day, but he couldn't be bothered to go and turn them all off either.

Despite the sunshine, the house felt cold. Cassie had probably not even ordered the heating oil yet, and even if she had, they would be lucky if it arrived in time for Christmas.

After breakfast, Kyle went out to get coal and timber from the shed to start a fire. He had never, ever lit so many fires in his life. It hadn't been any of his business. He had thought that he would be crap at it too, not being the most practical person around, but he was surprisingly good at getting the fire going.

Once the fire was happily burning away, he fetched himself a glass of orange juice and sat down on the floor in front of the fire, with Wanda retiring to her cushion a few feet away. It was comfortably warm next to the fire.

* * *

He woke up to frightened shouts from the sitting room doorway.

"Kyle! Kyle! Oh my god. Are you all right?"

There was a hand on his shoulder, ready to shake him. He opened up his eyes to avoid this further irritation that was threatening him.

"Are you all right?" Cassie was kneeling down next to him with a worried frown on her face and her handbag thrown on the floor with the contents bursting out.

He sat up slowly, the light in the room hurting his sleepy eyes.

"Yeah. Yeah, I'm OK. What's the panic?"

"I thought something had happened to you. I thought you had gone hypo or something... Are you sure you're OK?"

Ciara stood in the doorway holding her coat and looking down at him with a worried expression.

"Yeah... I must have just fallen asleep."

He turned to glance at the fire next to him. It was nearly dead. He must have been asleep for a long time.

"What's the time?"

"It's past three o'clock. Look, you're gonna have to eat something now anyway. Ciara's making some sticky chicken thighs, but it's gonna be a while. Fruit salad?"

"Whatever," Kyle muttered and started to get up as well, not liking sitting down at his sister's feet.

"You know, with you being at home all day now, I think you

147

should start to make yourself useful." Cassie chatted from the kitchen while preparing the snack.

Kyle made his way to the recliner without a word.

"I mean, with us working, someone needs to take care of the housework and cooking. You're not going to be a kept man, you know that?"

She arrived in the sitting room with a bowl of mixed fruit in her hand that she pushed towards him.

"You know I can't cook."

"Ciara seems to have a different opinion on that. She says you're not that bad."

Kyle reluctantly took the fruit salad from Cassie. He wasn't a big fan of fruit salad. He didn't mind eating fruit, but a fruit salad was an embarrassment.

"Not if you don't mind eating fish and chips every day."

"Bullshit. You can do better than that. After all, you can't just expect to meet a woman who will cook for you when you move out."

"Who says I'll move out? It's my house."

"Well, when we move out then, whichever way it goes. Anyway, we'll both be here tomorrow so you're off the hook for another day."

Cassie walked back into the kitchen, her hands confidently on her hips as if she were certain that he had bitten the bait.

* * *

They all went into town early the following day. The girls insisted that they needed to get supplies for Christmas as well as Christmas presents. Kyle was sorted out with his Christmas shopping, thanks to the internet, although he was still nervously waiting for a couple of the presents to arrive. His sisters had not allowed him to stay home on his own. Whether it was because of the fright they had got the previous day or because they just wanted to make him part of the household routine, he didn't know.

They all went their separate ways around town, not wanting one another to see what they were buying. Kyle was aimlessly walking around for the best part of half an hour because he really needed nothing. He was good at wasting money but didn't want to.

He had only just turned around a corner when he spotted Mel across the street. If he'd had the chance, he would have ducked behind a car or retraced his steps quickly in order to avoid her, but it was too late. She had spotted him. Did the girl never work?

She gave him a big wave and started across the street, making a couple of cars slam on their brakes. Kyle was less than pleased about the attention that she had caught, and for all the wrong reasons.

"Hello gorgeous," she cooed as soon as she got to his side of the street. She reached out to kiss him on the lips in a very familiar fashion.

"I don't have to go to work for another 40 minutes or so. Do you wanna go and grab a coffee?" She didn't even bother waiting for his reply; she just stuck her arm through the crook of his and started to pull him back the way she had come from. She had a couple of bags dangling from her arm. She was the type of woman who lived for shopping – and for mentally torturing any unfortunate men who had happened to find her attractive.

They were in the cafe that was practically across the street from GG's – no wonder since he had subconsciously been heading that way. He didn't like it though. He didn't want to run into Georgina when he was with Mel.

Mel didn't want anything to eat. He didn't either but forced himself to order a biscuit with his cappuccino and be a gentleman and pay for Mel's drink as well while she sat down next to the window with all her bags around her.

"So, you doing your Christmas shopping as well?" she asked with a huge smile when he sat down with their coffees.

"Sort of. The girls are and they dragged me along."

"Poor you. Where are they now?"

"No idea. We all went our separate ways."

Mel seemed to have lost interest in what his sisters were doing and started excitedly chatting about what she had bought. Most of the things meant nothing to him. She even pulled out a party top that he was forced to compliment.

He was gripped by light panic when he saw Georgina walking past the window. He tried to use his willpower to make her walk past the cafe, but of course she didn't. She walked right in and straight up to the counter. She hadn't seen him.

"You OK?" Mel asked with a chuckle. He probably looked like he was ready to wipe sweat off his forehead.

"Yeah," Kyle said and went back into his half-listening mode when she carried on talking about a St Stephen's night party that some of her friends were having. By the sound of it, she wanted him to go... He didn't know for sure. He couldn't take his eyes off Georgina, and he wasn't sure if it was because she was so damn hot or because he was afraid that she would see him.

"So, can you go then?"

"Umm..." Kyle turned to look at Mel's eager face again. He tried to recall what the last thing was that she had said. Something about the party. She was asking him to go.

"Erm... I'm not sure. The girls might have made plans."

"Well, will you find out? You don't want me to go dateless, do you? I mean, it's a good party, lots of cute boys there."

Judging by the look on her face, she was trying to blackmail him by making him jealous. It didn't exactly work.

"Hey Kyle, I didn't see you there. How are you?"

Hearing that voice, Kyle realised that he had much preferred the tight spot that he had been in to the one he now found himself in.

"Georgina. How are you?" Kyle tried to keep cool.

"Your hair is doing well. Give it another couple of weeks and you'll be able to get your highlights back if you want. After Christmas. I'll do them for you." There was an inexplicable, cheeky smile on her face.

"So, you're staying here for Christmas then?" Georgina carried on. She had only given Mel a quick glance when she arrived and had now blanked her out completely.

"Yeah. Just the three of us."

"I suppose you might be better off that way. Under the circumstances. It's going to be tough for you." She looked genuinely sorry when she said that, but then, Georgina was a genuine person.

Kyle didn't know what to say.

"Anyway, you guys have a good Christmas. You pop in after New Year if you want your hair done. See ya." She gave the two of them a big smile when wishing them a good Christmas before walking out the door with a cardboard tray full of paper cups.

"You're very friendly with her, aren't you?" Mel said with a critical look at Georgina, who walked past the window before disappearing out of sight.

"She cuts my hair," Kyle said, self-consciously running a hand over the stubble that was his hair.

"I could tell that. Do you know her outside the salon?"

"A little. I mean… I talk to her when I see her."

"She used to go out with this big black fella, a bouncer in Maccie's. You'd know him. Jay, I think he's called."

"Didn't know that," Kyle said, trying to sound nonchalant and stirring his cappuccino with the wooden stick.

"Yeah. They broke up a couple of months ago. I think he's a bit of a baddie really. Must be the type she likes."

Kyle gave her a suspicious look that she didn't notice, being too busy checking her phone. Was she trying to put him off Georgina? He had done nothing in the minute that they had spent chatting that could have been considered suspicious. He had barely spoken to her. Perhaps Mel still remembered him talking to Georgina in Juice that time?

"You know, there's going to be a really good crowd at this party. Eliza and Rose will be there, you know them. I don't know for sure, but Donal might be going. Unless they've a gig… Oh." She looked startled at that, and Kyle's head had jerked up upon hearing that.

"I don't think so though. I just thought they might. You're still not playing with them, then."

Kyle shook his head. He really needed to get talking to Donal. The whole band situation was cracking him up.

"You should talk to Donal. I don't think he really likes Tony anyway. This could be your chance."

"Yeah. I'll let you know. You know, I need to go, I said I'd meet the girls at 12."

Mel looked disappointed. "I suppose. I need to be at work in a few as well."

She stood up and grabbed Kyle's arm when he was trying to make his way towards the door. She put a hand on the back of his neck and pulled him in for a kiss.

"Happy Christmas," she whispered into his ear before releasing him.

"You too," he muttered before backing out of the door, almost walking into a middle-aged woman who was on the way in.

Kyle didn't understand when he had become such a loser. He didn't particularly like Mel, yet he was leading her on like there was no tomorrow. Sure, the physical side of things had a certain appeal to him, but she was shallow beyond belief and didn't seem to have much interest in anybody but herself. Maybe he was just getting old, but sure there must be more to it?

Cassie and Ciara were already waiting for him outside the supermarket when he showed up.

"There he is, our playboy of a brother," Cassie said indignantly when he stopped next to them.

"What have I done now?" Kyle groaned with a look at her and Ciara.

"Cassie tells me that they're fighting over you," Ciara said with a chuckle and grabbed him by the arm to bring him into the store.

"I saw you and your little girlfriend having coffee, with your hairdresser," Cassie made quotation mark signs with her fingers at the last word, "hovering over you like some chaperone."

"She wasn't…" Kyle started to protest.

"Now, now, we're women, we know these things," Ciara said, still holding on to his arm.

"She's not my girlfriend either."

"Which one?" Cassie retorted while pulling a trolley out of the bay.

"Georgina's just a friend."

"Yeah, and the other one is just a female friend who happily takes her panties off for you when you as much as look at her."

When had Cassie become so foul-mouthed?

"Cassie!" Ciara exclaimed in horror. "There are people around," she continued discreetly.

"She's just pissed off because Rob can't give her what she wants," Kyle said flippantly and released himself from Ciara's hold to get away from Cassie, who he was afraid was going to throw a raw potato at him.

"Oh yeah, and you're a regular Don Juan, aren't you?" Cassie said, tossing a cabbage into the trolley – much to Kyle's relief.

"Guys," Ciara hissed, "not here."

"Perhaps you should ask those in the know," Kyle said and walked away from them towards the fruit section. He looked at his two sisters while bagging apples. Ciara was effectively blocking Cassie's way and seemed to be talking to her in a calming manner while Cassie carried on glaring at him over Ciara's shoulder.

Kyle stayed well ahead of them for the rest of the tour around the store, but Cassie made no effort to speak to him at all – not even to insult him.

* * *

Kyle had been worried about spending two days in the house alone with Cassie while Ciara was at work. As it happened, they just kept busy and avoided any topics that might have resulted in an argument. They cleaned the house from top to bottom – Cassie's idea, not his – and Kyle did his best to help out with various Christmas dishes. Before any of them knew it, it was the evening of Christmas Eve and Cassie and Kyle were waiting for Ciara, watching TV while a pizza was cooking away in the oven.

Kyle had conveniently forgotten about Mel asking him to go to some party until his phone rang. It was the first thing on his mind as soon as her name showed up on the screen. He wanted to ignore the call but couldn't very well do it with Cassie eyeing him curiously.

"Hello sexy," Mel said in her usual chirpy, flirtatious tone when he picked up. He made his way into the study to make sure Cassie couldn't hear the conversation.

His response was a slightly more demure, "Hi, how are you?"

As expected, Mel wanted to know if he would be coming to the party or not. He wasn't given much of a choice without being a complete prick.

He hadn't thought about it. He didn't want to go, but Ciara would be working and he didn't fancy spending St Stephen's night alone with Cassie. So he said yes.

"That your girlfriend then?" Cassie said with a teasing smirk when he returned to the sitting room.

Kyle ignored the remark.

"I'm going out to a party St Stephen's night," he said instead.

"What? You're leaving me here all alone?" She sounded hurt.

"I'm sure you'll come up with something." Kyle took a gulp of the glass of Coke next to him.

"Ugh. I always hated going out for Stephen's night... Guess I'll have to."

The front door opened at that moment and a drenched Ciara soon appeared in the sitting room, practically pushing her hands into the fire in an effort to warm herself up.

"Does Ronan not have heating in his car?" Kyle asked and reached out for the peanuts.

"Have you any idea what the weather is like out there?" Ciara snapped over her shoulder.

Kyle shrugged. He didn't, really. He had been sitting comfortably indoors since returning from a walk with Wanda a few hours earlier – and that hadn't been very long either, neither of them being too keen on walking in wind, rain and occasional hailstones.

"When are you going to introduce me to this Ronan anyway? I'm starting to think he's avoiding me," Cassie said.

"He's not," Ciara said. She pulled her wet shoes and socks off her and left them by the fire while pulling her wet hoodie over her head. "I think he's avoiding Kyle."

Cassie had gotten up to go and take the pizza out.

"And what have you done to put him off you, Kyle?" she shouted from the kitchen. Kyle could see her carefully pulling the oven glove over her hands.

"He would probably call it a brotherly warning. I would just call it bullying." Ciara left the room, assumedly to go and get changed into something dry.

"OK, OK. I think we should all try to get along over the next 48 hours. Or whatever it is, a little less than that. Kyle, will you be a darling and sort the drinks out?"

He didn't want to be a darling at all but went into the kitchen and poured them all fresh drinks anyway.

It was the first Christmas Eve that they had dinner in the kitchen rather than in the dining room. It felt pointless to make a mess of an eight-seater dining table for the sake of a pizza.

Cassie still insisted on lighting two candles on the table – one for each of their parents.

It was, without a doubt, the most miserable Christmas Eve ever.

CHAPTER 13

He was up at eight o'clock on Christmas morning. He thought he would be the first one of them up – he had heard noises from both girls' rooms late in to the night, signifying that they had all been up late – and so was surprised to find Cassie in the kitchen, making rich-smelling coffee and scones.

"Good morning," she said with a huge smile. Kyle personally thought that there was no need to be so smiley at that time of the morning, especially not on the most depressing Christmas Day of their lives.

He muttered a hello and sat down. Wanda waved her tail from the floor where she was wolfing down her morning meal.

"Just butter for you, right?" Cassie asked. She held a knife in her hand, ready to cut through a steaming hot scone. He nodded.

"Is Ciara on the way down yet? We haven't got all morning if we want to get to church on time."

He was just about to say that he hadn't heard anything when footsteps sounded from the upstairs landing. Then they heard the upstairs bathroom open and close.

"I suppose that's a yes then." Cassie cut through another two scones and slid three plates onto the table. Kyle pulled his closer and eyed the other two scones suspiciously. The girls had theirs with butter and jam, which he found disgusting. He wouldn't take his with both even if it wasn't for him trying to balance his sugar levels – not that he was shy of sugar.

Cassie put a pot of coffee on the table and sat down.

"I assume you're not dressed for church yet then?"

He had not intended to go to church at all. He had dressed in tracksuits and an old jumper, considering this the best option for walking the dog – it would end up being his job, no question about it – and starting the fire. No point in getting any good clothes wet and sooty.

"Neither am I, yet," Ciara's voice sounded from the doorway. She was still in her pyjamas.

"Well, we better hurry up then." Cassie pushed a scone towards Ciara.

"Ooh, yummy," she said with a smile and sat down at the end of the table.

They breakfasted in silence. The girls started tidying up afterwards while Kyle took a reluctant Wanda out on a short walk. It was wet and cold, and there was still evidence of hailstones on the road. The weather forecast had promised snow for the Christmas weekend, but it seemed unlikely that it would stick to the ground, it being so wet.

Despite the weather, Kyle went for a longer walk than he had intended. By the time they returned home, Wanda was panting from her exertions and he was sweating. They were greeted by two unimpressed women in the hall.

"Where the hell have you been? We should get going by now." Cassie was tapping her foot on the floor.

"You can go without me."

"Oh no, we're not!" she exclaimed. "We're all going."

"Right. Let's go then." He knew he was annoying Cassie, and still he couldn't let it be.

"You're not going like that!"

Although it was Cassie who said that, the expression on Ciara's face said that she was in agreement.

"We'll wait for you in the car," Cassie announced and grabbed the car key off the hook by the stairs.

He sighed deeply before bending down to take Wanda's collar off and fetching her towel from the porch. The poor dog was drenched.

The dog somewhat dried, he marched upstairs and pulled on the first set of clothes he could find. They were not his Sunday best, nor did he want them to be. The jeans were purposely ripped and the top had a big, roaring lion on it, along with other cool prints. For a moment, he thought about wearing one of his rude T-shirts but decided against it. He only wanted to annoy Cassie, not the whole congregation.

He pulled on a pair of canvas shoes and grabbed his leather jacket on the way out. The car was already turned towards the road when he got out. Nobody said a word when he sat down in the passenger seat.

They arrived at the church about 15 silent minutes later. They only had about two minutes to spare and so they sat down at the back of the church. It was busy. It was amazing how many people decided to repent on Christmas Day when they had no interest in going to church on any other day. Kyle hated to think that he appeared to be one of those people. People probably thought that he was there to pray for his parents' souls. He wasn't. Their souls needed no help. Good people would be fine, no matter what happened to them after death.

He knew that people were staring at them. Ciara took it personally. She gave him a sideways look and hissed, "We told you you should dress smartly for church."

Kyle snorted but said nothing back. It was his own business how he dressed for church, or for anywhere else for that matter.

He was in a world entirely his own during the mass. He couldn't have said afterwards what the priest was talking about at all. His mind drifted from his parents to college back to his parents and sisters and to Mel and her unavoidable party. Then his mind drifted to worse things related to Mel that he tried to banish from his head – they were not appropriate for church and could have ended up being awkward. He stayed put while his sisters went for their communion, despite Cassie's unimpressed look at him while they passed, but she was not going to start an argument in church and in front of all those people.

They zombie-walked out of the church in the middle of the crowd. How they had ended up in the middle of it, he didn't understand, because they had been at the back and should have been among the first people out. Instead, he found himself swaying to and fro amid a mass of Christmas-cheery people.

Ciara spotted Ronan outside the front door and stopped to talk to him. Cassie, delighted of the chance to finally meet her little sister's mystery man, stopped too and didn't even notice that Kyle kept walking. He walked on a bit away from the crowd and stopped at a tree near the church. He leaned his back against it, hoping for some shelter from the wind which blew cold air over the uncovered patches of his legs and sleet that was now falling heavily.

Lots of people walked past. Many of them eyed him curiously. It was a small town, and no doubt people knew who he was, this helped by the horrid picture that had appeared in the papers some weeks earlier. It was one of those times when he wished that he had smoked. He could have looked a whole lot cooler puffing on a cigarette. Now he was just trying to keep his head down. His head felt cold. He should have worn something to cover it. He was not used to having mere millimetres of hair covering his head, and now it felt very vulnerable.

The crowd started to dissipate, and a few minutes later Cassie and Ciara appeared on the path in front of him. Their arms were linked and their heads bent together. It looked like they were sharing a secret.

"You ready, Kyle?" Cassie asked when they reached him. Her breath formed a cloud of fog in front of her face.

He nodded. They started walking away from the church, but not towards the car as he had expected. He should have known, but he hadn't given it any thought until now. To his horror, they were walking towards the graveyard.

They soon reached their parents' bare-looking grave. All the flowers that had been left on it had been removed. There were some candle remains, but they did not look particularly impressive. However, Cassie pulled out two identical candles from her handbag, along with a box of long matches.

To the two girls, lighting the candles seemed to be some sort of ritual of relief. He felt nothing. Well, he was cold and hungry and needed to use the bathroom, but emotionally, he was just numb.

He looked around at all the other graves. Several of them already had fresh candles lit on them. Some had heather and other sturdy plants on them. A lot of people were at the graveyard at that precise moment, looking solemn and mournful while lighting their candles. Was there something wrong with him? Why did he not feel anything when standing at their graves? The girls were crying, Ciara wiping her nose on a tissue while handing one to Cassie.

He directed his attention, once again, to the gravestone. The names were on it, in clear, precise writing.

MARCUS DONALD ABRAHAM FRENCH

15.6.1964 – 6.11.2010

MAUREEN LOUISE FRENCH

Née Callaghan

31.1.1965 – 6.11.2010

And still, no matter how carefully he looked at the writing, it meant nothing to him. It was like two entirely different people, not his mum and dad, not the people who had raised him, made him, loved him.

He looked at the two candles, now burning steadily in their glass containers. The girls stood beside him, each of them with their hands clasped together with a crumpled tissue, sniffling. Ciara was shivering. Cassie's eyes and nose looked red, almost the same colour as her coat. He felt a pang of sympathy for them, as if he was an outsider, but he couldn't make himself feel anything more.

Cassie looked at him enquiringly, nodding towards the direction of their car. He nodded, and the three of them turned around to head towards the car park.

The house was cold when they got home. Nobody had thought of turning the oil heating on before they left, let alone lighting a fire. Kyle hurried to fetch timber and coal from the garage while the girls started on the turkey and ham. He was better off staying out of their way anyway while they were in the kitchen.

Ten minutes later, the fire was happily roaring away. Wanda had curled up in front of it, unimpressed that she had been left alone in the cold house. Kyle sat down to look for the usual Christmas Day favourites on TV and was surprised when Ciara appeared in front of him with a glass of what looked and smelled like mulled wine and a slice of Christmas cake. He gasped at the sight of the cake.

"I'm sorry. It's not what you think it is. We bought it." Ciara smiled apologetically.

Of course it couldn't have been. It never would be again. From now on, Christmas cake would be just another item to throw in the trolley in the days approaching Christmas. Their mother had spent hours in an effort to get it right. The making of the Christmas cake had been a real countdown to Christmas, at least when they had been kids.

"And what have I done to deserve this?" he asked, trying to hide not just his disappointment but also the gripping pain.

"I think she just wants you to stay out of the way," Ciara said with a smile and a nod towards Cassie before heading back towards the kitchen.

Kyle balanced the mulled wine on the armrest of the recliner and took a bite of the cake.

It was a bitter disappointment. Compared to his mother's sumptuous, juicy Christmas cake, this one was dry and floury. It didn't crumble in his hands the way the real thing did. Instead, the pieces broke off neatly.

He looked towards the kitchen, where the girls were busy chopping vegetables, basting turkey and turning the ham over. The sight was all wrong. Normally, their mother had told everybody else to stay out of the kitchen while she cooked the Christmas meal, despite their offers to help. She had liked cooking it. She had loved Christmas, and seeing his sisters instead of her was just wrong.

He turned his eyes towards the fire and sat staring into it, blinking away the tears until they eventually subsided.

* * *

The phone started ringing in the afternoon. They all took

163

turns answering the calls from worried relatives, asking if they were OK for everything and why they hadn't gone down to Cork and if they were finding it hard. The three of them responded in as few words as was politely possible.

Kyle was asked to set the table, and he duly did so. It seemed pointless to set the big dining table for the three of them, but the girls insisted that everything should be done in the usual manner. So he put out the fancy candle sticks that only came out at Christmas and folded serviettes – he was no expert at that.

The dinner was ready around four, and they certainly had spared no effort in making it a feast. There was a turkey – much too big for three people – and a ham – more modestly sized. There was a big bowl of roast potatoes and lots of carrots and Brussels sprouts. There was a boat of gravy and their own Christmas speciality, Yorkshire puddings.

They all sat down in their usual spots, Ciara and Kyle with their backs towards the sitting room and Cassie with her back towards the kitchen. It had always annoyed Kyle as a child – and Ciara too – because they had not been able to see the TV from where they sat, not that it was often on during a meal. Cassie had always sat next to their mother, who had wanted to sit on the kitchen side for practical reasons. Their dad had sat at the end of the table, jokingly saying that that was where the man of the house was meant to sit. Kyle wondered briefly if that was where he should have sat now.

Ciara and Cassie seemed in good spirits during the dinner. They both enjoyed a glass of white wine with the meal – well, several in Cassie's case – and handed Kyle a bottle of beer, knowing that he was not a wine drinker. The girls chatted away enthusiastically. Cassie seemed to have formed a high opinion of Ronan during the few minutes that she had spoken to him. Kyle rather thought it was because he was so like Rob – boring, predictable and goody-two-shoes – but kept his opinion to himself. He kept to himself altogether during the dinner, not having much to say, aside from the usual comments on the food, which was good, even if not the same as his mother's cooking.

They were all stuffed after the meal, but Cassie still insisted on Christmas pudding. This, like the cake, was straight out of the wrapping and into the microwave and onto their plates. She went to the trouble of scooping up lots of brandy butter next to it, but Kyle had a feeling that no amount of alcohol was going to get him into the Christmas spirit.

It wasn't until after the pudding, when they were sitting around the table holding their all-too-full stomachs, that they realised they had not opened their presents. They had not even made it under the tree yet.

Lazily they all got up and disappeared into their rooms to get their presents. Kyle was the first one downstairs. He piled the presents up underneath the tree and went to the kitchen to feed Wanda, who was eagerly looking forward to her pieces of ham and turkey.

Ciara showed up soon enough, but Cassie took her time. She eventually showed up in the sitting room with two huge bags and red-rimmed eyes. Kyle and Ciara exchanged glances behind her back as she started to put her presents under the tree but said nothing.

Handing out the presents was a bit of an anti-climax. There were so few of them. Their parents had always been very generous with presents while the three of them had collectively struggled to think of anything to buy for the pair of them. It should have been a relief not to have to buy anything for them, but it wasn't.

It was also not right watching the expressions on each other's faces as they opened the presents. Instead of the usual laughter and exclamations, there was only the occasional, stifled comment and only one shriek, emanating from Ciara when she found a book of baby names that Cassie had bought her. Kyle felt like his present of a TV box set was not particularly thoughtful, her circumstances considered, but she thanked him kindly all the same.

Cassie seemed to have the biggest pile of presents, including some from Rob and his parents. She smiled sweetly when opening a box of earrings with a matching necklace and bracelet and reached out for her phone, assumedly to text Rob.

Kyle was reasonably pleased with his share, which included a voucher for a music store, a new belt and a decent cardigan. He was less impressed by the two books that Cassie had bought him. He was not exactly known for being a keen reader.

"I figured you'd need something to occupy your mind now that you'll be home all day," she explained with a cheeky smile.

When they had opened all the presents, Cassie surprised Kyle and Ciara by walking into the utility and returning with a massive box, wrapped up in newspaper.

"It was too big for wrapping paper, I was told," she excused herself while putting the box down on the floor, where Wanda hurried over to have a sniff at it.

"Is this from you?" Ciara asked her eyes wide with surprise.

"God, no," Cassie chuckled, "it's from Aunt Lizzie."

"When did she drop this off?"

"She dropped into the office, the one day I was there. So, who wants to open it?"

They all dropped on their knees on the floor and started

ripping at the newspaper, assisted by Wanda, who tore at the loose bits like her life depended on it.

The newspaper, as expected, only revealed a box. It said that there was a deep fat fryer inside.

"What? She wouldn't have bought us a..." Cassie said with a horrified look on her face. It didn't seem the kind of thing their aunt would have bought.

"She didn't. Look." Ciara pulled open the flaps of the box and revealed a collection of matching photo frames, all bearing a picture of their parents at different stages of their lives. There were six of them in total, all carefully wrapped up in bubble wrap.

"Oh my god," Cassie gasped. Her hand flew up to her mouth, and her eyes welled up at the sight of the first photo. It was their wedding photo.

There were a further five – one of each of their parents as a child, one taken when their mother must have been pregnant with Cassie and two of them when they were older. One of them Kyle had never seen before, but it looked like it had been taken at some sort of family gathering. There were other people around them although their parents were clearly the target of the camera. The other one Kyle knew well. It had been taken only some months ago, when the two of them had visited New York. It was taken in Central Park where they had gone for a picnic. Their dad was sitting on the blanket, casually dressed, and their mother was lying on her stomach next to him, wearing a colourful summer dress and dangling her legs in the air behind her. They looked so happy in the photo that it hurt just to look at it.

"It's so beautiful," Ciara whispered, carefully lifting the photo out of the box.

Kyle picked up their wedding photo. He looked at his mother's face and glanced up at Ciara. Yes, they looked very alike. Cassie, on the other hand, looked more like their father with her fair hair, slim build and height. He didn't know who he looked like. He had heard mixed comments about it.

"Where do you think we should put them?" Kyle asked with a look at his sisters. He appeared to be the only one of them who was still able to speak. Cassie was staring at the remaining photos in the box with her hand still over her mouth and tears freely rolling down her face. Ciara was sobbing now, silently but not holding it back. Kyle had a lump in his throat too but didn't fancy crying in front of them. One of them had to remain strong.

"How about this wall behind the couch?" he asked with a nod towards the wall behind Ciara. Their mother had never been a big fan of paintings or photos on the wall, so the wall was empty. Above the fireplace would have been ideal, but there was a big and apparently expensive mirror in that space that he knew none of them would want to move.

"That would be perfect," Cassie responded. She wiped her tears on her sleeve and turned to look at Ciara, who only nodded.

"Grand. I'll do that tomorrow."

Kyle gingerly lifted the wedding photo back into the box and took the other photo off Ciara, who was obviously afraid that her shaky hands would not be able to slide the picture back into the box without breaking it.

* * *

Cassie gave Ciara and Kyle a lift into town the following evening, dropping both off at the top of the main street just before nine o'clock. Ciara was due at work for a very busy shift –one of the busiest of the year – and Kyle had promised to meet

Mel at the house where the party was to be held. Although he was not very familiar with the area, he had a general idea where the address was and had decided to walk. It was only going to be about ten minutes.

Cassie had not talked about her plans for the evening, but she had not seemed bothered by being left alone and had not minded dropping them into town. She was probably just going to enjoy her time alone with a bottle of wine and maybe a bath, the way girls did.

It was a chilly evening, but at least the snow of the other day had stopped. There was a cold breeze, but Kyle was glad to get some fresh air and just kept his head down inside his scarf and jacket collar with his woolly cap carefully pulled down to cover his ears.

He eventually got to the right street and started counting the houses. They all looked the same to him. It was a posh part of town, with the houses selling at ridiculous prices – well, when houses had still sold – to people who paid for the address, not the house. They were big houses and mostly detached with a garage at the side. He had heard that some of them had had swimming pools added to them at the back, but he wasn't sure he believed that.

Luckily for him, all the houses were numbered with identical labels that at least were clear to read: 35, 36, 37... One more to go. Past number 38, and 39 met him at the end of the street. It did look huge. It was one of those modern-type houses that seemed to have no logic to them at all.

He walked up the pathway to the door and rang the doorbell.

The door was opened within seconds by Mel herself.

"Aaaaah, Kyle!" she exclaimed in the annoying high pitch that girls used when they were excited to see someone. She threw her arms around him, kissed him on the lips and pulled him into the house.

"So good to see you. Here, I'll leave your jacket in here." She practically pulled it off him, and for a moment he wondered if she was going to carry on tearing his clothes off. To his relief, she didn't. Instead, she carelessly threw his jacket into a closet under the stairs.

"Let me show you around. You know the girls."

Kyle looked at her usual group of friends in astonishment. Rose – the one who had seen him more or less naked – was dressed in neon green and bright pink. There was Eliza – the fat one – dressed in big shoulder pads that made her look even bigger and the blonde, annoying one whose name he still did not know dressed in something that made him think of Abba. Giving Mel a closer look, he noticed that she was wearing shiny, silvery leggings and an electric blue dress. It was totally over the top – even more than was her usual style.

"Come on."

Mel was pulling him by the arm into the kitchen. The room was huge, open-plan and bright – well, it would have been in daylight. Currently it was dimly lit by some candles and what appeared to be dimmer lights.

"This is Paul, Mark," Mel said, stopping briefly in front of two innocuous-looking fellas who were also stupidly dressed. Paul, a fair-haired guy with a face Kyle would not recognise the following day, barely spared him a glance before returning to their conversation. Mark, a small dark bloke, eyed him up and down carefully while not bothering to even say hi to him.

"We'll get you a drink," Mel said and helped herself to a bottle of beer from the fridge. She had no drink for herself, which probably meant that she had left it somewhere.

She started to guide him back out of the kitchen towards what appeared to be the sitting room.

"I must have forgotten to tell you, it's an '80s themed party."

That explained why Wham! was blasting out of the speakers then, along with why people were so badly dressed.

"It's OK, nobody will mind if you're not dressed up," she said with a big smile at what must have been a gloomy expression on his face. He was not a big fan of the '80s. He had never seen the '80s, even though he knew he had been made in the '80s.

They entered the massive sitting room with a big, roaring fire in the posh fireplace. Kyle was not convinced that all these fires were such a good idea around a lot of drunk people, but it wasn't his house.

"Mark's my brother," Mel carried on, "they live here. They're so lucky. They're renting off this really rich bastard who bought the house for himself when things were great. Then the recession came and he lost his well-paid job so he couldn't afford to keep up the mortgage repayments. Now he's living in some little bedsit and renting this out. It's really cheap, like the rooms are huge and they only pay 60 quid a week."

With this introduction to the story of the house Mel burst into another round of names. They were standing near a giant bookcase next to the door when Kyle felt someone squeeze his bottom. A quick glance at Mel confirmed that both of her hands were accounted for – one was pointing at various people in the room and the other one was still on his arm. He glanced over his shoulder and saw a tall, skinny guy, entirely dressed in white, walking off with a big grin in his direction.

Mel had noticed that she had lost his attention and turned to look after the man in white.

"That's Darragh," she said with a cheeky smile that was obvious even though Kyle was still not looking at her. "I see he fancies you." She leaned in to his ear and whispered, "He's gay."

That was stating the obvious. Kyle felt uncomfortable although the culprit was already out of sight.

"It's OK, he lives here and he knows you're mine. You're not homophobic, are you?" Mel asked with a curious look at his face.

"No, no... I'm not." He tried to sound confident. He wasn't, he'd met gay guys before and worked with one in a previous summer job, but he'd never had his bum squeezed by one either. He hoped that Mel hadn't forgotten to tell him that as well as being an '80s themed party, it was also a gay party.

"Well, Darragh's the only gay guy here that I know of. He's just one of the flatmates, no biggie," she said with a shrug. Kyle started to have a feeling that Mel had not seen how cheeky Darragh could be.

"Come on, I left my drink with Sophie."

Sophie turned out to be the annoying blonde one, who was still hanging around the lobby area with the rest of her group. There were no other men around at all, which Kyle found slightly disturbing. He started to have a feeling that Mel's friends were not all that successful with men, which was odd. They were all OK-looking, with the exception of Eliza, but seemed to be lacking in the personality department – particularly Sophie.

With no part in the conversation to speak of, Kyle found himself downing his beer quicker than he was meant to. And then he realised that he needed the bathroom. Mel helpfully pointed him in the right direction, but when he found the bathroom, there were already three people queuing outside, so he quickly headed up the stairs. Surely there had to be at least two bathrooms in a house this size?

There were only a handful of people upstairs, and the overall atmosphere was much quieter. Nobody even glanced at him as he reached the landing. He was relieved to see the bathroom right in front of him – easy to spot, with the door slightly ajar and the lights left on.

Kyle looked at himself in the mirror above the sink while washing his hands. He looked flushed but tired, with dark circles under his eyes. He had not been sleeping well over Christmas. Actually, he hadn't been doing anything well over Christmas – eating, sleeping, exercising, talking, looking after himself, laughing, crying… No, he hadn't really been crying despite all the pain he felt. It was just tearing him up inside, quietly. It was like his insides were being ripped up by an angered tiger.

He stared at his mirror image and didn't understand what he was doing. Why was he in this house? He should have been home with his family, his parents. He never went out St Stephen's night. He didn't care for it. Christmas was family time. He had never once been out for the night, not even after he had turned 18 and could have. And now he was at this glitzy ditzy party with a girl he barely knew and barely liked and where he didn't know anybody else and was being grabbed by gay guys…

He didn't know where it came from. It just came out all of a sudden, like an unleashed monster, or maybe that unleashed tiger, even though it didn't stop tearing up his insides. The tears came flowing in big, loud sobs and hysterical screams. He was grasping the sink so hard that his hands hurt, but he didn't pay any attention. Then his knees gave up and he slid onto the floor.

He didn't know how long he was crying like that. Then he started hearing knocks and shouts from behind the door. People were trying to get in.

"Come on, guys, get a bedroom! There's plenty of them in here!"

"Other people need to pee too!"

"You've been there for ages!"

The shouts slowly penetrated his foggy mind. It sounded like someone was kicking at the door.

He pulled himself up, unlocked the door and pushed his way out of the bathroom. People were staring at him as he walked past, throwing more insults at him, but they didn't hurt him. No insult aimed at him would ever hurt him as bad as the pain inside.

He collapsed on the floor next to the railing, with his back against the wall.

People started coming over to him. Some were worried, some amused, some annoyed. Eventually Mel showed up and sat down next to him in a confident manner. She was asking him what was wrong, tugging at his arm. Someone asked her if he would need a glass of water and Mel said it was a good idea. Mel pointed out that he was diabetic and wondered out loud if this had something to do with it. Some smartass said that it had nothing to do with it and that he was clearly just hysterical. The glass of water arrived, was passed on to Mel, who offered it to Kyle, who didn't want it. Mel asked him if he wanted everybody else to go away, and he managed a nod. He wanted everybody to go away, including Mel, but didn't get the words out of his mouth.

People reluctantly left when Mel told them to, throwing curious glances in his direction. She handed him some tissue which he took but didn't use. He knew that his face was covered in dried-up tears and snot but didn't care.

Mel eventually gave up trying to talk to him and just sat there looking at him. There was not likely to be much to look at, apart from the red, puffy eyes, runny nose and the rest of the mess that was Kyle French. Certainly not the once good-looking young student that Mel had developed a crush on.

A lot of time seemed to pass. Everything went numb. His face was numb from the crying, his legs were numb from sitting on the floor and his arms were numb from being in the same position for too long. The pins and needles were going to be unbearable, but he tried to get up. He wanted to leave the house and the people who had been staring at him as if he had six heads.

"I'm gonna go," he said, hobbling on to his feet, more to himself than to Mel. His legs didn't feel strong enough to carry him, so he made for the stairs holding tight on to the banister – well, as tight as his arms were still able to.

He knew Mel said something, but he didn't listen. She took hold of his left arm while he leaned on his right arm to get down the stairs. There seemed to be a crowd at the bottom of the stairs, all staring at him. Kyle immediately turned towards the front door. Mel reappeared at his side a few seconds later, holding out his jacket. He hadn't even thought of a jacket. The cold outside would not even have hit him until his lips, toes and fingers had turned blue.

"Hold on, I just need to find mine," she said.

"No," he said louder than he had intended. She looked astonished.

"I'm going alone," he said in a more discreet tone. Mel opened her mouth to say something but did not seem to find the words. Kyle pulled his jacket on and walked out the front door, into the cold, breezy night.

CHAPTER 14

He woke up to the sound of giggles and an annoyed exclamation. He opened his eyes carefully. His head was not sore, so he was not hungover. He saw a set of wooden steps above him. Those in his own house, he realised. He heard the distinctive sound of somebody descending from the last step onto the floor.

"Kyle, what the hell are you doing?"

That was Cassie's voice. She sounded unimpressed.

"Huh?" was the only reply he could manage at the time. A lot more giggling followed. He went to sit up and bumped his head. It was the stairs. They were much closer to him than he had thought.

"What are you doing in the dog's bed, Kyle?" Cassie's unexpected question caused more giggles.

Kyle looked up at his sister with blurry eyes while rubbing the sore spot on his head. There was going to be a right bump there. What was she saying about the dog's bed?

He turned around and saw Wanda's bed around where his head had been.

That explained his stiff neck then, and the crick in his back.

"How exactly did you end up sleeping in the dog's bed?" Cassie repeated.

Kyle glanced at her again and then let his eyes move to her

companions. Iris stood next to her with a severe look on her face. She was dressed in straight black trousers and a pink cardigan. Jeez, did the woman never let her hair down?

His eyes moved on to the person next to Iris. She seemed to be the source of the giggles, judging by the cheeky smile on her face. She was dressed in a knee-length skirt, and Kyle was suddenly sorry that his eyes had been closed when she had come down the stairs. She wasn't good-looking, but he liked the saucy glint in her eyes when she looked at him.

"Well?" Cassie had her hands on her hips.

"I was tired. I was too tired to get up the stairs."

He kept rubbing at his head and neck.

"Yeah right. Too pissed, I'd say."

"No, no. I was quite sober. I was just so tired…"

He could remember it now. After he had left the party, he had walked into town and gone into a pub. He had had three drinks, nothing too serious. He had eventually managed to get a cab home, very late, and he had been so tired that he had just gone to sleep on the floor, with his head in Wanda's bed. His jacket was still on the floor next to him.

"Whatever. Get up. I'll bring you some breakfast." Cassie nodded towards his room upstairs, making it clear that his company was not required. She turned towards the kitchen, closely followed by Iris. The giggler waited a moment before turning around and going after them, more interested in his attempts to get up with a very sore body. Wanda stood in the sitting room doorway, wagging her tail in a bemused fashion.

He walked up the stairs, feeling every step in his bones. He went to the bathroom, took his injection and lay down on the bed in a half-sitting position.

There was a knock on the door a few moments later. It wasn't

Cassie as he'd expected, but the giggler.

"I said I'd come instead," she said with a big smile, "it's Kathy. I know, you're Kyle." The latter was to stop him from unnecessarily introducing himself. Cassie must have said his name a dozen times just before, not to mention the less than complimentary names that had probably followed after she had gotten into the kitchen.

Kathy laid a cup of coffee and two slices of toast with marmalade on his bedside table. Trying not to stare, Kyle looked at her curiously. She had big brown eyes, brown, shoulder-length hair and a slim figure. No, she was not his type at all to look at. She was a good bit older too, around Cassie's age.

"I've never seen anybody sleep in a dog's bed before," she said with a chuckle.

"And I wouldn't recommend it," Kyle said, straightening his back for the umpteenth time in an effort to try and get comfortable.

"I'd say most dogs would agree." Her eyes seemed to wander down to the undone top buttons of his shirt. He'd undone them because it was too warm, but was glad that he had.

"Wanda didn't mind," he responded with a tired smile. His face still felt strange from the crying the night before.

"Well," Kathy said, and leaned in closer to him, "I wouldn't mind you in my bed either." Then she stepped back, nodded towards his breakfast and said, "Enjoy." She walked to the door and turned around to wink at him before walking out.

Surely he had heard that all wrong? She hadn't really said… No, no. No. His mind was playing tricks on him and he was hearing what he wanted to hear.

He took a slice of toast and bit into it, suddenly ravenous.

* * *

He went downstairs a couple of hours later, descending the stairs carefully due to trying to balance the plate and mug in his hand and trying to avoid the soreness all over his body. He got to the bottom of the stairs and stopped to listen to the voices in the kitchen.

"Oh, she's had her fair share, has Kathy. She's just that type, a flirt and a tease. It's not her looks."

That was Cassie. She was right. It was not Kathy's looks. She was quite average-looking, but her teasing had certainly worked on him, enough to inspire him to a bit of self-release earlier…

"I hate that type. Just can't beat them."

Ciara. She had made her way back home then.

"Lucky you don't need to. You've got Ronan."

"You've got Rob."

There was a moment's silence.

"How many has she had then?" Ciara asked with a curious edge to her tone.

"I don't know. Lots. She's always got something going on with someone. I think it's an awful bad example for a primary school teacher."

So she was a teacher. That was not exactly a turn-off. Quite the contrary.

There was another small silence.

"What about you? If you don't mind me asking."

That was Ciara asking again. Very nosey of her, but Kyle was intrigued all the same.

"Four. That's including Rob." Cassie said it quietly but sounded sincere. Four? That was pathetic, at her age anyway. "What about you?"

"Just Ronan."

He nearly dropped the crockery at that. She had slept with one man and was about to be tied down to him forever by having gotten herself pregnant by him?

He figured that the following silence was too long for him to get away with standing on the bottom step. Besides, his hands were starting to cramp from holding the plate and mug. Kyle carried on into the kitchen.

"You slept well?" Cassie asked with an amused look at him.

In fact, he hadn't slept at all.

"Fine."

"Better than the dog's bed then?"

Kyle acknowledged that with a grunt and sat down.

"I thought you'd have had a more comfortable bed to sleep in last night." Ciara looked at him curiously.

"Nope."

"Did she kick you out then?" Cassie asked. Her eyebrows were raised at him while she poured more coffee out of the pot.

"Not that." He fiddled with the ring on his thumb – the only one he wore, having gotten it as a present off his mum after his leaving cert.

"She knows when she's got a good thing going, I suppose," Ciara said with an amiable smile.

"I'm sure Kyle here does too," Cassie said less amicably.

"Well, I've more to compare to than the two of you put together." It came out as boasting not ideal when talking to one's own sisters.

A quick glance up at them showed that both their faces had reddened – Ciara's in embarrassment, Cassie's in rage.

"You heard that?" Ciara asked. There was a look of disgust on her face.

Kyle shrugged.

"I was on my way down the stairs. No biggie." He attempted a faint smile.

"You bastard! It was between girls," Cassie rebuked.

"Well, next time you talk about how many men you've pulled, maybe you should make sure that there are no men within earshot."

"Next time you eavesdrop on one of our conversations like that, you will have no ears afterwards."

This was obviously a sore spot for Cassie. She was jealous and envied Kathy for her conquests. He couldn't imagine Cassie being comfortable and confident with men. She was tall, having inherited their dad's height, and slim with naturally mousey blonde hair that she kept dyed for a brighter colour. She was a conventional dresser though. It was unlikely that Rob would have had to do much work to bag her. He had no idea how they had met.

"But really, how did you end up in Wanda's bed?" Ciara looked for firmer ground.

"Like I said, I came home, was tired and went to sleep there."

"How much did you have to drink?" She looked concerned.

"It wasn't the drink. I was tired."

"Couldn't Mel spare you some space in her bed?" Cassie was looking for a comeback.

"I wasn't with her."

"Well, obviously not. I don't think she's that desperate for you that she'd shag you in a dog basket."

Cassie was full of hatred this morning. Kyle tried to think of something smart to say but couldn't come up with anything.

"I mean, I didn't spend the night with her."

That wasn't much better.

"I left the party without her. Early."

"Oh. You guys break up?" Ciara sounded sad. As if that would have been a huge loss.

He shook his head.

"No. I broke down is what happened."

"What?" That was Ciara.

He sighed. He ran his hand across his head and leaned forward, staring down at the table.

"I had a breakdown. I was a total mess last night."

"What exactly are you talking about?" Cassie asked. The expression on her face had softened.

Kyle took another deep breath.

"I just started to cry. It was bad."

There was a moment's awkward silence.

"I'm sorry." Ciara glanced at him from behind her long eyelashes. Ciara, now, had gotten the looks out of the two of them. She had a pretty face. In fact, he remembered one of his schoolmates having a crush on her a few years earlier although he had tried to hide it from Kyle. "Are you OK now?"

He nodded. He was mortified and hoped he would never have to see any of those people again, but it was not to be avoided. He would have to see Mel and her entourage.

"Wrong time, wrong place," Cassie said, reaching out to give his hand a squeeze.

* * *

It was a quiet week. Cassie wasn't due to start at the office until the New Year, and Ciara only worked two days. They spent most of the week moping around, eating leftovers from the Christmas dinner and trying to figure out what to do with their presents. They put the framed photos up in the sitting room, the girls busily giving instructions while Kyle did all the hard work. They looked well in the end.

New Year's Day descended upon them with light snow falling

on the surrounding fields and Cassie and Kyle suffering from major hangovers.

It was around 11 o'clock that they sat around the kitchen table. Ciara looked well-rested and fresh-faced in a purple jumper dress. She had already taken the dog for a walk and done some laundry and now laid plates of scrambled eggs and toast in front of them, along with coffee for Cassie – to wake her up, she said – and tea for Kyle, who preferred a more traditional approach to breakfast.

"I don't know how I'll eat that," Cassie said, with a suspicious look at the food under her nose. She looked like shit; she was as pale as a sheet with dark circles under her eyes. It was plain to see that she was suffering from a massive headache as well.

"You'll feel better after you do, trust me," Ciara said cheerfully. "And you," she said, waving her finger at Kyle, "will eat that even if I have to force feed you."

He was so used to having to eat even when he didn't feel like it that it was like pressing a button and going into eating mode. Once he got started, it didn't even feel like a chore.

"Quite a night that, wasn't it?" Ciara said, getting stuck into her considerably bigger portion of eggs. She was having her breakfast with orange juice. How healthy.

"Ugh," Cassie muttered. She was drawing circles in the eggs with her fork.

"Well, the two of you looked like you had a good time. And I did too, watching everybody around me act like monkeys. It's great to be the only sober person around."

Kyle tried to remember what Ciara had done all night. She had been drinking soft drinks, except the necessary glass of champagne. He remembered pouring most of his into Cassie's glass – not a great idea, in hindsight.

"Oh, Cassie, who was that fella you were talking to for so long?"

"Huh?" Cassie looked at her younger sister in total incomprehension.

"You know, that tall, dark fella. Good-looking, I'd say."

"Oh… Ooooh…" Cassie buried her head in her hands. "Oh no. Was I talking to him?"

"For ages! You seemed quite friendly with him."

Kyle was not sure if Ciara was just acting naive or simply that immature. He remembered it well. He remembered Cassie talking to the man in question. She had spoken to him on two occasions, first early in the night, when it had been quite civil, and then again later on. The second round had not been quite that pretty. She had been leaning very close to him, hanging on to his arm for support and offering him a considerable view of her assets down the front of her dress. He had not seemed to complain, and if Kyle had been more sober at that point, he would have interrupted rather than laughed uproariously.

"Oh god… Cathal Martyn. His name is Cathal Martyn."

"Did you go to school together or something?" Ciara's plate was emptying much faster than theirs, despite having much more on it.

"We both used to play basketball… I knew him from tournaments and practice about… what, ten years back?" Cassie buried her head even deeper in her hands. "Oh man. That's so embarrassing." She raised her head and took a big sip of her coffee.

"I used to have a massive crush on him at the time, to no avail." She glanced sideways at Kyle, as if warning him to keep quiet.

"I'd say he noticed you now, all right!" Ciara said cheerfully.

"I can't believe it… I can't remember what I said to him. Did I

184

say something stupid?"

Ciara shook her head. "I've no idea. We were too far away to hear what you were saying. Not that Kyle would have been much better either."

He grimaced. He knew he hadn't been, but unfortunately, he could remember the previous night.

"It looked to me like you were declaring your undying love to Georgina."

He felt himself flushing heavily.

"Georgina?" Cassie asked.

"Uh-um. Georgina Adams."

Yes. He remembered that. He had not quite proposed to her, but not far off it. She had looked stunning in a silver-grey dress and had caught his eye as soon as he had walked into the nightclub. He had spotted her talking to a tall, blonde guy who seemed very keen on her. He felt a twinge of jealousy even thinking about it. He had known straight away that there was no hope he would ever be considered a rival to him, the other guy being the type that would always get the girl. He was of the captain-of-the-football-team type that one saw in American movies.

"I know her! I went to school with her. She was a little bitch," Cassie announced unceremoniously. "How do you know her?"

"She cuts our hair. Mine and Kyle's. She's good." Ciara was taking no sides here.

Georgina had eventually turned around to look over her shoulder – he had no idea what for. In any case, she had spotted him and given a big wave and a dazzling smile. The captain had given Kyle a piercing look that had made him feel very small indeed. A short moment later, Georgina had walked over to him for a chat. It wasn't a long chat or anything crucial, but he had been pleased to see from the corner of his eye that the tall guy had eyed them with some concern. She had just wished him happy New Year before going, pointing out that it couldn't be worse than the year that had just passed, and reminding him to make sure to get that kiss.

"You're quite friendly with her, aren't you?" Ciara asked with a look at Kyle. He thought he was as red as a tomato by that point, but he nodded.

"But she's… coloured," Cassie pointed out.

"That's very racist," Ciara sounded insulted.

"Yeah, but… She is black."

"She's none the worse for that," Kyle defended.

"Well, I've heard nothing good about her," Cassie concluded and proceeded to cut a huge chunk of eggs and toast.

He had run into Georgina again later in the night, and that was where it had gone horribly wrong. By that time, he had had way more to drink than was necessary. He had told her that she looked great, which wasn't all that bad, but then he had grabbed her hand and told her in no uncertain terms, in a way that left no room for guesses, that he thought she was amazing. She had laughed at that, carried on with the conversation – he had no idea what it had been about – and kissed him on the cheek before she left. He had been heartbroken when she walked away, confident as ever, even if she clearly was not leaving to go over to another man.

"She seems nice. Very genuine." Ciara gave Kyle what looked like a look of approval.

"Well, she's too old for you as well, so you stay well clear of her," Cassie said with a nod towards him.

Oh god, if he would. There was another person he did not want to see in a while – although, on the other hand, he really wanted to see her. If only he could manage to see her without having to be seen by her… He was quickly running out of women that he was not ashamed to meet, with the disaster at Mel's brother's party, Kathy having caught him sleeping in a dog's bed and now Georgina having found out that he worshipped the ground she walked on… He was going to have to widen his search area.

CHAPTER 15

While everybody else returned to work the Tuesday after New Year, Mel didn't. They had spoken over the phone at the weekend, and she had told him she was off for another day. She had been disappointed that he had not shown up for another house party that she had invited him to on New Year's Eve, but there had been no hope of him making a fool of himself again – even though he had, but not in the same company. She hadn't seemed to consider this and hadn't even mentioned the fiasco of the week before.

He had the car for the day – which unfortunately meant that he had had to get up early to drop Cassie into work for nine o'clock, then drive back and come back into town for 11 when Ciara was starting work. After that though, he was free until three o'clock when Ciara was finished work and he had promised to meet her so that they could go and do the shopping before having to pick Cassie up at five.

He had the four hours pretty much planned out. He drove over to Mel's house, parked the car, walked up to the door and rang the doorbell. She showed up a moment later with an oven glove in her hands.

"Kyle! What are you doing here?" She was surprised and excited.

"What do you think?" he asked and leaned down to meet her

kiss. "You on your own?"

"That I am," she said with a big smile and started heading back towards the kitchen.

"What's that smell?" he asked, being met with a smell of something freshly baked and sweet. Chocolatey.

"I'm making brownies."

That much was clear. There was a big pile of dirty utensils in the sink and a big plate of brownies on the worktop.

"No need to look that surprised. I'm not just a goddess in the bedroom; I'm also a goddess in the kitchen."

His eyes wandered from the tasty-looking brownies to the baker. She was, again, casually dressed in a zipped-up cardigan that just hid her entire cleavage, to his disappointment, and in a pair of jeans. He had never seen her in jeans before, but he liked it. They showed off the curves off her bottom in an entirely different way than any dress ever had, the pockets drawing attention to the rounded cheeks. He longed to just go and squeeze her…

"So, which skills do you want to test first?"

He must have been staring at her, and she had pretty much read his mind. There was a cheeky glint in her eyes as she leaned back against the kitchen counter. He walked up to her, forcing her to lean back further, enjoying the physical power he had over her that way. He went in for a long, hard kiss, the pleasure of it heightened by her hands making their way under his top. He eventually pulled back, reached for a brownie off the plate behind her back and responded, "Both," before stuffing a piece of brownie into his mouth.

"I've another load in the oven. You'll have to hold off for a few minutes. Coffee?" She gently pushed him out of her way and went for the kettle.

Kyle sat down at the small kitchen table. It was square with four seats. What was the point in a four-seater table when the house slept five people?

A moment later, Mel put a cup of coffee in front of him and pushed the plateful of brownies right under his nose.

"I didn't know you like to bake," Kyle said carefully, not wanting to offend her.

"Oh, I do. I go through phases. I just don't like eating the stuff I bake. It's bad for you, anyway."

He was just after taking a big bite of his first brownie. Of course it was bad. He should have watched out, more so than most people, but he had never been particularly good at fighting temptation.

Mel grabbed the oven glove and went to fetch the second tray of brownies from the oven. He found it hard to focus on his coffee with her bum sticking out right in front of him. The sight of it sent tingling shivers up his spine. He was relieved when she stood up and placed the tray on top of the cooker, not that his loins seemed to relax much after that either.

She poured herself a cup of coffee as well – very small, he noticed – and sat down opposite him.

"So, are you all right?" she asked with a serious look on her face.

He looked up at her in confusion.

"I mean, after the other night. It was about your parents, wasn't it?"

He had to look down again, in an effort to try and hide his reddened face. He had at one stage, in his late teenage years, had long hair, and he missed that now. It was such a handy way to cover one's face when needed.

"Yeah. It's OK."

"Aaaww. Poor baby. Sometimes I forget how tough it must be on you. You know you can always talk to me."

No, he couldn't. Mel wasn't the type of person he would open up to, if anybody. Whatever he told her was bound to be all over town within two days.

He had started to stir his coffee with the spoon, not able to look up at Mel or say anything.

"I told everybody at the party. They're OK with it. After all, most people don't know what it's like to lose parents, especially both at the same time."

If she was not going to shut up about this soon, his mood was going to be ruined and he was going to start crying again. He downed the rest of his coffee in one go.

"Do you want more coffee?" Mel asked, and took his cup without waiting for his reply.

He shouldn't have. If he had another cup of coffee – his third in two hours – he was going to start bouncing off the walls. Not that she would mind that a little later. He found a smile creeping up across his face.

"There you go."

She sat down across from him again. He decided that if he was having another cup of coffee, he might as well have another brownie as well. At least he'd have something to do while Mel kept talking, not seeming to notice that he barely responded. On the other hand, once her socked foot reached out under the table to rub against his thigh, it didn't matter what she was talking about.

* * *

It was around two o'clock that Mel asked if he could give her a lift into town when he went to meet Ciara. He agreed. He was too tired to think of an excuse and just wanted to sleep.

He hadn't slept well the night before, and his exertions in the bedroom had left him sleepy. After he agreed, Mel jumped up from the bed, leaving the duvet hanging only halfway over him so that he had to go and pull it back over him to save himself from the chill of the room.

He was in some sort of a half-slumber state while watching Mel get ready for going into town – a considerable effort, that, by all accounts. She got into a sort of long jumper type of thing and a pair of leggings, along with another pair of massive heels – after much careful consideration, it seemed. He must have snoozed for a while because the next time he saw her, she was fully dressed and applying eye make-up. She had let her hair down and brushed it, having gotten rid of the cute, tousled look that she had gained during their session. She had also put on a pile of jewellery and had overall gone from the nice girl-next-door look to someone so groomed to perfection that she seemed unattainable. He didn't feel proud for having attained her – quite the opposite, in fact.

"What's the time?" he asked drowsily.

Mel was applying lipstick and glanced at the alarm clock on her desk.

"It's a quarter to three."

He let out a groan and fell deeper back into the pillows.

"You better get dressed. You're not going out to meet your sister like that, silly," she said with a condescending smile at him. She didn't mean to patronise him, but that's how she came across. She was right, of course. He needed to get dressed.

He pulled himself up and started to gather his clothes.

"On the other hand," Mel said from beside her mirror, which undoubtedly gave her a great view of his naked backside, "you could just stay here like that."

He tried to laugh at that even though he didn't find her comment particularly funny. He pulled on his clothes, aware of her eyes on him, and headed out to the bathroom in the hall.

They were in the car five minutes later, and he dropped Mel off on the main street, where she caused the traffic to stop dead in its tracks while she passionately kissed him goodbye. He drove off red-faced, hoping that none of the other drivers knew him.

He met Ciara at the back of the supermarket. She hooked her arm through his and started guiding him in, leaning in as if she was about to tell him a big secret.

"You've spent the day with Mel, then."

Kyle pulled away from her, as far as he could, considering their linked arms, trying to get a good look at her face. There was a smug smile on it.

"How do you know that?"

"It's that look on your face." She grinned at him. He frowned in disbelief, and she burst into laughter.

"It's not, really. Although you should have seen the guilty look on your face just there. I ran into her."

"Oh." He relaxed at that, but only for a moment. That couldn't be a good thing.

"Don't worry. I didn't care to hear all the dirty details. Your secrets are safe. She thinks the world of you though."

There was something about the smirk on Ciara's face as she pulled a trolley out of the bay. Something conspiratorial.

CHAPTER 16

Cassie's first day had not been great. She had found the day horribly long and boring. It was not a busy time in the property market, the times being bad in general and particularly quiet with the holiday season that had passed. She had spent the day in the office with Iris, trying to figure out where everything was kept and how things worked. She had also come across her first nasty client, an elderly lady who had placed an offer on a house before Christmas and still not heard back. There had been no explaining to her that the office had been closed over Christmas and the vendor had been abroad and out of reach most of that time.

"I don't know if I'll ever get used to it. I don't know how dad did it. I don't have a clue about anything."

"In fairness, dad did it for, like, 25 years or something," Ciara said reassuringly.

"I know. I just hate starting in a new job. I'm sure it will be really interesting once I get my head around it."

"And how did our chauffeur spend his day today?" Cassie asked with a smile in Kyle's direction.

"Oh, I'm sure he kept himself busy," Ciara said, with a smile towards him.

"Well, you obviously didn't do much in the house anyway. Plus, we had to cook dinner."

"I think he had other things on his mind," Ciara carried on and got up to put her plate in the dishwasher.

"Did he now?" Cassie asked, looking at him with a cocked eyebrow. "I don't think I care to hear the details. Anyway, with me and Ciara working all day tomorrow, I'd like to see some improvement in this mess that we call our home and have dinner somewhat ready when we get home. No canoodling around when there's work to do."

* * *

He woke up to a confused and strange feeling. It was late in the morning. He was well able to tell that by just a glance towards the window. It was sunny outside, but his mind felt less bright.

He had been awake for a while when the girls had been getting ready to leave for work. After that he had drifted off again and had all kinds of wild and blurry dreams, which were now the cause of his bewildered state. First, he had been having the most delicious dream involving Mel and brownies, but that had suddenly changed into something a lot more sinister. In fact, that part did not appear to be a dream but a memory.

He had been walking down the wide front steps of a bar. He was walking next to his mother, holding on to her and with her arm around his shoulders. They were walking towards his dad's car in the largely empty car park – well, it was a huge car park and looked empty even though there was a good crowd inside. His dad had pulled up as close to the door as was possible. He had a serious, unreadable look on his face. Kyle avoided looking at both of his parents, preferring to keep his eyes averted, to the ground. He was staring at his mother's purple shoes. They had been expensive and only came out on special occasions. She wasn't speaking to him. He knew that she was sort of pissed off with him but at the same time concerned and sympathetic. He felt guilty.

It was the feeling of guilt that he had carried with him to the daylight of January 6th. He felt guilty. That was the only way to put it. Two months had passed, but the reality still had not changed. It was his fault.

That was the worst thing about this dream – or whatever it had been. He wanted to wake up from it and realise that it had been a terrible nightmare, but no matter how many times he had woken up, it didn't change anything. He wished so hard that his head hurt that his mixed-up dreams had been the other way around – the bit involving Mel should have been true and the bit with his parents only a dream. He turned it round and round in his head, but it all remained the same. His parents were dead, and he was to blame.

* * *

He had managed to rustle up chips and chicken Kievs without burning them. Cassie and Ciara were so far not overjoyed by his efforts in the kitchen but dutifully ate whatever was put on their plates – Ciara in ever increasing amounts.

After dinner, while the kettle was boiling away with a mind-numbing noise, Cassie walked determinedly into the hall and pulled something out of her handbag. She returned with something in her hand and laid it on the table in front of Kyle. He looked up at her and then back down at the piece of card in front of him.

"I got you an appointment with the therapist."

He could see that. It was for the following Thursday at 11 in the morning. Dr Martin Mooney.

"I'm not going," he announced.

"The hell you aren't!" Cassie exclaimed while vigorously shaking what appeared to be a sachet of cappuccino powder.

"I am not." He could not be bothered to raise his voice. This was not a matter up for discussion.

Ciara sat quietly at the table, looking at Kyle from under her eyelashes.

"I've booked an appointment, you're gonna have to."

"I don't have to do anything, and I'm not going."

"What is so bad about seeing a therapist? Are you too macho to talk about your feelings?"

That he wasn't. At least he didn't think so. There was just nothing the therapist could do, or any therapist, or anybody else for that matter. Their parents were dead, and no amount of talking was going to bring them back.

"There is nothing he can do for me."

"Well, if you won't talk to us, you're gonna have to talk to somebody else," Cassie tried to negotiate.

"I don't. Thank you." He wasn't sure what he was thanking her for, having made the dinner himself, but it was a done thing when leaving the table.

"Kyle! Come back. I need to talk to you!" Cassie shouted after him when he was making his way up the stairs. He didn't listen though. There was nothing more he wished to say on the topic.

* * *

He took the car the following evening, threw his bass guitar in the boot and left Cassie alone in the house. Ciara had been picked up by Ronan an hour earlier to go to work.

He drove off to Donal's place and pulled up next to John's battered Fiesta. When he stepped out of the car, he could hear the music grinding on inside. There was a sliver of light shining across the lawn from the garage window. Both the shutter and the little door next to it were closed, but he knew the door wouldn't be locked. He pulled his instrument out of the boot and walked to the door. He noted with approval that the band was rehearsing a System Of A Down song.

John was the first one to spot him. His fingers slowly slid off the guitar strings, and then he loosened his grip on his instrument and let it rest against his hip.

Sam quickly followed suit and let his drum sticks gently fall against the drum kit. Donal was so focused on his vocals that he had his eyes closed and only realised that something was going on because the other two had stopped playing. When he opened his eyes, they took a moment to focus on Kyle and then seemed to grow in astonishment.

Tony carried on playing, although he must have noticed Kyle's arrival. His bass playing sounded pathetic, particularly with all the other instruments silenced in surprise. Eventually he gave up trying to carry the entire weight of the song on his own and laid his bass guitar down on the floor.

"This is a surprise," Donal finally managed to say. Kyle nodded with a brief smile. It shouldn't have been; he had been talking about returning to the band. He laid his case down on the scrubby couch that was blocking the shutter and threw his jacket on the backrest. He then sat down on the armrest of the couch, pulled his instrument out of its case and started tuning it.

"So, you're coming back then?" Sam asked with a hint of hopefulness in his voice.

"Yep." It wasn't a matter of asking to come back. The role of bass player in Ulterior Motive was rightfully his.

"I didn't think you were ready."

It was kind of pitiable to watch Donal. He was torn in two, nervously running his fingers through his hair and making it a mess. Kyle didn't know what the original deal with Tony had been, but it was about to cause Donal some trouble.

"It's been two months," Kyle reminded him light-heartedly.

"Have you even touched that thing in two months?" Tony looked suspicious.

Tony apparently thought that he was the real thing. Sure, he had the rockstar looks with his long, straight, dark hair, a narrow face with a straight nose and the slim build that was perfect for skinny jeans and tight T-shirts, but from what Kyle had heard, he was not a talented musician – at least not a talented bass player.

"Would it matter if I hadn't?" he responded with a straight look at Tony. Then he got up from the couch, walked past Donal and went to stand next to John.

"So, are we gonna have a go?"

"Do you even know the song?" Tony asked in a patronising tone. He was not going to give up his place without a fight.

The song was clearly new to the band's repertoire because they had never played it together while he had been in the band. Kyle was pleased with himself for knowing the song really well. He particularly liked the sound of the bass in the song, which made him think playing it was Tony's idea. The man had been trying to make himself sound good – although that was unlikely to happen with his skills.

"One of my favourites," Kyle said with a grin and pulled the strap of his bass over his head. "Shall we have a go?"

"Man, you don't know what you're doing," Donal said discreetly.

"I'll figure it out as we go along." Kyle smiled back at him. John was keen to go, getting already started into the intro. Sam soon picked up. Donal looked panicked, as if he had realised that he didn't know the words, but got ready to start singing anyway.

It didn't take Kyle long to get into it. He had a good ear for this kind of thing and quickly started to figure out what to do. Halfway through the song, Tony picked up his long, black, rockstar leather coat and bass off the floor, muttered something under his breath and walked out.

Kyle was back in the band.

* * *

They had decided on a celebratory night out in honour of Kyle returning to the band. Well, John and Sam were celebrating it, but Kyle wasn't so sure about Donal. He seemed to be in a right gloomy mood, preferring to chat to Irene rather than his band mates. On the other hand, Kyle couldn't blame him – Kyle himself would rather have spoken to Irene, if she had ever made the effort to speak to him.

"You know, me and John are so relieved to be rid of Tony," Sam said, leaning in closer to Kyle to be heard above the music and general noise of the bar and – Kyle assumed – to avoid being heard by Donal, who sat right next to him.

"Really?" Kyle asked, raising his eyebrows in question. He had always thought that Sam was the easy-going type of guy who'd get on with everyone.

"Hell yeah. It was like," he paused for a moment to consider, "it was like when Tony was in there, the band was all about what he and Donal wanted to do. Nobody ever asked me or John what we thought. That man's ego is way too big for a bassist. He behaves like he's the lead singer of a band on a sell-out world tour."

"Is he any good?" Kyle asked.

"Are you kidding me? He could be good at a number of things, but playing bass is not one of them! I'd be better at it than he is, and I've never played anything but drums!"

The two of them burst into laughter.

"So no, we won't miss him much. You should never have left. Except, I suppose, you needed the break," Sam said with a more serious look on his face.

"I don't know," Kyle said, staring at the quarter pint of beer that he had left, swirling it around, "I missed it."

Sam nodded with a knowing look on his face although he probably had no idea what Kyle was talking about. Then he pointed at Kyle's pint and when he responded with a nod, got up to go to the bar.

John was deep in conversation with his missus, Mildred – a horrible name for a young woman, Kyle had always thought. She wasn't much to look at either, which was just as well because she had been off the market for a long time anyway. She was a nice girl though, and she and John seemed to have eyes for nobody except each other – something which proved to be wrong a few minutes later.

Kyle had texted Mel about half an hour earlier, asking whether she was out. It wasn't that he wanted to see her, but it was a hassle-free way to get laid. She would have gone into hysterics if he had tried to approach another woman with the view to chat her up.

She arrived, noisily, followed by her group of friends – flatmates, he had learned – and stood in the doorway to look around for him. Kyle was somewhat stuck to his seat, aware that most male eyes in the room had turned to the group of young women who had just entered the bar and that Mel was one of them. He felt a surge of pride at the thought that she would shortly walk over to him. Then he felt ashamed. It was nothing to get big-headed about, especially when he didn't even like her much.

While all these thoughts were going through his head, she

had started to walk towards him. He took guilty pleasure in watching her walk towards him, swaying her hips in a confident fashion, eyes fixed on him from across the room. She knew well that people were looking at her and seemed to enjoy it. Kyle started to feel self-conscious realising that once she reached him, all eyes would be on him too. He could hardly duck under the table either.

"Hello handsome," she said from beside him, putting a gloved hand on his neck. It felt cold though soft, and an ambiguous shiver went down his spine.

"Hi," he said, scrambling up from his stool as he realised what she was expecting him to do. As soon as he was up on his feet, she seemed to shrink, only reaching his shoulders despite her shiny red heels. She reached up for a kiss – and not just a peck either, but a lingering, wet, sloppy kiss with tongue and all that left him feeling dizzy. What a show-off.

"I'll just go and get a drink. Are you all right?" She pulled off her coat to reveal a bright-red dress, the kind that kids wore to the prom on American high school movies.

"Yeah, yeah. Sam is just…" He looked over to the bar to see where exactly Sam had disappeared to. He was leaning against the bar, chatting to two women that Kyle didn't recognise. They seemed to be having a good time, and the blonde kept swirling a lock of her hair around her fingers in an almost seductive way. In fact, it would have been seductive if it had been aimed at anybody but Sam. Sam was of an average height and average build, had long, blonde, slightly wavy hair and a protruding nose – usually not a hit with the ladies.

Noticing Kyle looking at him, Sam caught his eye and seemed to remember the fresh pint that was resting next to his elbow. He reached over to hand it to Kyle but swiftly returned to the conversation.

Kyle sat back down on his stool. Eliza, one of Mel's friends, pulled up a stool next to him and whispered with a nod in Sam's direction, "Is that his girlfriend?"

Kyle felt a need to laugh and nearly spat his beer out of his mouth, managing in the last minute to swallow it instead.

"Certainly not. There is no such thing."

"Oh. Really?" The girl looked delighted and concerned at the same time. "How come?"

"Have you had a look at the man?"

That was such a rude remark that Kyle couldn't believe it could have come out of his mouth until he realised that it hadn't. Donal had butted in. Irene seemed to have disappeared, which must be why Donal had decided to look for company elsewhere.

"What's that supposed to mean?" Eliza looked offended.

Kyle wanted to remind Donal to have a better look at Eliza but could hardly do that while she was within hearing distance.

"Well, he's hardly Brad Pitt now, is he?"

"Neither are you," Eliza said with a dirty look up and down Donal's upper body.

That caught him unawares. Donal was used to women falling at his feet, for a reason Kyle had never been able to understand.

"He's a sound fella. A bit shy. You should talk to him." Kyle tried to patch things up. He glanced over his shoulder. "Maybe not just now. Some other time."

Eliza pursed her lips with a distinct look of disapproval and disappointment on her face, but turned away to face her friends who had gathered around on a random selection of stools and chairs.

Kyle was surprised – and intrigued – by Mel not returning directly to him. She went and sat down next to her friends for a while. He felt abandoned in a weird way that he didn't like but threw himself deep into conversation with John instead, Sam having decided that he preferred the company of ladies for the time being and Irene having returned to Donal.

It must have been at least twenty minutes later before Mel returned to him. She sat down on the bench left unoccupied by Sam, turning sideways on it with her back towards Donal and Irene and facing Kyle.

"I heard the good news."

For a moment, Kyle didn't have a clue what she was talking about.

"You're back in the band. That's great news, Kyle!" She was beaming at him.

"Oh, yeah. That's right."

"It's brilliant. I don't know what it is," she said in a lowered voice and leaned in closer to him, "but there's something about a man being in a band that makes him instantly more attractive."

He felt all possible responses getting stuck in his throat. She probably didn't want a response anyway. She leaned in to kiss him again, laying one hand on his thigh, dangerously close to that part of his body that was sure to respond, and one on his neck, pulling him closer. He felt clumsy and awkward with his friends around him but couldn't push her away. He didn't need to anyway because she pulled away with a smug look on her face and told him she'd be back in a minute. She got up from the bench and walked towards the bathrooms.

Kyle heard a hissing sound from his left. It turned out to be from John. Realising that he had caught Kyle's attention, a huge grin spread across his face.

"Hot you are, the two of you."

Kyle attempted a smile at that but was too flushed to say

anything.

"Particularly her. She's one hell of a woman," John carried on, his eyes darting towards the door of the ladies' where Mel had disappeared.

"Hey!" Mildred elbowed him in the ribs in what Kyle took to be mock offence.

"I'm just saying," John said, lifting his hands up in surrender. "She's a good-looking girl and Kyle here is one lucky guy."

Mildred gave Kyle an exasperated look that was followed by an exaggerated sigh.

Mel returned a moment later. By that time, Kyle had somewhat returned to his senses, gulped down the rest of his beer and stood up to greet her. He grabbed her hand as she was about to go over to Sophie and pulled her towards him instead. He wrapped his arms around her waist, putting his hands on the small of her back. He was about to kiss her when she pulled away.

"So, that's how it is, is it?" she asked in a teasing manner, pushing her hands into his back pockets.

"It is," he whispered hoarsely.

"Do you wanna go now?"

Her fingers were gently rubbing his buttocks through the material. He was sure to burst if they didn't get out soon.

He nodded certain that if he was to open his mouth, the only sound that would come out would be a moan.

"Right so. I'll just get my coat." She pulled away, kissed him on the lips and turned away from him with a knowing smile on her face.

CHAPTER 17

Kyle left his room lured out by the wonderful scent of roasting chicken, feeling slightly dizzy after having spent the last couple of hours on the PlayStation, delightfully engulfed by an alternative universe. He was relieved to have a day off from his cooking duties. It was Thursday, so Cassie was working, but Ciara had had a day off and made the most of her time by slaving away in the kitchen – not Kyle's idea of a relaxing day, but then, women were strange like that.

He glanced at the clock on the hall wall – quarter to six. Taking a few steps down the stairs, he could hear Cassie's voice from the kitchen, and a few steps later, he could make out the words.

"He talked about all these things, post-traumatic stress disorder, survivor's guilt, all that…"

"Survivor's guilt?" That was Ciara. Kyle could picture the confused look on her face, eyebrows shot up in astonishment.

"Yeah. You know, Dr Mooney thinks that Kyle feels guilty because he survived the accident and mum and dad didn't. Like somehow it would have been better if he'd died too, or instead of them. Apparently, he could even think it was all his fault."

That was a direct punch to the jaw. No therapist could have a clue about how he felt. He grabbed the banister, suddenly covered in a cold sweat and feeling even dizzier.

"Are you gonna tell him that?"

Kyle heard the oven door open and close, then the sound of the switch being flicked.

"I don't know. Dr Mooney says we should try to talk him round to going in himself."

"Good luck with that! Doesn't he do home visits?"

There was a moment's silence that probably included Cassie shaking her head.

"No. He doesn't believe in trying to help people who don't want to be helped."

"Well, you know what Kyle is like. A typical man – doesn't talk about his feelings. I don't get that about men. It's no less manly to talk about stuff than it is to keep it all in."

There was a lot of shuffling for the next while. He could hear the chink of glasses as one of the girls looked for glasses in the cupboard, then the fridge door open with the usual sucking sound. He carried on down the stairs, having relaxed a little.

"Will you go and get him?" Ciara asked when he reached the kitchen doorway.

"Don't bother," Kyle said to their backs. Cassie was looking for cutlery in one of the drawers and Ciara was trying to carve the chicken.

"Oh, there you are. Dinner's just ready."

Kyle sat down at the table. There was a big bowl of salad on the table next to an equally large bowl of boiled potatoes and a full gravy boat. A moment later Ciara laid a plate down in front of him, covered in thin slices of roast chicken.

"Are you OK? You look a little pale," she noted with a worried frown on her face. She was going to make a great mother.

"I'm all right," Kyle huffed and reached over for the potatoes.

"Are you sure? Do you need something to…" A flush reached Ciara's cheeks as she realised she had been about to ask a stupid question.

"I'm about to, ain't I?" Kyle asked with a smile that he couldn't quite stop.

Cassie sat down opposite him and got stuck into her meal.

"You know I had to go and see Dr Mooney today."

Kyle wasn't sure if she said that as a statement or a question. He shrugged.

"Someone had to. You obviously weren't going to go."

"I told you I wasn't."

Ciara sat down at the table with a worried expression on her face.

"And I wasn't going to pay for an appointment that nobody went to. He would like to meet you."

"I am most flattered," Kyle noted with a smug satisfaction at which Ciara sniggered a little, not able to help herself.

"He knows you're not coping well," Cassie said, totally ignoring his remark.

Kyle said nothing. Ciara was much more focused on her plate than was necessary.

"You're obviously not how you used to be. You're even more of a pain in the arse than you were before. You're cranky, you don't sleep right, you drink too much…"

"Remind me," Kyle said, laying his fork down on the plate, "how long since you moved to London?"

Cassie looked baffled for a moment, then straightened her face.

"Five years."

"Five years. How exactly do you know how I've been in the last five years? I was fifteen when you left."

"I think I would know. I'm your sister."

"She's only trying to help," Ciara said. She reached out her hand and briefly touched Kyle's arm.

"I don't need help," he hissed. This was like an electric shock to Ciara, who quickly withdrew her hand.

"I think you do," she said quietly but put her head down again, not wanting to get involved.

"Well, don't come complaining to me when you wind up drunk in a ditch with no job, no home and no friends. I did try."

It was a miracle that nobody walked away. Instead, they finished their dinner in silence.

* * *

Kyle spent most of the following afternoon around town. Mel had texted the night before and asked to see him for a coffee around four. He'd agreed, knowing that he would have to head in for rehearsals at Donal's at seven. He had spent the last hour bumming around town after dropping Ciara in for work and leaving the car for Cassie at the office.

He was just heading towards the cafe when he saw a familiar face a few metres ahead of him. There was nowhere to hide. He wished that the ground would just swallow him up, but tarmac was not in a habit of doing that. It was going to be so awkward, even more awkward than the previous Sunday morning at Mel's place.

He had woken up in her bed, alone and naked. There was no sign of Mel around, so he had gotten dressed, used the bathroom and headed downstairs in search for her. In hindsight, it was odd that four girls could sit so quietly around a breakfast table, but he had not had a clue that they were all in the kitchen until he had stepped inside.

Normally he would have loved the idea of four young women sitting around a table in their pyjamas, nighties and bathrobes, but it was different when he had spent the night in bed with one of them and the rest of them knew it. Even if they hadn't, it was obvious from his dishevelled look that morning – the dark circles under his eyes, the wrinkly clothes, untied shoe laces and undoubtedly the smell of sex lingering in the air.

Mel, on the other hand, seemed to rejoice in her tousled look, bed hair and all. What's more, she was not wearing anything underneath her dressing gown. He'd realised that with a nervous gulp and looked away. Luckily, she had gotten up at that point and walked him to the porch where she had given him a promising farewell, pinning him against the doorframe and giving him a long, dirty kiss.

There was no such escape here. Georgina was approaching him, fast, with a delighted smile that he hoped was because she had spotted him. More than likely, though, it was because she was amused by his recent foolishness.

"Hi Kyle. How are you?" She stopped in front of him, still smiling widely.

"Ah, good. You?" The words seemed to stick in his throat, but she didn't seem to notice.

"Not a bother with me. All quiet."

Unusually for her, she didn't carry on talking. Why wasn't she talking?

"Erm… About the other night…" He couldn't bring himself to look at her. When he did though, she looked confused.

"New Year's," he clarified.

"Oh, that. Ah, don't sweat about it. You were slightly worse for wear that night. I know you didn't mean it."

Ouch. He wasn't sure he had wanted to hear that. Not all of it, anyway.

"Besides," she said, leaning in a little closer to him, "it was really sweet."

He just about looked up at her at that, but she had pulled away and was waving towards the shop.

"I need to go, I've an appointment at four. I'll see you soon."

Kyle remained on the footpath for a while, cheeks burning from embarrassment. He wasn't sure if he was relieved or disappointed. Georgina thought that he had only said what he had said because he was drunk. That could be a good thing or a bad thing. Was it better to be considered a drunk than just a complete idiot?

He shook his head and set off towards the cafe. He would have to shake Georgina off his mind if he was to have coffee with Mel.

She was already sitting in a corner, her back towards him, facing the window towards a little alleyway that ran between the cafe and the health food store next to it. She had a cup of what looked like a cappuccino in front of her.

Kyle ordered a tea and a sandwich and went to sit down opposite her. She looked up, surprised. She hadn't noticed his arrival and was startled when someone sat down at her table. When her eyes fixed on his face, her face lit up, her gaze wandering up to the top of his head when he pulled off his cap.

"Hi Kyle. How are you?"

"I'm all right. You?" he said while pulling off his jacket. It was a cold day, and he felt like he had about six layers on – a tank top, T-shirt, shirt, cardigan, jacket… Well, that was only five, but still, the weather outside was ridiculous.

Mel, on the other hand, did not seem to suffer from such issues. She was dressed in a big, long jumper with a high neck. For its size, it still gave him a good view of her figure while seemingly keeping her warm. He noticed that she had a beret perched on the back of one of the empty chairs at the table, along with her coat. She looked as well-kept as ever – not even a give-away red nose to prove that she had been out in the cold.

She burst into a fit of chatter, telling him all about some film that she had been to see the previous night and about a new flatmate that was about to move into the empty bedroom in her house over the weekend. Kyle nodded at what he thought were appropriate times in the conversation while getting stuck into his BLT. He was ravenous, and he hadn't realised until he had started eating.

"Kyle, there's something I wanted to talk to you about."

He looked up at Mel and saw that her expression had sobered. "Yeah. What is it?"

She fumbled with her serviette for a while and then looked up at him again.

"My friends think that you're not really into me. They think that you only ever want to see me when you want sex."

Hallelujah. So somebody at least had seen it.

"Is it true?"

Kyle looked up from his plate. She had that expression on her face that told him that he would be in big trouble if he didn't tread carefully. Luckily, he had his mouth full so he had a moment of grace before having to come up with an ingenious answer. He lifted his hand towards his face to point out that he was chewing. Her expression relaxed a little, but her eyes remained on him expectantly. He swallowed, twice, just to get a bit of extra time. He desperately wanted a gulp of his tea – preferably something stronger – but that would have looked like he was buying time to come up with an explanation. Maybe he could pretend to choke?

"It's not... It's just that I..." Oh Jesus. He wasn't going to do the old "it's not you, it's me" crap, was he?

"I mean, I'm a mess right now. I can't really... My feelings are all over the place. I don't think I can focus on anybody else just now."

He forced himself to keep looking at her. The severe expression on her face remained, and then a hint of sadness wiped over it before it was replaced by what looked like a – it couldn't be, could it? – smile. Then she reached her hand across the table and laid it gently on his arm.

"It's your parents, isn't it? I forget about it sometimes. You hide it so well. Normally." The last bit was probably a reference to his recent breakdown at her brother's party.

She looked more serious again.

"Does that mean we will not be seeing each other again?"

He felt such a surge of relief go through him that he was certain she was going to see it.

"It's probably better. It wouldn't be fair on you."

She sighed deeply. It sounded like she was holding back tears.

"I know. Not you either. I'll miss you though," she said with a squeeze of his arm before pulling her hand back. "When you do get over this... this trauma, make sure you let me know?"

"You'll be the first to know," he said with a smile although that was a downright lie. She would be one of the last to know – hopefully.

She sighed again but more cheerfully.

"There won't be anybody quite like you." She stared past him for a moment, then turned to look at him again and said: "Sure we'll still see each other. I'll still come to see the band play."

Oh joy.

"How exactly do you know Donal, anyway?" he couldn't help asking.

A wicked smile crossed her face.

"Jealous, are you?" Then she got more serious again. "Sophie's Donal's cousin. You know, she's an only child, so she's always been really close to him and particularly his sister."

Well that explained it then. Sort of.

"Right. I better get going then. I'm heading out tonight. I don't suppose I'll be seeing you then?" Mel got up and started pulling her coat on. There was a note of triumph in her voice. She thought he was going to be jealous.

He shook his head. "Band practice."

"Well, say hi to Donal and the gang then from me," she said and grabbed her hat. "I'll be seeing you."

Kyle was left on his own with his half-drunk cup of tea and half-eaten sandwich. He felt a little sad, but that was swallowed up by a great sense of relief.

* * *

He walked in to Donal's garage, frozen to the bone from the 20-minute walk from town centre. He found Sam and John already in there, Sam sitting behind the drums and John on a stool, tuning his guitar. It wasn't warm in the garage, but Kyle still proceeded to take off some of his layers. He would never be able to play if he was shaped like a sumo wrestler.

"You know, man, I just don't know what to do now," Sam said, exasperated.

"What's up?" Kyle asked curiously. He sat down on the couch and pulled his instrument out of its case. "And where's Donal?"

"He's gone in to get some beers," John replied.

Now that sounded like a good idea.

"And I just don't know what to do. I've never had this kind of a problem before."

Kyle looked over to Sam, who was clapping his drumsticks together.

"You know that gorgeous blonde I was speaking to last Saturday?"

Kyle couldn't remember seeing her face properly, and if he had, it hadn't been that impressive, but he nodded.

"You see, she actually seemed quite keen and we swapped numbers. The crazy thing is, she texted me."

Kyle raised his eyebrows. Now that was unusual – particularly when Sam was concerned.

"That's good, right?"

"That's brilliant! Only the thing is, there was this other chick…" Sam made a frustrated sound. "You know, one of Mel's friends. She is really keen."

Stupid fool. Had he not told her to leave it for some other time?

"And she texted me too. I've been texting them both, and I don't know what to do now. I mean, Jill is way too good for me, she'd never stick around, but she's totally hot. Eliza mightn't be a stunner, but she's a nice girl and we've a lot in common. Argh!"

"Why don't you just date both?" John said logically, even though Kyle knew it was morally wrong.

"I can't do that! They'd find out. This never happens to me. To you, maybe," Sam said with a look towards Kyle, "with your cherub face and all," – Kyle blinked at him in astonishment – "and Donal, whatever it is women like about him. What would you do?"

Kyle realised that Sam was waiting for his opinion.

"Erm…"

"Come on, you can't ask him. He'll obviously say Mel's friend, he would have to. His girlfriend would kill him," John butted in and put his guitar down, rubbing his hands against his thighs.

"Actually, we broke up," Kyle said quietly, returning his attention to his bass guitar.

"What? Oh man." Sam followed this up with a dramatic drum solo.

Donal walked in at that point, carrying two six-packs of beer that he planted on a cardboard box by the window.

"I've some good news for you."

The three of them looked at Donal expectantly.

"We've been asked to play a gig next month. Club Boulevard, Saturday night. How about that?" He opened a bottle of beer and raised it for a toast. The garage was filled with loud cheers and general excitement for a moment while they asked for more details and uncorked more beers.

"You know, I've been thinking... Do you think we should get Tony to play guitar?"

John gave Donal a murderous look.

"I mean, second guitar, instead of me, so that I could focus more on my performance."

"Not a hope," Sam announced with a bitter look on his face. "He couldn't play bass to save his life. What makes you think he'd be any better with a guitar?"

Donal shrugged. "He's pretty good with both, I think."

Sam rolled his eyes.

"I think we should just stay the way we are," John said peacefully. "It was working fine before."

Donal looked quizzically towards Kyle. "What do you think?"

"I agree. It should be just the four of us."

Donal looked disappointed and defeated.

"Fair enough then. We'll carry on as we are. Let's get going."

John, Sam and Kyle exchanged a victorious look behind Donal's back when he bent to pick up his guitar.

* * *

Kyle woke up to confusion, a sore neck and a stiff body the following morning. The sun was shining in through uncovered windows, but it was cold in the room. Everything seemed oddly yellow and orangey red in colour. He shook his head like a wet dog to get an understanding of where he was. Then he realised what had really woken him up.

His phone, which was uncomfortably lodged underneath him in his pocket, was ringing. He shifted himself enough to pull it out of his pocket and pick it up. It was Cassie.

"Where the hell are you? Me and Ciara want to get going."

"Going where?" he asked drowsily. He was trying to figure out what day it was.

"What? We want to get started with this thing. We waited ages, and when you didn't show up, we checked your room and there's no one there. Will you just make your way home?"

Cassie hung up. He couldn't tell for sure if she was pissed off or worried.

He made himself sit up and look around. He was tired, and his head felt like he had been drinking although he didn't really feel hungover. After a moment, he realised that it was Saturday. He was at Donal's house. Yes, that was it. John and Sam had gotten a taxi home after all the drinking, both living in town centre, but Kyle hadn't had any money and he was going in a different direction anyway, so Donal had offered him the couch in the sitting room.

He got up and made his way to the bathroom. What the hell was Cassie talking about? Saturday, Saturday... Ciara was off. Her hours had been cut down after the Christmas rush – nobody could afford to go out in January, so people weren't eating junk food either.

He moved on into the kitchen, found an opened bottle of orange juice in the fridge and finished the contents in one go. Then he spotted a pack of chocolate chip biscuits on the countertop and grabbed a couple before heading out the front door.

He called a taxi and started making his way towards the local shop where he had asked to be picked up. There was an ATM in there – and food.

Once he had gotten €20 out of the cash machine – his last, as far as he knew – it hit him. They were meant to be going through their parents' stuff today. The wardrobe mainly, but there was a pile of other things they needed to sort out.

When he made his way out of the store with a hot breakfast roll, his taxi was already outside. The driver issued him with a warning not to touch his breakfast while in the cab, so Kyle wasn't able to eat it until he stepped out of the car in the driveway and was halfway through it by the time he got into the kitchen.

The girls were both in the kitchen, obviously annoyed. Cassie was emptying the dishwasher and Ciara was sitting at the table peeling potatoes.

"Finally!" Cassie exclaimed upon seeing him.

"About time! You want a cup of tea with that?" Ciara asked with a nod towards his roll.

"Please," he just about managed to say through the sausage, egg and bacon in his mouth.

"One could get the idea that you were avoiding this," Cassie said, hanging the tea towel back over the oven door and kicking the dishwasher closed.

"Well, I'm not looking forward to it. I just want to get it out of the way," Ciara said.

"Me too," Kyle sighed and sat down at the table, grabbing the

TV guide that someone had left in the wrong place.

"We are not putting it off any longer. Once boy wonder here has his breakfast over and done with, we'll get going." Cassie sat down with her own cup of tea and wrinkled her nose in disgust. "Except that you might want to get changed first. You stink!"

That didn't surprise him much. Donal's garage was not a smoke-free zone, not to mention the spilt alcohol, sweat and whatever may have been on the couch. He didn't want to think about it.

"I hope your girlfriend keeps her place cleaner than that," Cassie continued.

"I don't have one," Kyle replied.

"Yeah right. Don't tell her that," Ciara muttered.

"No, really, I don't." Not like he had ever considered Mel that anyway.

"What is she then?" Cassie asked disinterested.

"Single," he replied smartly.

"Semi-single at the most," Ciara said.

"No, she really is single. We're not seeing each other anymore."

"Since when?" Cassie seemed slightly more interested.

"Yesterday."

"Did she throw you out?" Cassie seemed amused by that possibility.

"No. After that I went to rehearsals like I always do on Fridays."

"Hence the stink," Ciara concluded.

"Well, Donal could certainly clean his act up too. No smoking in the house. Right, can we now get going? You can bring your tea with you."

The girls made their way upstairs while Kyle went into the utility to get changed. There was a pile of clean clothes on the counter, and the dirty ones could just wait in the basket for now.

His sisters were well organised. There was a roll of black bin bags and a couple of empty cardboard boxes on the floor near the wardrobe. Ciara sat on the floor with her legs crossed under her and Cassie had the doors open, carefully starting to pull stuff out.

"Why are we doing this?" she said quietly, more to herself than to anybody else.

"Because we need to move on," Ciara said softly.

Cassie looked up from the cardigan that she was holding on a hanger.

"No. I mean, we shouldn't have to do this. They should be here."

Nobody had anything to say to that. Kyle took a sip of his tea. Ciara patted the floor next to her to signal for him to sit down. He did.

It was a painful task, and it took them ages. They didn't want to throw everything out. They wanted to keep some pieces to remember them by. The girls wanted some of their mother's clothes for themselves. Kyle had no use for his dad's things, being considerably smaller than he had been. The girls insisted that he should keep one of the ties.

"What am I ever gonna do with this?" he asked, eyeing the blue tie with rain drops and umbrellas on it. It was hardly going to do for job interviews.

"It's cool. You'll figure something out," Ciara said with a convincing smile.

"You know, there's one thing I can't find here," Cassie interrupted. She sounded worried. "I can't find those purple shoes. I wanted to keep them."

"Oh yeah, they were lovely. I would have wanted them; only they would be too big... Where are they?"

Kyle looked at them in sudden horror. It was like all blood drained from his face. It probably had, because they both looked at him with concerned expressions, expecting him to say something.

"She was wearing them."

There was a moment's silence.

"Was she? Are you sure?" Ciara asked.

He nodded.

"I remember them... I remember staring at them. When we were walking out..."

"She was wearing them," Cassie repeated, her attention elsewhere.

He didn't remember much about the journey. He had been sort of dazed, his mind foggy from the drink and the hypoglycaemia. He thought he had been sort of dozing off, but his mother had kept talking to him – to keep him awake, he thought, to make sure he wouldn't faint and they wouldn't realise, thinking that he was just asleep. The music had been on, some classic rock – the kind his dad liked, but it had been playing very quietly in the background. He'd felt cold although the heating was on in the car. He had no idea how fast they had been going. Dad was a good driver, and the roads were slippery, so he would have been careful. He remembered hearing a frightened curse from him. That was unusual because his dad rarely cursed – he was a mild-mannered business man. His mum was more likely to let out the occasional expletive. But it wasn't the use of bad language that had alerted him; it was his tone. Kyle had lifted his head. It was in that fraction of a second that he realised something was wrong. The car didn't feel right, it wasn't gripping properly and the tyres sounded wrong. He could see his dad clasping the steering wheel with both hands. The engine sounded weird too.

The car wasn't in gear. It was in neutral.

Then there was a huge bang, he flung forward in the backseat and there was the sound of glass breaking. Then there was complete silence.

"Kyle, are you OK?"

He shook his head and realised that Ciara was looking at him. She had her hand on his shoulder, as if she had been shaking him. No sign of the ambulance man.

"Uhum," he managed to utter.

"It looked like... like you were somewhere else," Ciara said in an odd tone that she did not normally use.

"I was." He swallowed hard, then reached for his tea and took a sip.

"OK," Cassie said cautiously. "They are gone, then."

Kyle looked at her in total confusion.

"The shoes, Kyle. They are gone," Ciara came to his rescue.

"Right. Right."

Cassie had already moved away from the wardrobe and into the en suite. When Ciara realised that Kyle was all right, she followed her in. They were going through their mother's make-up, dividing it into three piles according to their usability. Kyle got up from the floor, his legs numb from sitting on them. He waited for a while until the feeling returned and walked up to the bathroom door.

"What I wouldn't do to have an en suite," Ciara sighed, looking around at the decently-sized room. "It's so unfair that I don't have one. I mean, what does Kyle need one for?" She looked at him over her shoulder. Here we go again.

"It's because I have diabetes," he sighed.

"The blessed diabetes. Aren't you lucky?"

"Not a bit," he muttered.

"I never understood it either. Such an excuse," Cassie said, picking up the towels off the little shelf under the window.

"They thought you should have some privileges to make up for it, didn't they?" Ciara said in a joking tone.

"It was a practicality." That was the truth. They had decided that he needed to be able to keep his supplies at hand – whether it was the medication or food and drinks.

"Hah," Cassie declared but didn't push further.

"There would be no harm if you had been born a girl," Ciara grinned.

"You would have been called Kylie if you had been a girl," Cassie informed them.

"Would I have been called Ciaran then?"

"As a matter of fact, yes." Cassie moved back into the bedroom with her arms full of towels and bathrobes.

"And what would they have called you? Casanova?" Kyle couldn't help asking.

Cassie gave him an offended look.

"They hadn't considered it. Mum knew she was expecting a girl with me."

Ciara sat down on the bed, carefully, as if worried that it might break. She looked thoughtfully at her siblings.

"Wouldn't it be odd if we were three girls instead?"

"I would hate to be a girl," Kyle said, bending to pick up his empty mug of the carpet.

"You would make a pretty girl though," Ciara said in a contemplative tone, looking him up and down.

"She would be a horrible slut," Cassie said a lot less wistfully.

"Good point. You should try a girlfriend, Kyle." Ciara leaned back on the bed.

"Too much hassle." He picked up the bagful of clothes that they had decided to give away.

"Not that you've tried too hard. You were seeing Mel for about two weeks."

"She wasn't worth the hassle," he grunted.

"I thought she was lovely," Ciara admitted. Kyle gave her a sideways glance. What planet was she from if she thought Mel was lovely? Well, she had a certain appeal at times, but most of the time she was just a pain in the ass.

"It's hardly a good time now anyway. Too much baggage."

"Well that's for sure. You should try the luggage storage at Dr Mooney's," Cassie retorted before disappearing out the door with a box full of shoes.

CHAPTER 18

Time went by slowly. Cassie was starting to get the hang of her job, although she still spent most of the time answering the phone and taking messages for Iris and James. When she wasn't doing that, she was dealing with personal affairs more than anything – talking to the solicitor, therapist, bank, her old employer, Social Welfare, Rob. Kyle was a lot less excited than Cassie and even Ciara when Cassie announced that Rob was coming over for a weekend in early February.

It was one afternoon that he descended the stairs to the kitchen to have some lunch that he heard Ciara crying in the sitting room. When she noticed him in the sitting room doorway, she quickly wiped her eyes and pretended to be all right.

He moved into the room and sat down next to her on the two-seater.

"Are you all right?"

She nodded, but he could see her red-rimmed eyes and wet cheeks. She couldn't hide her sobs either.

"You're not. What is it?" He put an arm round her shoulders in a way that he had not done in a long, long time. They weren't a huggy family.

"I just started thinking... My child will never meet mum and dad. He'll never meet them, or she. And they won't get to meet

225

their grandchild either."

He could feel her pain, in a way. He hadn't thought about having children, but the thought of having children who only knew his own parents by their names was unbearable.

"They'll only be names," Ciara said as if reading his thoughts, "just names and photos on the wall and in albums. Memories, not real people."

"They'll always be real to me. And you." Kyle squeezed her shoulder a bit. He tried to see her face, but she had her head down. What he saw instead was her rounding belly, despite the '70s style wide top she was wearing. He felt a sudden lurch in his stomach, a very strange sensation that they were the grown-ups now, almost as if they no longer needed parents. Inside he was screaming; he felt nowhere near old enough to get by without parents, not yet, not ever, and not now of all times when he needed them most. It was ridiculous, of course, because he wouldn't have needed them if they weren't gone.

"What if we forget?" Ciara looked up at him and wiped her nose on a tissue that she was holding. "What if we forget what they were like? Sometimes I can't remember their voices."

Kyle doubted that he could ever forget, but unfortunately, his last memories of his mum's and dad's voices were not happy ones.

"We have them on video. And tape. Remember when mum did that thing on the radio?"

Ciara almost smiled at that, remembering the time their mum had been talking about tarot cards and other weird stuff on the local radio station.

He leaned his chin on her shoulder and said almost into her ear: "There will still be grandparents. Ronan has parents, hasn't he?"

"Yes. I envy him for that. Sometimes I hate him for it." Ciara sounded guilty saying that, but Kyle knew what she meant. He often felt angry about that, how other people much older than him still had both their parents. Some even had grandparents left – he did too, but horrible as it sounded, he would much rather have kept his parents than grandparents. He was almost sure that they would rather have gone before their children too.

"They would have been so happy to have a grandchild." Ciara wiped her nose again.

He doubted that slightly. They would have loved a grandchild, but not from Ciara – not for many years to come, anyway. Still, he knew they would have gotten around to the idea and been happy for her and adored the child when eventually it arrived.

He lifted his head and pulled his arm away, squeezing her shoulder closest to him instead.

"I think they would have much preferred if it was Cassie."

Ciara sniggered.

"Yeah, you're probably right. I still wish they could be here and see the baby."

"They will see the baby. It's just that we can't hear what they would say."

Ciara nodded. She wiped her eyes on the back of her hand again. Then she laid a hand on his arm for a moment.

"Thanks, Kyle."

She got up then and headed towards the kitchen.

"I'm starving. Do you want lunch?"

* * *

It hadn't been a great day overall. The post had brought them letters advising that the estate documents had now been completed and that all the funeral costs had been covered, meaning that it would not take much longer before they could

227

receive their inheritance. This, as such, should have been good news because they needed the money and because they wanted everything to be wrapped up and over and done with. On the other hand, it was another nail on the coffin – just another reminder and confirmation that their parents were gone and not coming back.

After practice that night, Kyle headed out with Donal. Sam was in a hurry to go and see Jill – he had gone for looks over personality after all – and John had announced that he was too broke for a night out and that Mildred would not appreciate him spending his last few quid on a night out.

It wasn't a busy night in Juice. Tony was there, and they had run into another couple of guys that Donal was friendly with and Kyle half-knew. Kyle was planning on taking it easy. He had gotten himself sorted out with some dole money, but it was by all means not much and he did not intend on drinking it all. Cassie would not have been too pleased if he did. He was only half-way through his first pint when there was a tap on his shoulder.

He turned around and froze for a moment. It was Kathy. He immediately felt awkward but also excited. There was a certain promise about her, but there was also the small issue of her having caught him sleeping in a dog's bed…

"How are you, Kyle?" she asked with a flirtatious smile. He liked the way she said his name.

"I'm good," he said, although he wasn't really. It had been a tough day with his emotions up and down, and now he was ridiculously nervous, like a teenager.

"Umm. You're looking well. Grey suits you."

For one brief moment, Kyle had the time to be pleased with his choice of clothes, but that was quickly wiped out of his mind when she lifted her fingers to the zipper on his top and gently pulled it down – only an inch at the most, but her intentions were clear. A little voice at the back of his mind tried to tell him that he should have returned the compliment, but no words came out.

"It's kind of boring here. I was going to head on." She looked into his eyes. Then he felt a hand squeeze his shoulder, which was followed by Donal's voice in his ear.

"If you don't go with her, I'm gonna kick you out of the band with immediate effect, and your balls will follow tomorrow."

Kyle realised that Donal was handing him his jacket. He saw Kathy giving Donal an approving look, then Donal grabbed Kyle's pint right out of his hand and Kathy took his now free hand. Before he knew it, he was out the door.

* * *

It was nearly midday before he got home the following day. The girls were both in the kitchen. It looked like they were folding tea towels, but that seemed the most pointless household chore ever, so they were probably doing something else.

"And where the hell have you been?" Cassie scolded him as soon as he entered the kitchen, having left his wet jacket in the hall to dry.

"Looks like the walk of shame to me," Ciara said teasingly.

"I said I was heading out," Kyle said defensively. "Did you need the car?"

"No. I just needed to know where my little brother was." Cassie said that in a mocking tone, as if he wasn't able to look after himself and knowing fine well that he was shorter than her.

"I'm quite safe. And I was in good company."

"I'm sure you were. So, who was it?" Cassie lifted a pile of tea towels of the table and put them back in the cupboard.

Kyle scratched his neck uncomfortably.

"Well come on, spit it out."

"Ah come on, Cassie. He doesn't want to kiss and tell," Ciara said good-humouredly.

Why, oh why couldn't Ciara be the older sister? She would have been so much easier to deal with.

"There are no secrets in this town. We'll find out sooner or later," Cassie pointed out. She just stood there, staring at him and expecting him to spill the beans.

He didn't say anything, but there must have been a look of guilt on his face. Cassie's face reddened, and she leant her hands on the table.

"Oh Jesus. You didn't." It wasn't a question. It was a statement. What was she thinking? She couldn't know…

"What's going on?" Ciara asked, eyeing them both in amazement.

Cassie turned her head to look at her sister.

"I got a text off Kathy this morning."

Ciara nodded.

"She said, 'you should have seen the stud I picked up last night'."

Ciara looked confused. Kyle was mortified. Then the look on Ciara's face started to clear up.

"Oh, do you mean that she… that Kyle…" She looked at Kyle, her pupils turned into question marks. "Oh."

"Oh god… It's sickening. To think of what I said back… Ergh!" Cassie grabbed her head with both hands as if worried it was going to fall off. "No wonder she didn't text back. It's disgusting!"

Ciara looked amused.

"How could you? How could she? I can't believe it…" Cassie stood up abruptly and walked out of the room.

"Oh dear. I don't know which one of you is in more trouble, you or Kathy." Ciara seemed to be enjoying all this in a smug, I'm-so-glad-I-don't-have-to-deal-with-any-of-this kind of way.

"I'd safely say it will be me," Kyle muttered. Even though none of it had been his idea…

* * *

A week later, Kyle dropped in to see Georgina before heading to Donal's house for rehearsals. Although he was still embarrassed about his behaviour on New Year's Eve, Georgina hadn't made a big deal out of it and it was over a month ago. He would just have to face the music if he was ever going to… Well, whatever it was he was going to do.

To his surprise though, she did not seem pleased to see him. It wasn't because it was so busy – it was quiet, particularly for a Friday night when she normally complained that the place was full of people wanting their hair done in the last minute. She came straight over to him, a comb in hand, arms crossed in front.

"What can I do for you? I'm still not cutting your hair yet."

"I don't want a haircut," Kyle said and took a seat on the couch. She sat down on the armrest and reached over to examine the scar on his head.

"You know, if you comb your hair down like this, put a bit of gel in it, you could hide the scar. There's not much I can do about this one," she said, touching the scar on his forehead. "If you ever end up on TV, they'll have to use make-up for that one. Unless, of course, you want a fringe."

The thought didn't appeal to him even though lots of blokes in bands had a side fringe– it seemed to be all the rage. He shook his head.

"Well, that's all I can tell you." Georgina made to get up from the armrest.

"Is something wrong?" Kyle couldn't help asking.

Georgina nodded.

"I'm disappointed."

"In what?"

"In you," she said and stood up, straightening her bright pink shirt.

Kyle stared at her in confusion.

"I thought you had better taste than that."

He must have looked more baffled because she elaborated. "It's a small town, Kyle. Everybody knows. You were seen leaving with her." Then she lowered her voice a little. "One of my girls here saw you."

"That means nothing," Kyle said defensively but in a small voice.

Georgina laughed out loud.

"Oh, Kyle, this is Kathy Donnellan we're talking about. She has never left the post office with a fella she didn't sleep with."

Kyle didn't know what to say. He couldn't deny it.

"She is such a slut. I can't believe that people like that are allowed to teach kids in school. I really thought you would have had more sense than that."

Kyle started to feel a sense of relief that she was only carrying a comb and not a pair of scissors. He had a feeling he might have ended up losing parts of him more precious than his hair.

"Sure, no harm to you, though, is there?" he asked carefully, sort of testing the ice.

She grunted.

"So you think."

Then she took a deep sigh.

"She stole my boyfriend. It was years ago, but it doesn't mean

I've forgiven her."

Kyle couldn't understand why any man in his right mind would have preferred Kathy to Georgina, but then, maybe he hadn't been in his right mind. Or perhaps it was his own twisted preferences.

"Anyway, just don't get involved. She's trouble. I gotta go."

And she did, just disappeared towards a customer with a big hair dryer around her head.

* * *

Sam was in big trouble. He said so himself, and it was quite obvious to the rest of them when they were having a well-deserved drink after rehearsals.

Basically, he had been over to Jill's place the week before, stayed the night – this causing his mates to cheer and toast to show their appreciation – only to run into Eliza the following morning when he was heading downstairs on his way out. According to Sam, his exit had been completely acceptable, having told Jill that he was going and having promised to text her later, but Eliza obviously had not expected to see him there. Nor had Sam expected to see her in the house. As the story unfolded, Kyle did remember Mel talking about a new flatmate, but he had not had any idea who it was. It was just an impossible coincidence that it was Jill.

Anyway, Eliza's face had first lit up with surprised delight, then fury and then eventually horrible disappointment and despair, and she had run up the stairs to what Sam assumed to be her room without a single word.

That would have been all fine, Sam said, if it wasn't for the fact that Jill had not answered his calls or texts after that.

"Were you still texting her? Eliza, I mean," John asked.

"Yeeaaah," Sam responded, scratching his head. "And no. I

233

wasn't, but she was still texting me, and I hadn't exactly told her to piss off."

"So, she thought that she still had a chance," Donal concluded.

"Possibly." Sam looked heartbroken, and Kyle wasn't sure if it was because he had hurt someone or because it looked like he was going to lose Jill.

"But what's that got to do with Jill?" John wondered out loud.

"I have no idea. I mean, none at all." Them Sam turned to look at Kyle. "I was thinking if you could find out… I mean, your Mel lives in the same house. She's bound to know what's going on."

"She's not my Mel," Kyle pointed out.

"Yeah, well, whatever. You've still got her wrapped round your little finger. Could you ask her? I mean, I don't know what to do."

Three pairs of eyes were intently staring at Kyle. He was in no position to say no although he had no idea how he was going to go about this.

"Right. I'll try. But not now."

"Cheers man. I knew I could count on you," Sam said with a big grin and raised his bottle in toast.

* * *

It was a weird weekend having Rob around. Kyle got up on Saturday morning to what seemed an empty house. He had managed to avoid Rob the previous day, having headed into town before Rob had gotten to the house from the airport and having spent the evening with the band. It was late in the morning before anybody showed up downstairs. Then it was Ciara first, shortly followed by Ronan. About half an hour later Cassie and Rob showed up, looking like they were on honeymoon. Supposedly they sort of were too. Kyle left the four of them to fend for themselves and took the dog for a walk instead. He would only have felt like the fifth wheel, and not being very fond of Rob and not getting on with Ronan wasn't going to help.

Rob insisted on taking the family out for dinner that night. It was bound to be an uncomfortable evening, but Kyle couldn't refuse without coming across as a brat, particularly when he had no plans.

Luckily, the weekend went quickly. Cassie wasn't happy about it and seemed even moodier after Rob left – in fact, she had hardly been moody at all when he was around. Kyle thought that Rob might have some special powers.

He texted Mel on Monday evening to try and figure out why Jill had jilted Sam. He had no idea how to go about it, so he decided to just ask if Mel knew if Jill was all right because Sam hadn't been able to get in touch. Mel called him about five minutes later.

She was full of sweet-talk. The way she spoke to him, anybody would have thought that they were still dating. Kyle was not convinced that she had realised that they no longer were.

At long last, Mel told him much the same as Sam had about Eliza running into Sam on the stairs and getting upset by that. What Sam did not know was that the girls had had a huge argument later that day. Sam was going to be pleased to hear that girls were fighting over him. Anyway, it appeared that since Jill had realised that Sam had also been texting Eliza while they were going out, she had gotten very upset and decided that he wasn't worth the trouble.

Kyle was sure that he was meant to stand up for his mate and figure out a way to convince Mel to persuade Jill. It wasn't going to be easy because Mel was firmly on Eliza's side, as expected. She didn't seem to have much time for Jill at all. In the end, he thought he had managed to convince Mel to at least ask Jill to

235

talk to Sam to hear his side of the story. He thought it best not to imply that Eliza was making things look worse than they were for her own benefit – if he did that, Mel would give up on the cause altogether.

CHAPTER 19

Two weeks after Rob's visit, the band packed up their gear and piled it up in the back of a van belonging to a friend of Donal's. They were headed for a small, alternative-type night club in Dublin called Club Boulevard. Kyle had never been in there before and neither had the rest of the band except Sam, who said it was mostly a dodgy-looking venue with good music and reasonably priced booze.

It was only about an hour's drive, but Donal asked their driver to stop at a petrol station just outside town. He returned with a boxful of bacon and cheese chips which he handed to Kyle.

There was a look of confusion on everybody's faces.

"I am just making sure that you eat," Donal said while returning to his seat. "Oh, and as well as that, you are absolutely not drinking until after the gig."

John and Sam sniggered at this.

"I mean it. After the last disaster, I'm not taking any risks. Kyle is going to be well-fed and sober when he goes on stage."

* * *

So he was. He was so nervous while they were setting up their gear and before they got on stage that he thought he was going to get sick. He was also envious of his band mates, who were all happily drinking away to drown their nerves.

When he got on stage and started playing the first song, though, the nerves disappeared. He forgot about the audience – not that it was particularly big or loud – and let the music take control. Everything seemed to go quite well. Everybody seemed happy, and the only hiccup was when Donal's microphone stopped working, but the problem was quickly resolved.

Afterwards they all filed into the tiny space backstage that consisted of a toilet cubicle, a cramped space with two torn couches and a narrow dressing room with seats on either side of it as well as hooks for clothes. The whole place was grubby and had not had any work done to it in years.

Kyle took a seat on one of the benches below the hooks, out of everybody else's way. He probably had been nervous after all, because he now felt like the tension was letting go. He felt empty somehow. It was like something wasn't right even though everything had gone perfectly.

He missed his parents. That's what it was. He missed them in horrible, engulfing spasms. He wasn't going to go home and tell them everything about the gig. His mum had always been very supportive of his music, his dad less so but being a keen classic rock fan had never complained either. Now they were never going to know how his actual first show with the band had gone. He had screwed up badly, and they were no longer around.

"Here, mate." Donal had shown up in the tiny space and handed him a bottle of beer and a pack of biscuits. "You deserve it. Good job."

"Cheers," Kyle said quietly, raising the bottle in a reluctant toast.

"You all right?" Donal asked with a concerned frown.

"Yeah, yeah. I just need a moment."

"Right. You make sure you eat something. We don't want you fainting."

Kyle snorted at that but tore open the pack of digestives.

"It's only diabetes, Donal."

"So you say." Donal started to make his way back towards the couches.

"You know, Ian Curtis was epileptic. That's a much worse problem to have in a band, with flashing lights and all."

"Who?" Donal looked at him quizzically.

"Ian Curtis."

Donal still looked baffled.

"He was the singer in Joy Division."

"I've heard of them," Donal said, as if that was something to be proud of.

"So, you know, it could be worse."

Kyle thought it best not to mention that Ian Curtis had killed himself. It was unrelated.

Donal shrugged.

"We'll go back in in a few and sort out the gear." He disappeared around the corner.

They did just that. The crowd had moved away from the stage and was now dancing to some shitty remix of a Green Day song – horrible.

Kyle was on his own on the stage the moment he heard someone behind him.

"Hello sexy."

He turned around in hope of figuring out that Ulterior Motive had groupies. Evidently they did, but not the kind he had hoped for.

"Hi Mel."

She tried to look the part, bless her. She was dressed in a tiny, black denim miniskirt with fishnets. If she was to bend over in that thing, everything would be on show. This was accentuated by her black, very high-heeled what he had heard Ciara call ankle boots and a low-cut top. She really didn't have much class. She was accompanied by Sophie, who was at least more decently dressed.

"You were great tonight. You all were, but you're really great with that thing."

Kyle assumed that by "that thing" she meant his bass guitar, which had already disappeared into the van a long time ago.

"Thank you." He carried on winding up an extension reel. Nobody had ever told him there was so much work involved before and after a gig. Bring on the stadium gigs where someone else does the work for you, he thought. Still, Donal's mate who owned the van and the friend he had brought along for company were doing their best to help, presumably wanting to get home before lunchtime.

"You know, we have a favour to ask," Mel said with a glance towards Sophie, who was standing slightly to the side with folded arms and eyeing him suspiciously. She really didn't like him much.

"What's that?"

"I think we need a lift back. Simon – that's Sophie's brother – dropped us off, but he's staying here with his girlfriend for the night and we can't because Sophie has to work in the morning."

Kyle glanced at Sophie. It was well past midnight, she was still an hour's drive from home and she had to work in the morning?

"Right, I'll find out for you."

* * *

It was rather crowded in the van on the way back. Unbeknown to the rest of the band, Sam had asked Jill to come to the gig. They had obviously made up, then – another thing that they hadn't known. Jill also wanted a lift back but it appeared that this wasn't out of necessity but because of Sam. There were six seats in the back, but Jill and Sam only took up one seat with Jill sitting in Sam's lap and the two of them unable to keep their hands off each other. Sam hadn't spoken a word to them since they sat down in the van, and it would have been hard for him to do so with Jill's tongue constantly down his throat.

"Where's Irene tonight?" Mel asked from across the narrow aisle that separated the seats.

"She's at home. At mine, I mean, keeping the bed warm for me," Donal responded with a cheeky grin.

"Same as. Better that way anyway. Mildred would just complain," John said with a laugh.

Kyle stared out the fogged-up window, not wanting to look ahead at the pair of lovebirds in the seat opposite him. He didn't want to talk. He was still partially gripped by the panic that had struck him straight after the set.

"Anybody keeping your bed warm, Kyle?" Donal asked with a laugh.

"Nope," he said without turning his head. He didn't want anybody in his bed. He just wanted to sleep and forget about it.

"Ah come on, someone, go and keep poor Kyle company, will ya?" Donal encouraged with a nudge at Mel's foot.

She didn't need much encouragement. She got up and stepped over to him, squeezing herself into his person-and-a-half seat. She laid a hand on his thigh and looked up at him.

"Are you OK, Kyle? You're quieter than usually."

"I'm fine," he said. He didn't look at her. He wanted to push her hand away but didn't want to be rude.

"Would you prefer Sophie?" Donal asked. He was pissed, thinking that everything was hilarious. "She's a good-looking girl. I mean, I can't have her, she's my cousin, and anyway, I've

Irene."

"No thank you," Kyle responded. He shifted in the seat to get away from Mel.

"Are you sure? You know I still like you."

That was blatantly obvious.

"How about a threesome?" John asked. This was followed by uproarious laughter from the singer and guitarist.

"Really, I just want to be left alone," Kyle said gruffly and proceeded to take Mel's hand off his leg.

"Suit yourself," she said and removed herself from the seat and went back to Sophie.

It was quiet for a while. The girls were whispering to each other. Kyle had a feeling that everybody was looking at him, but he didn't care. He was quite content staring out the window and drinking his beer.

* * *

He woke up to a burst of late morning sunlight and a cold draft. He pulled himself up on his elbows and squinted at the open window. Ciara was standing there, trying to tie back the curtains.

"Morning, sleepyhead," she said with a big smile when she realised he was awake. "How are you?"

"Tired," he breathed out. Despite the strong need to fall back into bed, he pulled himself further up to lean against the headboard.

"I brought you breakfast," Ciara said, with a nod towards the bedside table, and started walking towards him.

"Ugh," he said ungratefully, with a look towards the tea and scone next to him. He knew he would have to eat even though it was the last thing he wanted.

"You're getting skinnier," Ciara pointed out when she sat down on the edge of his bed.

Kyle was surprised to hear that. He thought he had been gaining weight recently, but then, Ciara was not used to seeing his bare chest and stomach either.

"Unlike you," he said with a nod towards his sister's ever growing stomach while reaching out for the mug.

"Haha. How polite of you," she responded with a smirk. "How was the gig?"

"It was good. Really, really good," Kyle said with renewed enthusiasm. After a night's sleep, it seemed the gig had gone really, really well indeed.

"Cool. How was the crowd?"

He grimaced at that.

"Not very big, and not very loud either. But I think they liked us."

"No groupies then?" Ciara reached to fold a piece of his scone. Kyle gave her a displeased look. He might not have been hungry, but he liked his scones, and it was his after all.

"Not really," he said nonchalantly and stuffed a big piece of scone into his mouth.

"I couldn't believe you turned a pretty girl away last night." Ciara took a moment to bend her leg underneath her other one. She was not as nimble as she had once been – supposedly her belly was getting in the way.

"You were either really drunk or… I don't know what else it could have been, really."

"It wasn't a pretty girl. It was Mel."

Ciara looked at him quizzically.

"Mel is pretty."

Kyle frowned at his sister.

"Not that it should matter to you anyway, should it?"

"Not like it should matter to you," Kyle said, with emphasis on the last word.

Ciara shrugged and got up to leave the room.

"Aunt Lizzie called a while ago. She's coming over. I'll be gone to work by then, and Cassie's giving me a lift."

Kyle grunted. With a hangover and otherwise horrible day ahead, he wasn't sure that seeing Aunt Lizzie was at the top of his wish list.

CHAPTER 20

Aunt Lizzie did turn up, luckily on her own. As usual, she brought a big bag of groceries with her along with an armful of concerns.

"You don't look too well today, Kyle," she said as she came into the kitchen and started reorganising the place like she always did. "Are you hungover?"

"A bit," he admitted.

"Ciara said you were away in Dublin with your band. Late night?"

Kyle nodded.

"Come on, be a sweetheart and make us some tea, will you? I brought some freshly baked scones."

Scones. More scones. Kyle would have preferred something more substantial at that point, but if they were fresh, he could hardly refuse them. He went to boil the kettle and set about making tea.

"I wish you had someone more grown up to look after you. Ciara's so young, and the poor soul's got a bun in the oven to worry about now. I don't know how much good that boyfriend of hers will be. Don't worry, I don't expect you to step in and help her. Cassie can do that, but she can't look after you either. Men need a bit of guidance at your age…"

She turned around from the fruit basket still holding a bunch of bananas in her hand. She was frowning.

"Your mother was so worried about what would happen to you."

There was a moment's silence, and then her eyes widened. She turned around again and busied herself with the bananas and then grabbed a knife to start preparing the scones.

"What do you mean?" Kyle was holding the jar of teabags in his hand. He was frozen to the spot and staring at his aunt's back.

"Forget it, Kyle. It's nothing."

Kyle wasn't prepared to let it go.

"You didn't just say that she was worried about us. You said she was worried about what would happen to us."

Lizzie stopped buttering the scone in front of her. Kyle could tell because she stopped moving. It only lasted a moment before her shoulders started shaking.

"Not to all of you, Kyle, just you. She was worried about would happen to her darling boy when they were gone."

Kyle put the jar back on the countertop before he could drop it.

"Yes, she was worried about all of you, of course she was. She knew you'd be hit the hardest. She knew you would feel guilty and you'd think it was all your fault."

She turned around slowly, and there were tears in her eyes. Kyle noticed his own vision getting blurry too. He needed to sit down, but he couldn't move.

"She knew." It came out in a hoarse whisper.

His aunt nodded. Kyle grabbed the back of a chair for support.

"She knew, and she did nothing? Did dad know?"

Lizzie took a step towards him, arms reached out to give him a hug, but he pulled away.

"She knew, but she also knew that there was nothing that she

246

could do about it. The universe has a way of course-correcting, she said. It was always going to happen. She just wanted you to be safe…"

There was a big loud sob. Kyle thought first that it was his aunt, but then he realised that it was not. It was him. Then he felt his knees give way, and he was on the floor in tears, with his aunt's arm around him.

"Your dad didn't know. She didn't want to tell anyone. I don't know why she told me. She must have had closer friends. I don't know. Maybe she figured I'd look after you when they were…" She stopped to wipe her nose. "She knew I'd take care of you. I never meant to tell you. I thought it would be too much. She planned the night carefully. She wanted her and Marcus to have a good night before it happened. She hoped that you would too, but she didn't know…"

There was another sob, and this time it was from her.

"She wanted you to know that she would rather you lived and they went than try to keep changing it. One can't keep running from one's destiny, she said. She loved you so much."

* * *

It was so confusing, so real, so tangible and so painful. There was the rock, his mother's face as she turned towards him to look at him and to say something soothing, and there was that loud noise, then the physical pain and the smell of blood and a slight smell of burning. There was a crunching sound of glass being trod on. He could hear his father cursing. Then everything was quiet.

Clearest of all, though, was the scene outside the car while it was parked outside the bar. He got out with his bass, then his mother got out from the passenger side and walked over to him. He was embarrassed when she put her arms around him and hugged him tightly. Then she stepped back, with her hands still on his shoulders, almost as tall as he was. She looked into his eyes with deep affection.

"We've got you this far. Now it's up to you."

Even when he opened his eyes, he could still hear those words in his head. He could hear the exact tone of her voice when she said them. He had thought at the time that she had meant his first time playing a show with Ulterior Motive.

He wiped at the corners of his eyes to get rid of the tears that kept coming. He had tried his best all day to hide from Cassie. Ciara had still not returned from work when he went to bed, so avoiding her had been easy. There was no way he would ever tell the girls. It would break them. He wasn't sure Lizzie had done the right thing by telling him either, although his mother had wanted her to. Was he supposed to feel less guilty for drinking too much when having practically nothing to eat, when he was old enough to know how to control his diabetes, just because his mother had thought it was a case of fate?

Kyle wasn't sure he believed in fate. He thought there would have been something she could have done. She could have tried to make him stay at home, but he knew he wouldn't have listened. She could have made sure he had eaten properly before going. She could have refused to come and collect him. There were taxis, after all, even ambulances, and there had been other people present... These were all ifs, he knew it, and none of it mattered now. He didn't know if he believed in fate, and he was even less sure that he believed his mother had been a clairvoyant. How could she have been? Yet, the proof was there. She had known the date and approximate events. She had told Lizzie a week in advance.

There were so many questions, but the one thought he kept

coming back to was that he had not noticed anything wrong with his mother in the last week or two. He had been too busy with his college work, the band, his friends, chasing skirt and generally being too self-absorbed to realise that she was hiding a secret. He knew he hadn't seen Lizzie during that week, but she had had to hide it too. She had had to hide it after the crash too, but everybody was upset then. Had she done anything about it before it was too late?

He sat up and slid his feet into his slippers. He picked up a hoodie from the end of the bed and quietly left the room.

Kyle walked into his father's study. His mobile phone was still in one of the desk drawers, the top one, along with the charger. Nothing happened when he pressed the power button, so he plugged the phone into the socket nearest the desk and waited.

At least his dad hadn't known. He was a bit of a cynic too and had been more amused than anything by his wife's interest in all things spiritual. She couldn't have told him about it, and that was for the better. She had just done the one thing she could do for him, and that was to give him a nice goodbye. That brought the tears flowing again.

The phone finally had enough power to switch on. Kyle browsed to the call history. There wasn't much activity on the day. There were two calls. There was one in the afternoon from one of his golf buddies. In the morning, though, there was one from Aunt Lizzie. They had spoken for four minutes and 35 seconds.

There was no way to tell what they had talked about, but Kyle hoped that they had made that time count.

* * *

Kyle came home the following Friday night after rehearsals. It was near enough to midnight, so he was surprised to see Cassie sitting at the kitchen table. She was on her own, with Ciara working late and him having been gone all evening.

He left his coat in the hall and entered the kitchen. Cassie was leaning her chin into the palm of her hand and looked up at him in a drunken fashion when he walked in. There was a half-empty bottle of white wine on the table next to her, and she was twisting an almost empty glass in her free hand. Some female singer wailed out at the top of her voice on the stereo in the sitting room.

Kyle pulled up a chair opposite her and sat down. Cassie gave him an amused smile. It was like the tables were turned for once; he hadn't had a single drink all night, whereas Cassie had clearly had more than was necessary – more than she was able for.

"What's up?" he asked testily, worried that she might lash out at him. It was when she focused her eyes on him that he realised that she had been crying.

"I hate work. I just can't get my head around it, I don't understand property. Nobody's buying or selling anyway, thanks to this bloody recession. If it wasn't for the rentals, we'd be absolutely fucked. I miss my old job. I miss mum and dad. I miss Rob."

She let out a stifled sob and took a sip of her wine to hide it.

"I know. I miss them too." Except Rob, of course, he thought.

Kyle started fiddling with the strings on his hooded cardigan.

Cassie gave him half a smile. "I bet you do. You probably more than anyone."

Kyle wasn't sure what she meant. It was probably a hint at the guilt she wanted him to feel – and he did, especially after what Aunt Lizzie had told him.

"What do you do with yourself nowadays anyway? You have no purpose in life, no goal."

Kyle stared at his sister. He was offended and wanted to come up with a real smart-ass answer, but he couldn't think of one. The truth was that she was right.

"It's like you just drift around day after day after day after day. I don't know how you do it." She shook her head, finished her glass and poured herself another one. She was having trouble getting the wine into the glass rather than on the table, but he didn't want to interfere. She would have snapped at him.

"I saw Kathy for lunch today," she said then. She was trying to push the cork back into the bottle but eventually gave up.

Kyle looked at her expectantly. They were on thin ice here, and he didn't want to seem too enthusiastic about the mention of Kathy. Not that he was, even if he wouldn't have minded seeing her again.

"She was asking about you." Cassie giggled at that, in the drunken, girly kind of way. "And that's OK, she was asking about Ciara too. It's just the look on her face when she talks about you that I don't like."

Kyle wished that he could have seen the image of Kathy's face inside Cassie's head.

"Oh, it's so awkward. I don't know if it's more awkward with you or with her. I would have thought of all the men in this town she could have found someone else to shag… But no, it had to be my little brother. Maybe it was just pity. You know, with mum and dad and your guilt and all…" Cassie made a wide-reaching gesture with her left hand that left her wine glass in danger. She missed it by half an inch.

"Then, on the other hand, maybe there aren't enough men in this town. I mean, I didn't have too much luck. And Iris, you know Iris from work?" She looked at him as if he had never heard of Iris before.

"Of course you do, the poor woman who caught you with your hand on some girl's bare backside… Anyway, she has developed a crush on James. You know James from the office?"

He did, just about. He had met the guy a few times. By his recollection, he was an average-looking, tallish, stocky fella with dark hair and a quiet demeanour.

"Is he not going out with someone?" Kyle asked.

Cassie shook her head with a stupid grin on her face.

"No, they broke up a couple of months ago. He's fair game now."

"So, what's the problem?" Kyle could imagine what the problem was, Iris not having an attractive face or dress sense, but there was always the small chance that James would disagree. There was also the possibility that she was a nice person.

"She can't tell him. She's just so awkward around him. I told her she should have done something for Valentine's Day, but did she? No." Cassie took another big gulp of wine.

"What's happening with that laptop anyway?" Kyle had been painfully reminded of the occasion when Iris had come to collect it and realised that the laptop had never returned. "She's had it for nearly three months now."

"Oh yeah. She's done with it. I just need to bring it back. Whenever I remember." Cassie made another gesture with her hand, this time towards the bottle. It started to rock, and Kyle reached out to steady it. He pulled it closer, pushed the cork deep into the bottle and put the bottle on the countertop instead.

"You need to go to bed," he said and walked over to Cassie.

"Hmm? I'm not tired."

"You can't sleep here. Come on, I'll help you up the steps." He reached out to take her hand, which she reluctantly grabbed. She got up from her chair unsteadily.

"I need to pee," she winced when they started making their way towards the stairs.

"You can do that upstairs," Kyle said uncomfortably. Here was where the en suite came in handy.

They slowly made their way up the stairs – he was worried that she might slip or stumble and fall and break her neck. Eventually, she was holding on to the doorframe of her bedroom, the room obviously swaying in front of her.

Cassie stared at him in that drunken fashion that makes it so hard to concentrate on anything for a long time before she broke into a flood of tears. Then, to Kyle's amazement, she leaned her head on his shoulder and carried on crying right there. She cried there in his arms for several minutes. He had never known how many tears a woman could hold.

"Are you all right?" Kyle asked when Cassie stopped sobbing and pulled away from him.

"Yeah, yeah. Thanks," she said with an un-Cassie-like kiss on his cheek and stepped into the room.

"You won't be alright in the morning," he muttered at the closed door and headed downstairs.

Once back in the kitchen, Kyle looked at the almost empty bottle of wine and decided that it would be best to hide all wine from Cassie in the future. It didn't agree with her. He slid the bottle into an empty space in the wine rack and went to let Wanda out before heading to bed.

* * *

The following day, Kyle went into town. He had reason for going in; no errands to run and nobody to see. Still he found himself heading towards GG's. He wasn't sure why. He had lots of reasons not to want to see Georgina – and she had lots of reasons not to want to see him – but he felt like he should.

So he walked into the salon. It was a Saturday afternoon, so it was busy. Georgina, as well as all the other girls, seemed to be up to her elbows in shampoo, conditioner and loose hair.

He knew she spotted him coming in, although she made a point of ignoring him. She didn't even nod or smile at him to acknowledge his arrival but just carried on with her customer. He knew it was stupid and childish to be offended. She knew well that he wasn't a paying customer, which – he hoped – the middle-aged lady she was looking after was.

He stopped at the counter and waited. A few minutes later she came over to him, wiping her hands on one of those towels they used for drying people's hair.

"What do you want?" she asked somewhat bitterly and threw the towel into a laundry bin behind the counter.

"I wanted to talk to you."

He was surprised by his own words. He hadn't known he wanted to talk to her, but now that he had said it, he knew what he wanted to talk to her about.

"Right. You know I'm busy."

It wasn't a question. It was a statement. She was trying to belittle him.

"I know," he replied in a small voice. Her intentions were working.

She sighed, staring at him with her hands on her hips.

"OK. I can give you a few minutes. We can go in the back."

There was something about the way she said it that made it sound like a promise, and he was aware of Georgina's staff's curious eyes on him as he followed her into the backroom. She closed the door behind them.

The room was tiny. Immediately next to the door was a fridge, and a microwave was directly over it on a small shelf. The rest of the space was taken up by what acted as a desk; essentially just a piece of timber along the wall. A small safe sat in one corner under the desk. There were piles of files everywhere, along with diaries and notebooks. There were boxes of hair products piled up on shelves all the way to the ceiling and on the floor. The little space that was left at the corner of the desk was taken up by a kettle, standing precariously on the corner of a pile of papers.

"Tea?" Georgina asked, holding up the kettle.

He nodded, and she disappeared through the door in front of him to what appeared to be a tiny little bathroom. At least the tea would give his shaking hands something to do.

She set about sorting out teabags and sugar while the kettle was boiling.

"Sugar?" she asked again. He shook his head.

"Right. So, what did you want to talk to me about?" She leaned back against the desk expectantly, and he did the same, trying to avoid the heat of the kettle right next to him.

"I just wanted to… Make sure that we're all right, really. You seem pissed off with me."

She snorted at that.

"I'm not pissed off, just disappointed. I thought you had higher standards than that. And anyway, I thought you had a girlfriend."

He frowned at that.

"I haven't."

She gave him a doubtful look.

"Let's hope not, for her sake. I just think you could do much better."

Kyle wasn't sure if she was referring to Kathy or Mel.

"But it's not any of my business anyway, so I'm not sure why we need to talk about it."

The kettle clicked, and Georgina rushed to pour the water

into two cups next to him. She was so close to him. The fluffy material of her pink jumper sleeve brushed against his hand as she started squeezing the teabags, clearly in a rush to get away from him. She left them in while she fetched milk from the fridge and poured it in.

"I just wanted to make sure we're OK," he said again when she handed him his tea. He couldn't bring himself to look at her. The small space was getting to him. It was impossible to watch someone so attractive so close to him, yet so far out of reach.

"Of course. I just don't know what men see in her," Georgina shook her head. She, too, was avoiding his eyes.

"Yeah, well, I'm not proud of it." He looked coyly up at her. She was staring into her tea. "I'm just kind of a mess just now... Easy prey or something."

"Yeah, right," she said loudly. "You're very proud of it and as easy as ever."

Then she looked up at him and smiled. "Don't worry. I like you that way."

He could feel his cheeks redden at that.

"Anyway, I need to get going. I've customers waiting."

She put her empty cup on the desk next to him. Kyle looked from her to the empty cup and to his own cup. He had only barely drunk a third of it.

"You can finish it in there," she said and moved towards the door. "I'm used to drinking my tea quickly." She pushed the door open and entered the salon. "I have a few quick ones in there every day."

This last comment was followed by a burst of giggles. The ambiguity of her words had not gone unnoticed by her employees. Kyle felt the flush on his cheeks deepen further.

"Ah come on. Don't embarrass the poor fella," Georgina said

with a friendly pat of his arm before walking back towards her customer. "He's having a tough enough time as it is."

Then she turned back towards him with a quick smile. "I'll see you later."

CHAPTER 21

Her smile still warmed him when he walked in the door and entered the kitchen. The temperature in the kitchen, however, was a lot lower.

The two girls were at the table. Ciara looked tired and fed up, while Cassie had her head buried in her hands and dark circles under her puffy, red-rimmed eyes. They didn't bother looking at him when he walked in, in contrast to Wanda, who jumped and bounced around him until he bent to scratch her fluffy ears.

"What's going on?" he asked. Kyle walked over to the kettle and re-boiled it. It had obviously been used recently because it clicked off almost immediately.

"It's one of those days," Ciara explained.

She didn't need to elaborate. They all knew what those days were like. Kyle, on the other hand, was not having one of them.

"And Cassie has a massive hangover," he said cheerfully while reaching for the coffee jar.

"Oh, shut up," she muttered. Cassie seemed to be sliding further down onto the table.

Kyle sat down at the table and eyed the croissants in front of her. He was, in fact, quite hungry.

"Are you gonna have them?" he asked with a gesture towards the croissants.

"Do you think I want to eat?" Cassie gave him a disbelieving look.

"You need to eat," he said in a mocking tone, imitating Cassie at her best – or worst, in fact.

"Will someone please just shoot him?" Cassie asked in Ciara's direction.

"Be nice to her. She's having a tough day," Ciara said with a sympathetic smile.

"Apart from the obvious, what exactly is wrong?"

Kyle reached out and pulled the plate of croissants closer to him.

"It's everything," Cassie announced dramatically. "I miss them so much today."

And last night too, Kyle thought, remembering all the times he had tried to drown his sorrow. It never worked. He could never mention to his sisters that their mother had known what was going to happen. It wouldn't be right.

"And I hate work. I just don't get it. It's boring, and I still don't have a clue how everything works. I worry about everything. I miss Rob, and what the hell is going to happen when the baby comes? I mean, where are we all gonna go with a screaming baby, two teenage parents, a troubled diabetic and a nervous wreck in the same house? Sometimes I think Wanda is the only sane creature in this house."

Wanda looked up at Cassie with hopeful eyes when her name was mentioned. Kyle broke off a piece of a croissant for the dog.

"It's just a disaster. I hate everything. I can't see how it's ever going to be good again." Cassie rubbed at her temples.

"Jeez. The optimism in the room is suffocating."

"And what are you so happy about?" Ciara asked with a sleepy look in his direction. "You're the one who's been moping around for months with no purpose at all."

Kyle thought about it for a moment, then said philosophically: "Maybe that's just it. Maybe it's easier with no purpose."

"I should give that a go," Cassie responded.

* * *

Kyle was not sure why he was wanted for the occasion, but Mel had asked him along to Rose's birthday at their house the following Saturday. He barely knew the birthday girl, was no longer seeing Mel and did not get along with the rest of the housemates. He would have come up with some excuse if it wasn't for the fact that both Donal and Sam were going. Kyle was surprised to hear that Sam was invited, since it could cause nothing but trouble between Jill and Eliza. Donal wasn't exactly a friend of Rose's either.

In fact, it looked like Mel had invited more people than Rose had. All the housemates were there, as could be expected. Rose opened the door for him and looked surprisingly glad to see him. Kyle was surprised to see how well she looked in a knee-length black and red dress. He gave her the compulsory birthday kiss on the cheek and made his way in to the sitting room.

He had barely gotten in when Mel pounced on him and gave him an unnecessary kiss much closer to his mouth than was required. Then she launched into her usual chatter about unimportant things.

He finally managed to get rid of her and made his way into the kitchen to get himself a drink. While in there, he ran into Donal and Sam, accompanied by the never-disappointing Irene.

They launched into a conversation about the lack of John's presence. He had not been invited, as they had found out at the previous night's band practice. There was no reason why he would have been, since he didn't have connections to anybody in the house, but it seemed unfair since they all hung out in the same circles.

A little later, Kyle was returning to his mates after a visit to the bathroom when he ran into Jill in the dining area. She stopped to say hi, then cocked her head and smiled at him while examining his face.

"You must be Kyle."

Kyle thought that this was an odd comment. They had not been introduced before but had been in the same place at the same time on more than one occasion, so he thought it was rather a case of stating the obvious. Still, he had to admit that he was guilty to the accusation.

"Sam calls you cherub face, although I can't see why," Jill said, still peering at him as if trying to solve a mystery.

Kyle was too stunned to make any comment. He wasn't sure if he was more stunned by the nickname that Sam had created for him or by the blatant remark that Sam's girlfriend had just made.

Then, much to Kyle's surprise, Jill reached out and touched the scar on his forehead. Kyle flinched a little but did not move away.

"You've got a nasty scar here, and another one on your head." She moved her hand further up to touch the bald spot on his head.

Was she flirting with him? She wouldn't want to be. Or would she? Did he want her to be? He had never found her attractive, but still, she was… Kyle gave himself a mental slap. It wouldn't do, not with her going out with Sam and the hassle that already existed between the flatmates...

"Yeah, well, they're recent," he said to bring the conversation back on track. If it ever had been on track.

"A fighter, are you? You don't look the kind." Jill said this with thoughtful, teasing consideration. She sounded proud of having thought of it.

She knew how to pick her words. Kyle was self-conscious of the scars he had acquired. That aside, Jill obviously had no idea what had caused them or she wouldn't have brought them up at all. He wasn't sure if he should tell her or let her carry on thinking that he liked to pick fights.

She let out a deep sigh.

"Look, Kyle, Sam may not be the best-looking fella around, but he's a sweetheart. They're hard to come by, you know?"

She leaned against the doorframe and kept on looking at him with that conspiratorial smile. She was flirting with him. She was insinuating that she found him more attractive than Sam. It almost sounded like she was trying to convince herself that Sam was the man for her.

"Which is why I think I'll stick to him," she added. It sounded like an afterthought. It didn't come across as a realisation, but more of a reminder to him to keep away.

Kyle made his excuses and returned to the spot in front of the fridge where he had been speaking to Donal and Sam. Irene was nowhere to be seen.

He picked up his bottle of beer off the table and turned towards Sam.

"I can see the attraction," he said sarcastically, only barely stifling the need to roll his eyes.

"Yeah?" Sam said enthusiastically. "I knew you would. She's great isn't she, so honest. I'm a lucky man."

Kyle didn't have the heart to say anything back. Sam was so obviously beaming at the thought of his new missus that Kyle couldn't bring himself to ruin it for him. When Sam looked away, though, Kyle gave Donal a horrified look and a nod towards Jill, which made Donal chortle and almost choke on his drink.

It wasn't an exciting evening overall. Kyle found that he didn't have an appetite for drinking and found himself annoyingly sober as the night wore on and everybody else was getting drunk. There were no interesting women to speak of, so he found himself starting to goggle at Mel again in a desperately hopeful manner that he didn't like and had no intention of mentioning to her. Just as well he was sober.

The kitchen had gotten quiet with everybody moving into the tiny sitting room, so there was nobody about when he went to get himself another beer. He stood there for a moment, enjoying the relative silence of the room and not being pushed about.

His eyes caught Eliza in the sitting room doorway. She looked rather worse for wear. Her eyes were focused on something that was happening at the end of the hall. Kyle stretched his neck to look towards the front door. Jill and Sam were having an intimate moment. She was twirling Sam's long hair around a finger, and his hands were possessively around her waist.

Kyle was so focused on them that he didn't notice Eliza walking into the kitchen. It was obvious that she was holding back tears.

"Is something wrong?"

She looked at him as if she hadn't even noticed he was there.

"No," she muttered then and went back to trying to open the wine bottle. Her hands were shaking and slipping.

Kyle stepped over to her and grabbed the bottle and corkscrew. He wasn't sure why he did it because he was useless with corkscrews. He set the bottle on the worktop and started drilling into the cork. He was making decent progress with the bottle when he realised that Eliza was again lost in her own little world. He followed her glance and realised that she was looking at the lovebirds in the hall.

"I wouldn't waste my time pining for him," he said in a cheerful tone. It caught her attention, but she looked annoyed more than anything else. "He's not all that, you know."

The screw was now steadily stuck inside the cork. He lifted the bottle off the worktop and started prying the cork out.

"And what do you know?" Eliza said, offended. "He is the nicest, most gorgeous fella I have ever laid my hands on."

Kyle couldn't help raising his eyebrows at that. He hadn't known that hands had been involved in their brief... whatever it should have been called. Then he was struck by the rest of what she had said.

"You mustn't have laid your hands on many then."

It was out before he realised. He had not meant to say that.

"I mean, he's not exactly a pin-up, is he?"

He knew it was too late to try and recover from his slip-up. He had certainly diverted her attention now. She stood there, hands by her sides, staring at him, ready to strike. He took the precaution to put the open bottle back on the worktop.

Then he received a slap.

It wasn't a gentle warning either, but a full-blown angry one that left his right cheek stinging. His hand flew up to touch it, not that it helped. He stepped towards her in what he assumed was meant to be a calming gesture, but she was already on her way up the stairs.

It was at that moment that he noticed Mel in the doorway. She looked after her upset friend, at Kyle's reddened cheek and clearly came to some conclusion.

She stepped towards him with blazing eyes.

"I can't believe it," she breathed out and took yet another step closer to him.

"You know what, Kyle? You're a twat," she announced loudly

but then changed her mind. "No, no, you're a prick. A bollocks! I don't know what I ever saw in you! Piss off!" She put out both arms and pushed him in the chest, sending him staggering against the kitchen table before she walked off and headed up the stairs after Eliza.

"Lovely," Donal pointed out from the doorway and walked to the fridge to get another bottle of beer, which he started opening. "You sure have a way with women, Kyle."

Kyle was trying hard to regain his composure and what little pride he had left.

"What did you do to deserve all that attention?" Donal asked with a cool nod towards him and took a sip out of his bottle.

"Nothing," Kyle muttered.

"Right," Donal said with a meaningful twitch of his eyebrows and, realising that Kyle was not in a chatty mood, left the kitchen.

Kyle decided that a change of scenery seemed like a good idea and headed for the back door leading into the garden. He was relieved to see that there was nobody about.

He sat down on a pillar that decorated the steps leading down to the back of the garden, right next to a lamp. The stone was cold to sit on, but he didn't mind. The atmosphere inside wasn't exactly blistering hot either.

It was almost quiet outside. He could hear the thumping of dance music from inside, but he couldn't even tell what was playing. The air was crisp and dry. There was a slight feeling of spring in the air, even though it was only early March and late at night.

He lifted his beer to his cheek to ease the burning a little. Man, the girl knew how to hit. Possibly she had laid her hands on more men than he had thought after all. Mel had probably given him mighty bruises as well, if not from the shove then from the way he had slammed into the table. It was turning into a great night. He should just head home before anything worse happened.

"Don't you look lonely." It wasn't a question but a statement.

Before Kyle had a chance to turn around, he saw movement out of the corner of his eye. Then someone leaned against the pillar on the opposite side of the path. It was Rose.

"It was just what I wanted."

"To be lonely? Fair enough."

She didn't make a move to leave him alone. Instead, she lit a cigarette. She offered him one too, but he shook his head. It was the kind of moment that asked for a smoke, but he had never taken to it.

"Not a great night then?" she asked.

Kyle looked over at her, but she was not looking at him. She was staring at some point in the distance and puffing away.

"No. You?" he asked politely.

She gave a dirty-sounding chuckle. "No."

Kyle thought he had seen her with a potential boyfriend earlier that he hadn't known existed. And it was her birthday…

"No, it's not a great night. People always think you will magically have a good time just because it's your birthday, don't they?" She turned to look at him, and he made a point of nodding.

"I saw the commotion earlier. I don't know what you did, but I sure hope it was worth it."

"It wasn't," Kyle said with an attempt at a smile that seemed to hurt his cheek.

Rose took another puff of her cigarette.

"She loves you really," she said playfully.

Kyle must have looked confused because she carried on with a smile. "Mel. She's crazy about you."

266

"Or just crazy," Kyle muttered under his breath, thinking that the two things might be mutually inclusive.

His comment hadn't gone unheard.

"Quite likely. I never liked her much anyway."

Kyle looked at Rose in surprise. She gave him a conspiratorial smile.

"She just annoys the hell out of me. They all do, really. That's why I'm so glad I have the only downstairs bedroom. It gives me some privacy, at least." She pointed at the dark window directly behind his back.

"You know, Kyle, I think sometimes we all need a change of scenery. Some more than others. I think you need it more."

She dropped her cigarette butt on the concrete path and carefully crunched it with her shoe.

"You should think about it. You've had a really shit few months."

* * *

There was something bothering John at the band rehearsals on Friday night. Although he played well, his mind did not seem to be on what he was doing and he lacked enthusiasm. Nobody said it while they were playing, but when they sat down to enjoy a few drinks afterwards, Donal gave him a quizzing look which John could no longer ignore.

"OK, guys. There is something that I must tell you."

Everybody quietened down and turned their eyes on John.

"Good news or bad news?" Sam asked.

"Both," John said with a nervous smile.

"Come on man, spit it out," Donal said impatiently.

John took a deep breath.

"Well, the good news is that I am going to be a daddy."

The news was met with a silence that was not followed by the customary round of congratulations and clinking glasses.

"And the bad news is that I am leaving the band."

This was met with another stunned silence.

"Why the hell would you want to do that?" Donal eventually whipped out. "What's wrong with the band now?"

"There is nothing wrong with the band," John hurried to explain. "It's just, with the child and everything, I won't really have the time. And in any case, I must face the facts. I'm much nearer to 30 than 20. I'm not going to be a rock star at my age. I'm better off focusing on a real job and earning some money."

"While you can," Sam agreed, somewhat bitterly, before taking a swig of his drink. He had been unemployed for a long time – much longer than Kyle, who hardly even considered himself unemployed. He was a college drop-out for perfectly understandable reasons and he kept himself busy.

It was sad, though, what John was saying. He was willing to let go of his dream for a life with a child, more than likely soon-to-be-wife and bills. He had a point with the age thing, but becoming famous at an older age was not unheard of, if unusual. Kyle was not sure he ever wanted to be famous. In fact, he thought it would be uncomfortable. His brief spell of fame when his parents died had been extremely awkward. Of course, it had not been for an achievement – unless surviving a fatal accident was an achievement – but he did not like people he didn't know coming up and talking to him as if he was their best friend. All he knew was that he enjoyed playing, but he was just as happy doing so inside Donal's freezing garage as in front of a crowd.

"So, is this effective immediately?" he heard Sam asking. "Is this our last rehearsal together?"

"I guess it is."

John looked sad, and he looked guilty.

"Well, don't worry about us. We'll be fine." Donal looked at his remaining two band mates. "We can get a replacement."

"No!" Sam and Kyle shouted at the same time, obviously both thinking the same. Donal looked taken aback.

"All right. I suppose we won't then. I'm not sure how we'll work as a three-piece though."

"A lot of bands work as three-pieces. What about Muse, Green Day, Nirvana?" Kyle pointed out.

"Yeah. I guess." Donal scratched his head, looking thoughtful, as if he wasn't sure what Kyle was talking about. More than likely he just wasn't sure how he was going to make the noise of two guitars with just one.

"We'll be grand. You'll be a great dad. Congrats."

With those words, Sam was the first one to get up and congratulate John with a hug.

* * *

They had postponed the following rehearsal until Saturday night because Donal had to stay back at work on Friday evening for stock-taking. Neither Sam nor Kyle was too bothered. The first rehearsal without John was bound to be odd, and it was. There did not seem to be enough noise coming out of Donal alone, and he got annoyed and eventually announced that he wanted to quit early that night and head out. There were no objections to that, particularly after Donal promised that he would buy them a drink as well.

To Kyle's surprise, they did not head into Juice as normal but a small, new bar on the main street that Kyle was not very familiar with.

They got their drinks and gathered around a high round table. It was not all that busy, but none of them fancied the idea of sitting at one of the large tables and couches that were the only other option.

After only a few minutes, they were joined by John. Donal grinned cheekily.

"I was not going to let this man leave the band without a proper goodbye."

Kyle could not believe his eyes when a few minutes later he saw his older sister walk into the bar, all dolled up for a big night out, followed by none other than Kathy, who had also gone to extreme lengths to look good. They immediately headed their way. Cassie threw her arms around him and held him tight for a moment while whispering into his ear: "Happy 21st, Kylie."

He had never been happy about his feminine pet name but didn't get a chance to remind her about that. Kathy sneaked up close, planted a wet kiss on his cheek and quietly said: "Happy birthday, gorgeous." She batted her eyelids flirtatiously before the pair of them disappeared up to the bar.

"If that isn't a promise, I don't know what is," Sam said with an envious look at the two women. "I don't know how you do it." He shook his head for emphasis.

"Well, I suppose now that he is all legal, there is no stopping him," Donal said and raised his glass for a toast that everybody eagerly joined in.

Within the next half an hour the group expanded with the appearances of Mildred, Jill and Irene. Cassie said that she had also asked Iris and James to come out for Kyle's birthday, but she was not sure if they were going to appear.

Ciara did though. She looked extremely pregnant, although she was dressed nicely and looked glad to be out. She was joined by Ronan, who kept a wise distance from Kyle and only shook his hand to congratulate him.

It was turning into a great night out, even if Kyle had not prepared himself for it –or maybe that was why. Iris and James did show up, but separately. Iris was awkward around James, who seemed unaware of her affections for him and seemed to take a shine to Kathy instead. It was easily done, Kyle knew that, even though Kathy seemed to be giving James no encouragement at all. Her eyes were mostly on Kyle, and he knew he should have been pleased. For some reason, he felt more resigned to the fact that he was probably going to go home with her. It almost seemed that Cassie had planned it that way.

Then he noticed Georgina uncertainly approaching the group at the back of the bar. She looked amazing in a short denim dress that perfectly accentuated her dark skin. Then she stopped dead in her tracks to stare at Kathy.

"What is she doing here?" Cassie hissed at nobody in particular.

"I invited her," Ciara cried out.

"Why on earth did you do that?" Cassie glanced nervously around.

"She's friends with Kyle. I didn't know she," Ciara glanced at Kathy, "was going to be here."

"You should have warned me when you realised."

By this time, Georgina had plucked up her courage and walked up the steps to join the group. She came straight over to Kyle, and he was quietly praying for a spotlight to shine on them so that everybody could see they were talking.

"I shouldn't be here," she said first, barely looking at him while she eyed in Kathy's direction. "I just wanted to come and wish you a happy birthday." She leaned over and kissed him on the cheek in a mechanical fashion. "You know I can't be in the same place as her," she said quietly with a nod towards Kathy. "I better go."

"No, no. Don't go." Kyle reached out and grabbed her wrist before she could escape down the stairs.

"I can't stay here."

A quick look at Kathy confirmed that she was indeed giving Georgina murderous looks. It didn't make sense. Kathy had stolen Georgina's boyfriend, not the other way around. Women were so complicated.

"We'll go and sit somewhere else. Over there." Kyle pointed at the window sill a few metres away. "I'll go and get you a drink. What do you want?"

Georgina quietly accepted his offer, and he went to the bar while she made her way to the padded window seat.

Donal grabbed Kyle's arm when he walked past on his way from the bar to Georgina.

"Frenchie, have you...?" he asked with a nod back towards Georgina, obvious astonishment in his voice. Kyle didn't acknowledge his question. He just carried on towards Georgina.

"Thanks, Kyle. I didn't realise she was going to be here. Ciara didn't say anything."

"She didn't know," Kyle explained. He found himself fiddling with his shirt sleeves. He wished he had dressed better, but he had only been on his way to rehearsals that evening; he had not been ready to go out on the pull. And there she was, the most amazing woman in the universe as far as he was concerned, and he was wearing a wrinkled shirt with an old Nirvana T-shirt underneath. How uncool and untrendy.

"Yeah. I can't stay long. Not with her staring at me like that."

Kyle looked over. Kathy was staring at them. She didn't look pleased, but it wasn't any of her business. A one night stand did not give her any rights.

"She seems to think she has a claim on you. Has she?"

Kyle hoped that there was a slight hint of worry in her voice. "Not a bit."

"I'd say she claimed you good and well that night," Georgina added, with an attempt at humour which neither of them got.

They settled into a quiet conversation for a moment. The bar seemed to quieten around them. Kyle forgot that he was badly dressed and that he was out for his birthday. He just wanted to carry on talking to her while admiring every visible inch of her and imagining the bits that were not visible.

She couldn't forget about her hatred for Kathy, though. She eventually brought it up again.

"She's making me so uncomfortable. I really need to go."

Georgina went to reach for her jacket.

"Oh no, please don't."

Kyle found himself reaching for her arm again to stop her. She turned around in surprise. Their faces were suddenly very close together, and he couldn't help himself. He leaned in and kissed her.

The first thing that happened was that he was filled with incredible excitement and fulfilment for doing something that he had waited a long time to do. Then he realised her surprise. Then, for a brief moment, she responded to the kiss. And finally, all too soon, she pulled away. He was left sitting bent slightly forward, unable to move.

"I really have to go," she muttered and grabbed her jacket. She got up and started towards the door before he had a chance to recover sufficiently.

"Georgina, please," he said, but too quietly, and with not much hope at all.

She didn't stop. She walked out quickly, jacket still in hand and not looking back.

Kyle glanced around. Nobody around him seemed to have any notion of what had just happened. Nobody was looking at him, nobody realised that he had just screwed up and embarrassed himself.

Then he looked up at the crowd of his friends in the upper part of the bar. They were all deep in conversation and seemed to have forgotten that the birthday boy had disappeared. All except Kathy. She looked at him long and hard, making sure he noticed, and then turned her back on him in a very final manner.

The strange thing was that he did not care.

CHAPTER 22

Ulterior Motive struggled on as a threesome. Kyle knew they struggled. They seriously missed another guitarist, and he started to come to the conclusion that Donal was not all that great with the instrument. He could sing and act the frontman, but he was not strong with the guitar. Kyle thought he would have been better, even though he did not have much experience with electric guitars and particularly not lead guitar, but Donal would have been useless with a bass guitar and they would not get by without a bass. So he said nothing, and neither did Sam.

Until about five weeks after John's departure, when Sam arrived at the garage, very late and with a serious look on his face. Kyle expected him to head straight for his drum kit, but instead he sat down on the armrest of the couch where Donal was sitting and tuning his guitar – an act that did not make his playing sound any better.

"I'm not going to bullshit here, lads." Sam wiped his long hair off his face. There was something about his tone that made Donal stop his fingers moving along the guitar strings and Kyle let go off his bass and leave it hanging off his shoulder, heavy as it was.

"I've got a job and I'm moving to England in two weeks."

"You're moving to England? What about the band?" Donal was

the first to speak.

Sam shrugged. "I can't turn it down. It's been a year and a half. I need the job."

"Where is it?" Donal asked.

"Manchester. Online sales and marketing. It's a good job, good money. It's what I should be doing."

"What about Jill?" Kyle found himself asking. He wasn't sure that it mattered.

Sam looked at him with a saddened expression and shook his face.

"Man, I don't think it was ever gonna work. She's not what I thought. She can be really rude, you know?"

Kyle resisted the urge to roll his eyes.

"So, you're leaving us," Donal sighed. He rested his chin in his hand and stared at the floor.

"You can replace me. Jeez man, there is no shortage of drummers in this town."

Kyle made towards the couch to put his bass guitar down. It was obvious that rehearsals were not going to happen that night.

"Until John left, I thought we were actually getting somewhere," Donal carried on as if Sam had not spoken at all.

"Let's face it, D, you and me are well past it. We need to start thinking about making an honest living. Kyle here, on the other hand, has his whole life ahead of him."

It was the first time that the age difference had come up. Kyle was a few years younger than the rest of the band, but it had never bothered anyone. They had just fitted in.

"I mean, look at us. We're losing our looks, and soon enough our hair too," Sam said jokingly, with a brush through his still thick hair. "But with a cherub face like yours, you're destined to be a rockstar." Sam made a playful punch at Kyle's face, which made him flinch even though it was only a feather-light touch on his cheek, and made Donal raise his eyebrows, presumably at Sam's nickname which had not come up in his presence before.

"I don't know about that," Donal said thoughtfully and straightened up on the couch. "I mean, I'm still on the better side of thirty, and if it doesn't work out with this line-up, and it clearly doesn't, then I will have to come up with another one. You're welcome to join us, of course." He nodded towards Kyle. "What are you going to do with your drums?"

Sam looked at his drum kit with an almost tender look. "I'll have to leave them here. Once I get somewhere to keep them, I'll ship them over. I won't stop playing."

"So, I guess that's the end of Ulterior Motive then," Donal said dramatically, clapped a hand against his thigh and got up. "Anybody fancy a drink?"

To everybody's surprise, they all shook their heads.

"No, I best get going. I've so much to do," Sam explained, "but we should meet up before I go. Bring John out too. Make it a proper burial."

Donal nodded. "Yeah. A proper piss-up to celebrate the death of a band that never was."

"Don't say that! We had fans in Dublin. Groupies, even," Sam said with a cheeky grin.

"Mostly everybody's personal fans," Donal said in a somewhat irritated tone. "But yeah, let's do that. Kyle, do you need a lift?"

Kyle shook his head. He preferred a bit of fresh air before grabbing a cab from town. He didn't want to get home too soon.
* * *
Kyle was making the most of his first Friday night without rehearsals. He had joined a few mates in the pub for a couple of games of snooker. He had not played in months and had

277

never been much good anyway. Besides, he had taken the car and could not drink. It was not a piss-up, though; it was just a chance to catch up with some people he had not seen in a long time.

They were halfway through their second game at about half nine when his phone rang. It was Cassie. He was so unimpressed to see that, he almost did not answer the call. She was checking up on him. Or maybe the two girls were not having so much fun in the house. Maybe Ronan had unexpectedly shown up and ruined their movie night.

"Kyle, you need to get here fast," she started in a panicky voice before he even had the chance to say hello.

"It's Ciara. You need to get to the hospital, fast."

Kyle was gripped by a feeling that could not quite be déjà vu, considering that the last time a family member had been taken to hospital it had been himself, but he felt the blood drain from his face and his friends staring at him even though he had not said a word.

"What's happened?" he croaked while he threw his snooker cue on the table and went to grab his denim jacket from a nearby stool.

"It's Ciara. It's the baby. It looks bad."

"Is Ciara all right?" he asked as he ran down the stairs and towards the door.

"I don't know. It's bad. Just get in here."

He was out the door without a word to any of his friends.
* * *

Kyle reached the hospital less than ten minutes later. He parked the car in a spot right next to the front door, not bothering to check if it was a disabled or reserved space or if he was supposed to pay for parking.

He half-ran through the building to where Cassie had explained they were. He nearly knocked a nurse over on the way, causing her to exclaim in irritation when the clipboard fell out of her hands. He didn't bother with an apology.

He ended up in a dead-end in a small waiting room with only a few chairs. There were big glass doors wide open into another corridor. At first, nobody seemed to be around, but then Cassie appeared from around the corner, saw him behind the doors and hurried towards him. She had been crying. His heart sank. She wrapped her arms around him. He hugged her back for a while and then gently pushed her away. They stood there for a while, looking at each other, Kyle desperately trying to figure out what was going on and Cassie sniffling and wiping her red eyes.

"What's going on?" he asked apprehensively.

Cassie shook her head.

"I don't know. It seems bad. They fear for both of them. They're running some tests…" She broke down in sobs again.

Kyle placed an awkward hand on her arm.

"Do we know anything yet?" He wasn't sure why he used the first person plural. He didn't know anything and he knew that much.

She shook her head again.

"Something about the placenta… I don't know. I don't have a clue of these things."

Kyle was certain that he didn't have a clue what a placenta was and he was in two minds about whether he wanted to know. It didn't sound promising.

"Ronan!" Cassie exclaimed in the direction of the corridor where Kyle had come in only moments before.

"Is she OK? I couldn't… I couldn't get over any quicker."

THE TRUTH ABOUT TOMORROW

Ronan looked shocked, genuinely shocked. He glanced from Cassie to Kyle and back again.

"I don't know, Ronan. They are doing tests..." Cassie was interrupted by the appearance of a nurse from behind the glass doors.

"Cassandra, do you want to come in?"

The nurse then looked at Ronan and Kyle.

"Is one of you the father?"

"I am," Ronan barged in.

"Kyle is my brother. Ciara's brother," Cassie hurried to explain.

"Right. Do you all want to come in?"

"Can we see her?" Cassie asked urgently.

"Not at the moment," the nurse said with an apologetic tone. "But Dr Granahan can now give you an update. He is particularly keen to talk to you," she said, with a nod towards Ronan.

They all started moving towards the glass doors. Kyle remained standing, rooted to the spot. He didn't want to go in.

"Kyle, are you coming?" Cassie sounded concerned.

"No, no. I want to get some fresh air."

"But don't you want to know what's going on?" She now sounded disapproving, and Ronan looked downright mocking.

"You can tell me later. I won't go far. I just..."

They all walked away without trying to convince him further.

He didn't know why he didn't want to go and find out what was happening with Ciara and her child. He just couldn't take it. He turned around and walked out of the hospital. He returned to the car, turned the key in the engine, reversed out of the parking space and left the hospital.

He didn't know where he was going. He was just driving, seemingly aimlessly, around town. He didn't know how long he was driving for, but in the end, he found himself at the graveyard.

He had no idea how he had ended up there or why he was there, but he parked outside the gates and left the car.

It was late at night. The gates were closed and carefully locked with a thick chain and massive padlock. That wasn't a problem, though. The wall around the graveyard was only about a metre and a half tall, and in places there were rocks right next to it that made climbing over it easy. He landed on the other side with a thump, lost his balance and nearly lunged into a gravestone. He missed it by inches.

There were no lights in the graveyard, but it being May, it was not that dark. It was a clear night too, so he found his way easily. The tree was easy to spot, as was the still-noticeable mound beneath it.

He stopped in front of the grave and stared at the stone for a while. He stared at the names and dates on it, stared at the candle that was forever burning in the lantern next to the stone, at the wreaths on top of the grave, at the recently planted small, pink roses.

"I'm sorry," he said quietly. "I am so, so sorry."

Then the tears came running down his cheeks.

"I'm so sorry," he sobbed. "It shouldn't have happened. It shouldn't have been you… I shouldn't have…"

He broke down and knelt down on the dewy grass. He looked up at the starlit sky.

"You can't take Ciara too. You can't have her! She can't… She cannot go. She is going to have her child and be a great mum. You are not taking her, do you hear me?"

He was shouting now, on his knees, beating the ground with his fists.

"You cannot take my sister! Isn't it enough already!"

He stopped shouting. He buried his head in his hands on the

grass, not caring about the soil or the damp or the cold. He just cried.

* * *

There were faces staring down at him. Two blurry faces that he couldn't see clearly. It was too bright behind them. The sun was behind their heads like a halo, making them look angel-like. For one bizarre moment, he thought they were his parents, calling out to him and looking down at him, and he was filled with hope. He had been dreaming, they were alive and the accident had never happened.

Then one of them moved a little, and he saw the face clearly. It was too old to be his dad's. This man must have been in his seventies.

"Are you all right, love?" An unfamiliar female voice said from above him. It was not his mum.

He made himself sit up. He looked around at all the grave-stones, full of pain. His neck was stiff. His clothes felt wet, and he was shivering.

"Have you been drinking, son?" This was a man's voice.

Kyle felt a protest growing inside him. He was not his son, how dare he call him that?

"Are you OK?" he said again.

"Yeah. I'm OK," Kyle said in a strange-sounding voice. He rubbed his neck and tried to flex the muscles in it a little. It hurt.

"Can we help you? How did you end up here?" The woman reached out towards him.

Kyle looked at her hand as if she was trying to slap him. He looked around some more, saw his parents' grave behind him and startled into reality. He groped around blindly for a while, found the car key behind his back and got up unsteadily.

"Young man, I don't think you should be driving," the man said behind him.

Kyle didn't heed him. He walked over to the car, opened the door and saw his phone on the passenger seat. He picked it up and checked the screen. There were twelve missed calls on it, all from Cassie. There were four texts and three voicemails.

He didn't check them; he just started the car and headed towards the hospital.

* * *

He arrived at the same ward as they had been in the night before. It appeared to be about half past seven in the morning. Cassie was sitting on an uncomfortable looking couch next to the window. There was no sign of Ronan. As soon as Cassie saw Kyle, she sprang up and came over to him.

"What's happened to you? I called you a million times and I couldn't get an answer. Where were you? I've been so worried. As if it wasn't enough…"

"I'm OK," Kyle stopped her. "How is Ciara? What's going on?"

"Did you not get any of my messages? They've done a Caesarean." Then a smile reached her lips. "I think everything is OK. It seems to have gone fine."

At that moment, the nurse that had spoken to them the night before came over. She looked tired. She gave Kyle a long, strange look and turned towards Cassie.

"You can come and see her if you want. She is very tired, so you can't stay long."

Cassie nodded. Then she turned towards Kyle.

"You best go and tidy yourself up, then. She won't want to see you like that."

Kyle frowned at her.

"You haven't seen yourself recently, have you? Go and take a look at yourself. The bathrooms are right across the hall."

Kyle glanced at the nurse. She nodded encouragingly.

"It's OK, we'll wait for you."

Kyle started towards the bathroom. Behind him, he heard the two women start a conversation about him, wondering where he had been.

Kyle got to the toilets and looked at himself in the mirror. They had a point. He had muck on his cheek, his clothes were wet and his denim jacket and jeans full of muddy grass stains. He had dead leaves stuck to his hair.

They were right; he shouldn't go in looking like that. Ciara would not be impressed.

CHAPTER 23

They were all standing there, looking nervous and gloomy. Ciara was holding little Mark in her arms, and Ronan had his arm wrapped around her. Cassie stood a little to the side, arms wrapped around her as if she was cold, and she couldn't be because it was 20 degrees outside.

"So, you'll let us know when you get there, won't you?" Cassie said for the umpteenth time.

Kyle sighed theatrically.

"I know, I know, you've said you will. But I want to make sure you do."

"You best go," Ciara said, with a look at Ronan's watch behind Mark's head.

"Yeah, I guess."

Now that it was time to go, he was reluctant to leave them. He didn't know when he'd see them again. Cassie had said that she and Rob would come over once she had settled in London again. Ciara obviously wouldn't, for a while. Mark was too young to travel for a long time yet, and she wouldn't go without him. Besides, she wanted to settle into her role at the office when the baby was a little older. She was so keen to learn everything that she was reading books and property magazines whenever she had a spare moment. Kyle didn't understand where she got all the energy from.

"We'll take good care of the house for you. And of Wanda," Ciara said when she leaned in to give him a half-hug, hindered by the child between them.

Kyle was awkward around Mark, but he made a point of touching the child's cheek gently before moving on to shake Ronan's hand. That was another awkward moment, but if Ronan was going to be living in his house, he supposed he had to get Kyle's approval.

"Oh god. I can't believe I'm saying this, but I'll miss you," Cassie said when she wrapped her arms around him. "Don't do anything stupid, will you?"

Kyle rolled his eyes at Ciara, a gesture that Cassie didn't see, having her arms around him.

He let go of his sister and lifted his sports bag higher onto his shoulder. He couldn't believe all the stuff he had. His checked-in suitcase had been ready to burst, and he could only hope that the zipper held until he landed. His hand luggage was heavy enough, and he hoped that he wouldn't have to walk too far to get to his gate.

"OK then," he said, with a look towards the queue snaking its way towards the security checks.

"Hold on, Kyle, hold on!"

They all swung around to see where the shouts were coming from. To his amazement, he saw Georgina running towards them in her work clothes, a blur of pink and black and panting from her exertions.

"I… I only just heard. I only found out this morning."

Kyle was staring at her like an idiot.

"I couldn't let you go without saying goodbye," she breathed with a smile. She had stopped in front of him, her face sweaty. She reached out and touched his hair. "You should have come in to see me before you left. You need a haircut."

Kyle couldn't help a smile forming on his face. "I'm sure I can get a haircut there too. Not as good as yours, of course."

She smiled again.

"Well, have a good time. Don't be gone too long. I'll miss you."

Then, to his astonishment , she wrapped her arms around his neck and planted a tender kiss on his lips. It was so quick he didn't have the time to be embarrassed about it in front of his family. Before he knew it, she punched him gently on the shoulder.

"Go, you're gonna miss your flight."

He nodded. He looked at Ciara and Cassie, both standing there with tears in their eyes. Then he lifted his hand to a final farewell, turned around and joined the queue without looking back.

It was up to him now. New York was waiting for him.

THANK YOU FOR READING.

I hope you enjoyed the book. If you did and you want to make sure you never miss a new release from me, please sign up to my mailing list by going to www.pamelaharju.com. When you sign up, I'll email you a free copy of my short story, CONNOR'S CURSE. I may occasionally send my newsletter subscribers other freebies too and opportunities to win cool stuff, so you don't want to miss out!

DID YOU ENJOY THE BOOK YOU JUST FINISHED READING?

I hope so, and if you did, wouldn't you like your fellow readers to get the opportunity to read it too? You can help other booklovers discover The Truth about Tomorrow by leaving a review on the retailer's website. It's straightforward enough, but if you need any help, please go to www.pamelaharju.com/reviews, where I explain the steps you need to take. I'm an independently published author, so reviews mean everything to me and my future career. I can't thank you enough for the time you take to write a review or leave a rating.

THE STORY BEHIND THE STORY

When I started writing this novel – many, many years ago as you can tell by when the story is set – I did so based on a dream I had. My dreams are weird, and the whole story was basically there, so all I needed to do was to write it. Even as I was writing, I wondered what I was doing. I knew nothing about my subject matter, having never lost anyone close to me.

Then, a few months into the writing project, completely out of the blue, I lost my mother.

From that point on, all the pain that Kyle and his sisters feel is real.

I would like to dedicate this book to my mother, Berit – so far away, yet always so close.

I also want to thank Francis and Angela for their feedback in the early stages, Katherine for editing and proofreading and – most importantly – you for reading.

Here's to many more novels!

40071436R00176

Printed in Poland
by Amazon Fulfillment
Poland Sp. z o.o., Wrocław